I0595784

Phebe A. Hanaford

The Life of George Peabody

Phebe A. Hanaford

The Life of George Peabody

ISBN/EAN: 9783337168674

Printed in Europe, USA, Canada, Australia, Japan

Cover: Foto ©Raphael Reischuk / pixelio.de

More available books at **www.hansebooks.com**

THE LIFE

OF

GEORGE PEABODY;

CONTAINING A RECORD OF

THOSE PRINCELY ACTS OF BENEVOLENCE

WHICH ENTITLE HIM TO

THE ESTEEM AND GRATITUDE OF ALL FRIENDS OF EDUCATION
AND THE DESTITUTE, BOTH IN AMERICA, THE LAND OF HIS
BIRTH, AND IN ENGLAND, THE PLACE OF HIS DEATH.

By PHEBE A. HANAFORD,

MEMBER OF THE ESSEX INSTITUTE, AND AUTHOR OF "THE LIFE OF LINCOLN," ETC.

WITH AN INTRODUCTION

By DR. JOSEPH H. HANAFORD.

"God loveth a cheerful giver."

AUGUSTA, ME.:

PUBLISHED BY E. C. ALLEN & CO.

1875.

Entered, according to Act of Congress, in the year 1870,

By PHEBE A. HANAFORD,

In the Office of the Librarian of Congress, at Washington.

BOSTON:
STEREOTYPED AND PRINTED BY RAND, AVERY, & FRYE.

To

ALL TRUE FRIENDS OF HUMANITY,

IN ENGLAND AND AMERICA,

THIS RECORD OF A CHEERFUL GIVER,

WHOSE BENEVOLENCE IS WORTHY OF WORLD-WIDE IMITATION,

IS NOW

INSCRIBED.

PREFACE.

A MERICA has been rich in great men whose intellectual superiority or moral excellence bade them tower above the masses, or whose vast possessions, wisely used, as in the case of the subject of this Memoir, entitled them to high place in the regard of a grateful and appreciative people. And it is now conceded, that

> " Among the few, the immortal names
> That were not born to die,"

is to be read in glowing characters the name of GEORGE PEABODY. A wide interest attaches to the events of his life and the record of his noble deeds, because he showed so truly that he valued wealth on account of the power it gave him to do good, and benefit others than himself and his immediate family or nearest relatives. His life is an example,

in some grand respects; and is therefore worth
reporting to future generations.

We do not present him as a perfect man, nor
yet as one who professed to be perfect. He was
remarkably unassuming; and by his deeds, more
than by his words, must he be judged. If we had
a larger store of materials, in the shape of letters
and private memoranda, the volume might be
larger; but the gist of the whole matter — the
points of his character most desirable to be known
in order to awaken the emulation of others — can
be presented in the compass of this smaller volume. Besides, a large volume would probably be
commensurate with the artistic skill of those employed to prepare it, and therefore be too expen-
sive for the million. To obviate this difficulty, this
book is prepared, and also because we hope to do
good by helping to spread abroad the record of a
life that was in some respects unique, but noble,
and a benevolence worthy of world-wide imitation.

As a member of the Essex Institute (whose
headquarters are in Salem, Mass., near the birthplace of Mr. Peabody), the writer takes the pen
with an emotion of gratitude to one who manifested so great an interest in the objects of our

association, and whose munificence, as will be shown in the following pages, so enhanced our means of prosecuting historical and scientific research, as to make his name illustrious, and his memory fragrant, among us forever.

READING, MASS.   P. A. H.

CONTENTS.

CHAPTER VI.

GOOD GIFTS CONTINUED.

CHAPTER VII.

STILL GIVING.

CHAPTER VIII.

GREATER BENEFACTIONS.

CHAPTER IX.

APPRECIATION.

CHAPTER X.

MR. PEABODY IN AMERICA.

CHAPTER XI.

MORE GIFTS FOR SCIENCE.

CHAPTER XII.

STILL HELPING EDUCATORS.

CHAPTER XIII.

YET GIVING CHEERFULLY.

CHAPTER XIV.

FILIAL DEVOTION.

CHAPTER XV.

RETURN TO ENGLAND.

CHAPTER XVI.

DEATH OF MR. PEABODY.

CHAPTER XVII.

FUNERAL IN ENGLAND.

CHAPTER XVIII.

FUNERAL IN AMERICA.

CHAPTER XIX.

DESERVED TRIBUTES.

CHAPTER XX.

THOUGHTS SUGGESTED.

ILLUSTRATIONS.

INTRODUCTION.

O F the myriads of human beings who flit across the stage of life, but few, comparatively, ever become really eminent; but few ever thrust themselves, so to speak, unwittingly, it may be, upon the popular observation, or organize and achieve a marked success. But few are willing to burst the shackles of sensuous thraldom, and gird on the whole panoply of a true and elevated manhood, and enter the arena of life's conflict, yielding to the nobler impulses of the higher nature, the intellectual and moral, necessitating the complete subserviency of the lower and mere animal nature. But few raise high the standard of attainment, basing the purposes of life upon clear and vivid ideas and potent aspirations, and then concentrate the developed and expanding energies of the soul with pertinacious and indomitable courage. These few stand out in bold relief, like the majestic oak on the hill-top, or like 'some " bright, particular star," suddenly emerging from the horizon, moving upward in majesty, full-orbed and radiant, increasing in size and brilliancy, and sending its beams of light to the remotest regions. Some of these remind us of the meteor as it dashes across the heavens, blazing with its own native fires; sometimes seemingly erratic in its course, yet true to its nature, and controlled by fixed and immutable laws, startling and awing the observer, or challenging respect and admiration. Such organize and decree success and distinction in obedience to the laws of mind, not only by unremitting effort and toil even, but by a wise adjustment of means to ends, having regard to principles as definite and undeviating in their applications as those which guide the chemist in the laboratory, the physician at the bedside, and the surgeon in the operating-hall. Their success is not the result of accident, " luck," unusual mental endowments, aid of friends, but rather the legitimate and necessary sequence of industry, perseverance, energy, clearness of perception, oneness of purpose, fixedness of effort, and strength of *will.* If the circumstances and surroundings are not favorable, no energies are squandered in useless hesitancy or unmanly murmurings, but are modified, and, if possible, made subservient to the great purposes of life, or may be utterly ignored;

while the aspiring candidate for distinction and an enviable pre-eminence determines never for a moment to entertain the idea of a " cessation of hostilities," —- never admits into his vocabulary the word *fail.*

Mr. Peabody was a marked man, a representative man, towering in giant proportions among the prominent and successful business-men of the age, — a model financier. He courted no special favors, no exclusive privileges, but was ready to enter business - life "single-handed," and become the architect of his own fortune, or personally share the fate due to those who ignobly fail.

His success as a financier is attributable rather to his inherent qualities of mind, and, to a certain extent, of body, — personal appearance, — than to any specially favoring circumstances. If there were any apparently favoring circumstances, we may claim that he either produced these, or adroitly availed himself of them ; appropriating whatever might be conducive to his advantage. Though not in abject poverty, as often stated, it is certain that he rose from the humbler walks of life, and, of course, is estimated more fairly by the *progress made* than by the simple fact that he rose to a high position in society, socially and financially, winning unequalled laurels on both hemispheres. No wealthy friend or relative ever furnished

funds to aid him in commencing a business-life, or exerted
in his behalf any specially favorable influence as a means
of giving him advantages at the commencement of his business career, when counsel and material aid are ordinarily
of great service. Commencing active business-life while
still in his minority, his education was necessarily limited, —
far more so than that of most young men of the same age at
the present time, with the educational advantages now possessed. His was only a " common-school" training, that
afforded, about a half-century since, only a partial course,
— but a fraction of the meagre facilities for a preparation
for a commercial life presented to the youth of an age far
less auspicious than the present. Yet, like all other obstacles, this was fairly and fearlessly met; self-culture compen-
sating, at least measurably, for these manifest disadvantages:
affording a fine illustration of the fact, that native good
sense, industry, and *will* are sufficient to insure victory
under almost any circumstances. Those who were familiar with him, who understood his conversational powers,
his general intelligence, would ordinarily have accorded to
him the advantages of a good, if not of a liberal education.
Indeed, his correspondence was remarkable for its compre-
hensiveness, its terseness of style, elegance of diction, and
chasteness of expression.

These most assuredly indicated culture and refinement, by no means usual in business-circles, in those more familiar with bonds, coupons, notes of hand, &c., than with science and literature. It is, indeed, a matter of surprise that one so devoted to his business-pursuits; one who personally attended to even the details of his financial transactions, — such duties often demanding nearly twice the number of hours of toil now required of the mechanic and artisan in this country; so methodically exacting in every thing relating to these duties; so remarkably devoted to his business, — it is surprising that such a man should have availed himself of the fragments of leisure moments, devoting them to self-culture, or that he should have had any taste for mental pursuits and literary recreations. This anomaly is only explained by the fact, that Mr. Peabody was emphatically a man of energy, decision of character, remarkably industrious, intellectually inclined; a man of method and system, scrupulously dividing his time as existing circumstances might demand.

Gentlemanly in his bearing, honorable in his transactions, genial in his intercourse with men, — with *honorable* men, — though his frown was sufficiently scathing toward the mean, fraudulent, conniving, and false, his indignation sufficiently marked, and his words of denunciation

2

sufficiently pointed and personal, towards those unworthy of confidence, — scrupulously honest as a business-man, he could not but command the respect of those engaged in similar pursuits, and enjoy the confidence of those familiar with him in the ordinary walks of social life. Prompt and methodical, he avoided many of the vexations and disasters experienced by men of the opposite business-habits. With him the appointments of business were sacred, the day and the hour to be observed with the most undeviating certainty on his part; while those who failed in these respects, if unable to offer a satisfactory excuse for such delinquency, would not ordinarily escape a decided reprimand, or more frequently forfeit confidence and business-relations. Financial obligations were promptly met at the appointed time, in strict accordance with the literal structure of the contract, when he was the obligor; while it was at least injudicious for others to be less scrupulous towards him. If there was sometimes seeming severity, such must be attributed to his marked methodical habits, and to an idea of commercial obligation and justice.

Mr. Peabody was a man of good natural abilities; had a large volume of brain, as the most casual observer may notice; his noble bearing well calculated to command respect, not less than confidence. His were clear perceptions, —

those of a careful and discriminating observer of men and things. His brain was neither beclouded by the narcotic influences of the " vile weed," as he was not accustomed to the use of tobacco in any of its forms; nor inflamed, set on fire, by the use of alcoholic stimulants. Such indulgences, indeed, would have been inconsistent with his large success, and incompatible with the performance of his manifold duties, his almost crushing labors, which would have exhausted the energies of almost any man less scrupulous and less consistent in his personal habits. Nor did he stultify himself with the indulgences of the gourmand, — a slave of appetite: far from it. He gave and attended banquets; yet, of all present, he was the most simple in his habits, the most abstemious, often partaking of but a single dish, and that of the simplest quality, though the table might groan under the weight of the luxuries of all climes. There was neither wasting of his energies in sensual indulgences, the gratification of the lower nature, nor a dissipation, a scattering, a frittering-away of his powers in unmanly amusements and senseless frivolity. He was no mere pleasure-seeker; though it is reasonable to suppose that he was not averse to a consistent "unbending," after exhausting and overburdening the mind by excessive effort. It is certain that he was conscientious in regard to the more usual amusements; not partial to theatricals, since, in the finish of the "Memorial Church," he gave special directions to avoid certain decorations calculated to "remind one of the theatre;" though that church was finished in elegance, taste, and beauty, without regard to expense, to "last one hundred years without a stroke of repairs," in the language of the donor.

The key to his marked success is seen in these prominent characteristics. Inheriting a firm physical constitution, a vigorous and discriminating mind, the energies of the one were husbanded by a remarkable abstemiousness and temperance, the normal vital forces not only retained, but increased in their powers of endurance by correct habits; while the other was called into harmonious activity, developed by effort, expanded by observation, and refined by self-culture, his personal habits being favorable to such physical and mental development.

As a business-man, Mr. Peabody had a single idea, a oneness of purpose, — success in financial pursuits. He was not only industrious, almost without a parallel in business-circles, but his energies were centred, concentrated with a marked persistency and vitalizing energy, upon this one object, this one life-pursuit. Finance was his study, — if the expression is allowable, — and success, eminence in his avocation, his great object; though an avaricious spirit, a mere love of money as such, were not fairly attributed to him. He was neither diverted from his chosen pursuits by the enticements of pleasure-seeking, nor by the allurements of fashion, nor yet by the blandishments of the court and the applause and attentions of the sovereign of his adopted land. It is a remarkable fact, that the kind regards of the Queen, the honors bestowed upon him, the many, many temptations to accept, not court, the favors and distinctions almost thrust upon him by those occupying the highest position in the realm, were not sufficient to captivate him. It was not until after he retired from business that he could be induced to specially notice these proffered distinctions and regards; never having been presented to the royal family until after his retirement from the harassing cares and labors of business-life.

Nor is it to be supposed that he never encountered difficulties or experienced disasters in his financial pursuits, since these are the necessary concomitants of a life of business. He is a wise man, worthy of success, who encounters difficulties without misgivings, irresoluteness, or murmurings, and boldly and resolutely attempts the removal of all obstacles; throwing himself into the *van*, in the conflicts of life, *expecting to become the victor*. After Mr. Peabody had passed the meridian of a business-career, misfortunes came, for a time jeopardizing his financial prospects. After the age of fifty years, — at which time his wealth was comparatively small, far less than that of many of our successful business-men of perhaps half that age, — most of his vast accumulations were acquired; the last few years of business being, probably, by far the most remunerative. His earlier life seemed to have been preparatory, prefatory; a time for the deposit of the seed afterwards to germinate, and yield its fruits; a time in which to lay the foundation on which prosperity was to be reared near the close of life, and the creation and adjustment of plans and instrumentalities by which success was afterwards made almost or quite certain.

But the "crowning glory," the brightest halo that encircles the brow of Mr. Peabody, is that connected with his munificent donations; those of a general character, but especially those intended for the lowly, — the poor of England and of this country. This benevolence was but the outgrowth of his compassionate nature, and was early developed; though but little was known of him, in this respect, beyond a certain circle, publicity not being sought. He was commendably devoted to his mother and many other relatives and personal friends; and on these he early bestowed favors, though, of course, not as lavishly as in after-life, when his means would justify generous bequests. With a son's devotion, an affectionate brother's solicitude and tenderness, he cared for those more nearly connected by family ties; while others were educated, that in business. relations, professional duties, &c., they might encounter less of the disadvantages than himself in the avocations of active life.

While cherishing these kindly impulses in early manhood, nurturing them by judicious bestowments, we may reasonably infer that the idea of these larger and royal donations, royal in magnitude and design, were contemplated long before their public recognition; reposing in his capacious and far-seeing mind,—an embryotic existence,—to be developed and assume vast proportions in due time. Cherishing a tender regard, an affectionate solicitude, for the lowly of both hemispheres,—the unfortunate from the force of circumstances, the peculiarities of government, &c., in the one, and the terrible degradation of slavery in the other,—may we not infer that this was the cherished benevolent impulse of his life; and that, with his far-seeing intellect, as he foresaw the magnitude of the results of such a gift in the elevation and the humanizing of the downtrodden, this was the one great aspiration of his life, long reposing in the bosom of the future, as the helpless infant calmly sleeps on its mother's breast, and nourished there for future activities ? This was indeed a munificent gift, worthy of the man who bestowed it. Yet its mere financial proportions do not constitute its most important significance. The design of reaching the lower stratum of society, educating those who must have remained in relative ignorance and degradation, aside from such gifts giving life, energy, and courage to the despairing, furnishing the means of self-elevation, self-improvement, these features overshadow all others; these aspects determine the magnitude and the true benevolence of these vast charities. Having no children of his own, he conceived the grand idea of adopting the unfortunate of his native and his adopted countries; wisely bequeathing to them, with an affectionate regard, the means more wisely granted than by personal bestowments, squandered or exhausted in a brief period as it might have been under some circumstances, by which future generations would be blessed, remembering the name of the donor as a father indeed, who had more regard for future benefits, real prosperity, and con-, tinuous fruitage, than for brief and temporary gratifications. Such a monument will outlive marble and granite; such a record is indeed *indelible.*

To the young men of this country, the noble example of Mr. Peabody as a business-man, a man achieving and deserving success; his remarkable prosperity; his brilliant career; his large-heartedness, as seen in the outcropping in his vast charities, almost prodigally scattered, all suggesting the idea of magnitude, vastness, — to such his whole life has a peculiar significance. In a country like ours and a government like ours, based on morality and universal intelligence, with the schoolhouse and the church-edifice as the " front-guard and the rearward," the foundations cemented with as pure blood as ever flowed in patriot veins, " large expectations " are peculiarly appropriate. While the invitation, " Go up and possess the land," seems imprinted in bold relief on our public institutions, or is rung out in the pealing notes of the bells that call the young to the halls of learning, — the humbler ones, the " people's colleges," not less than the higher institutions, — the youth of our favored country may well be emulous, raise high the standard of attainments, and aspire to enviable positions. Still in its infancy, by no means having reached the vigor, strength, and self-sustaining force of maturity, but even now joyous, exuberant, vivacious, and active, as if in the springtime of life, with a vast domain unexplored, and still more but partially developed,

with mineral resources unfathomed, natural advantages unparalleled and unappropriated, our country is peculiarly
the nursery of enterprise and industry, and the foster-
mother of generous and noble aspirations. Here the avenues to wealth, social eminence, enviable distinction in
science, literature, oratory, the professions, to a wide field of
research, — all are thrown wide open to the lowly as well
as to those occupying higher social positions, as our records
in the past amply demonstrate; the meed of praise and
the badge of honor having been bestowed upon the offspring of some of the most lowly of our citizens. A good
education, one far superior to that acquired by the young
Peabody, is attainable by every young man in New England, at least, if blessed with even medium capabilities and
a *will;* attainable, indeed, with but a slight expenditure of
funds, since the State has adopted the fundamental and
ennobling idea, that it costs less to educate the masses than
to punish crime. With such an education, not only wisely
and mercifully proffered, but almost thrust upon the recipient, success is attainable if merited.

It is important for the young men of this country to
remember that Mr. Peabody was not merely a man of
finances, not merely a business-man, and that wealth was
not obtained simply for its possession. As soon as relief

from his crushing cares and labors would admit, and probably far sooner, in some degree, at least, he cast about himself to decide what judicious disposition should be made of such vast accumulations; in what manner he might bless society, that the far-reaching results might more than compensate for the toils, anxieties, and unceasing efforts demanded for its accumulation. The mere accumulation, the mere possession, with no high and noble impulses, no characteristic philanthropic emotions, would dwarf the intellect, congeal the generous outgushings, make man a miser, the despised among men, instead of the philanthropist, the friend of the lowly, held in grateful remembrance in at least two of the most powerful nations of the globe.

Again : the avenues to distinction are open to the young, aside from those leading simply to wealth. There are higher honors than those usually merited by the financier (Mr. Peabody modified and added to his by his judiciously-bestowed charities), — those sought in paths of learning, in the labors of the philanthropist, &c. ; though financial success seems the basis of other enterprises, furnishing the means of producing great results.

An age may produce but one identical philanthropist-financier like Mr. Peabody ; yet the major part of the young of this age, if ready to throw themselves into the arena of life's struggles and *labors*, if willing to make a sacrifice of personal ease, if they will study the principles of success, concentrate effort, taking Mr. Peabody as a model, may make *their* mark, be remembered in succeeding ages for their noble deeds and their meritorious attainments. To succeed as he succeeded demands the same instrumentalities, the same temperance, the same favorable personal habits, the same industry, and the same business capacity.

I cannot better close this chapter than by transcribing the beautiful poem of Longfellow, so full of inspiration and encouragement to the young : —

" Tell me not, in mournful numbers,
    Life is but an empty dream ;
For the soul is dead that slumbers,
    And things are not what they seem.

Life is real, life is earnest,
    And the grave is not its goal :
. Dust thou art, to dust returnest,
    Was not spoken of the soul.

    .   .   .   .

In the world's broad field of battle,
    In the bivouac of life,
Be not like dumb, driven cattle ;
    Be a hero in the strife.

Trust no future, howe'er pleasant;
   Let the dead Past bury its dead:
Act, act in the living Present,
   Heart within, and God o'erhead.

Lives of great men all remind us
   We can make *our* lives sublime,
And, departing, leave behind us
   Footprints on the sands of time, —

Footprints that perhaps another,
   Sailing o'er Life's solemn main, —
A forlorn and shipwrecked brother, —
   Seeing, shall take heart again.

Let us, then, be up and doing,
   With a heart for any fate;
Still achieving, still pursuing,
   Learn to labor and to wait."

J. H. H.

THE LIFE OF GEORGE PEABODY.

CHAPTER I.

EARLY DAYS.

Ancestry. — Birthplace. — Childhood. — The Young Store-Keeper. — Newburyport.

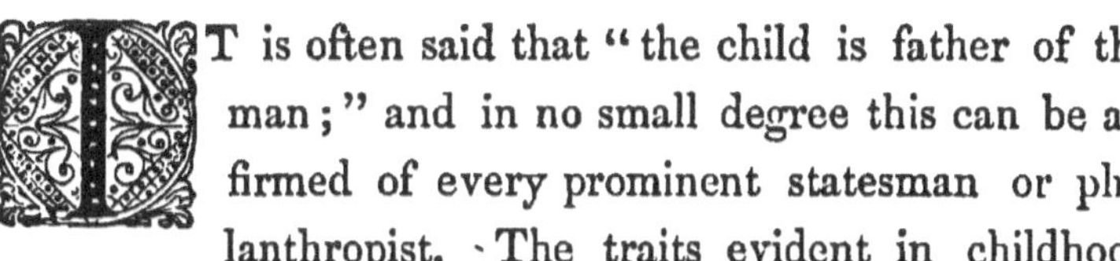

> " A flower, though offered in the bud,
> Is no vain sacrifice."— WATTS.

> " They that seek me early shall find me." — PROV. viii. 17.

IT is often said that " the child is father of the man ; " and in no small degree this can be affirmed of every prominent statesman or philanthropist. · The traits evident in childhood are often prophecies of distinction in certain paths then indicated, when the years shall have given gray hairs to the brow, and maturity to all the mental powers.

This was eminently true of George Peabody, the financier and the benevolent giver of great gifts. His childhood foreshadowed the glory of his later years. And yet his childhood was not marked by incident, or memorable for peculiarities. Whatever the little eccentricities of after-years, his childhood was not in any sense that of an odd-ity. Men and women thought of him as the good boy, the faithful son, the dutiful child, the industrious student, the honest youth; and, if they sometimes called him a "mother-boy," it was not because he was shy and effemi-nate, and wanting in boyish energy and daring, but be-cause he loved his mother; and it was the joy of his young life to add any thing to her happiness.

That he was brave and honest, upright and conscien-tious, is not at all strange when we consider his ancestry. However any may sneer at heraldic emblems, it is yet true, that, as the Scriptures declare, " the glory of children are their fathers; " and none may therefore rightfully de-spise a pure and noble ancestry. The genealogy of the Peabody family has been compiled by the late C. M. En-dicott of Salem, and revised by William S. Peabody of Boston, with a partial record of the Rhode-Island branch by B. Frank Pabodie, in the spirit of those who adopted the language of Job: " For inquire, I pray thee, of the former age, and prepare thyself to the search of their fathers."

In the same spirit, Nehemiah Cleveland, Esq., in his address at the Topsfield Bi-Centennial Celebration, thus spoke of the origin of the Peabody family in America: —

" From a very early period in the history of this town, the Peabody name has been identified with it. Thanks to the spirit of family pride or of antiquarian curiosity, great pains have been recently taken to dig out the roots and follow out the branches of the old Peabody tree. Old it may well be called, since it has already attained to a growth of nearly two thousand years. Boadie, it seems, was the primeval name. He was a gallant British chief-tain, who, in the year A.D. 61, came to the rescue of his noble and chivalrous Queen Boadicea, when 'bleeding from the Roman rods.' From the disastrous battle in which she lost her crown and life, he fled to the Cambrian mountains. There his posterity lived, and became the terror of the Lowlands. Thus it was that the name 'Pea,' which means 'mountain,' was prefixed to 'Boadie,' which means 'man.' There was a Peabody, it seems, among the knights of the Round Table; for the name was first regis-tered with due heraldic honors by command of King Arthur himself. At the period when the business transactions of this town begin to appear on record, Lieut. Francis Pa-body (this was the orthography of the name at that period) was evidently the first man in the place for capacity and influence. He had emigrated from St. Alban's, in Hert-fordshire, England, about seventeen miles from London, in 1635, and settled at Topsfield in 1667, where he remained until his death in 1698. His wife was a daughter of Re-ginald Foster, honorably mentioned by Sir Walter Scott in 'Marmion' and 'The Lay.' Of this large family, three sons settled in Boxford, and two remained in Tops-field. From these five patriarchs have come, it is said, all the Peabodys in this country. Among those of this name who nave devoted themselves to the sacred office, the Rev. Oliver Peabody, who died in Natick almost a hundred years ago, is honorably distinguished. Those twin Peabodys (now, alas! no more), William Bourne Oliver and Oliver William Bourne, twins not in age only, but in genius and virtue, learning and piety, will long be remembered with admiration and respect. The Rev. David Peabody of this town, who died while a professor in Dartmouth College, deserves honorable mention. A kinsman of his, also of Topsfield, is at this moment laboring, a devoted missionary, in the ancient land of Cyrus. The Rev. Andrew P. Peabody of Portsmouth, and the Rev. Ephraim Peabody of Boston, are too well and favorably known to require that I should more than allude to them. Prof. Silliman of Yale College is descended from a Peabody.

" The Peabody name has abounded in brave and patriotic spirits. Many of them served in the French and the Revolutionary Wars. One of them fell with Wolfe and Montcalm on the Plains of Abraham. Another assisted at the capture of Ticonderoga and of Louisburg, and in the siege of Boston. Another was among the most gallant combatants on Bunker Hill. Another commanded a company in the Continental army, and sent his sons to the army as fast as they became able. One more, Nathaniel Peabody of Atkinson, N.H., commanded a regiment in the Revolutionary War, and subsequently represented his State in the Continental Congress. In medicine and law, the reputation of the name rests more, perhaps, on the quality than the

BIRTH PLACE OF GEORGE PEABODY.- PHOT. BY BLACK. BOSTON.

number of practitioners. In commerce, too, this family may boast at least one eminent example, — an architect of a princely fortune. I need not name him."

With such an ancestry, how could any thing but honor and honesty be expected from George' Peabody? A "mountain man" was he, indeed, from his very boyhood: brave and noble in thought and action, lofty in purpose, and prompt whenever the call of duty came. Well said the editor of the published account of the "Danvers Centennial Celebration," "Might we invade the sanctuary of his early home, and the circle of his immediate connections, we could light around the youthful possessor of a few hundred dollars — the avails of the most severe and untiring efforts — a brighter halo than his elegant hospitalities, his munificent donations, or his liberal public acts, now shed over the rich London banker."

That rich banker was born a poor boy, in the town of Danvers, Mass., on the eighteenth day of February, 1795; not at all in abject poverty, but in circumstances which afforded him but little opportunity for education, save for the first decade of his life in the common schools. Hon. Alfred A. Abbott, at the laying of the corner-stone of the Peabody Institute in Danvers, remarked concerning this Danvers boy, "The character and history of Mr. Peabody have, by the natural course of things, become so familiar to us within the last year, that, like his name, they have almost come to be household property. How, nearly threescore years ago, in a very humble house in this then quiet village, he was born, the son of respectable parents, but in humble circumstances; how from the common schools of the parish, such as they were from 1803 to 1807, to use his own simple words, he obtained the limited education his parents' means could afford, but, to the principles then inculcated, owing much of the foundation for such success as Heaven has been pleased to grant him during a long business-life," — all this Mr. Abbott thought familiar to the Danvers people; and so it was and is. In his native place, as much as anywhere, George Peabody's memory is precious; and, however it may be with prophets, with this successful and beneficent merchant it is not true that he is " not without honor save in his own country and among his own people." In fact, the town where he was born is now called by his name. First it was a part of Salem; then, for a century, it was known as Danvers; for a season it was called South Danvers; and it is now known as Peabody, in honor of him whose brief and necessarily imperfect memoir is here presented.

On the occasion of his visit to Danvers in 1856, Hon. A. A. Abbott said to his fellow-citizens, " Here was Mr. Peabody's home; here slumbered the honored dust of his fathers; here, ' native and to the manor born,' he passed his youth and the pleasant days of his early life; here were many of those who had been his schoolfellows and playmates; and when young ambition, and devotion to those whom misfortune had made his dependants, and the first stirrings of that great energy already indicating the future triumph, led him forth to other and broader fields of labor, the eyes of his townsmen, like their prayers and best wishes, followed him ; and, from that day to this, the events of his life and his whole career have been a part of the public and most treasured property of the town. And, all along, what returns have there been ! and how warmly has this regard been reciprocated ! There has been no time when we have not been in George Peabody's debt. Separated from us by the wide ocean, living amid the whirl and roar of the world's metropolis, engrossed with the weightiest concerns, flattered and caressed by the titled and the great, that ' heart untravelled ' has yet clung steadfast to its early love. While, wherever his lot has been cast, every worthy object of charity and every beneficent enterprise has received his ready aid, in an especial manner has he remembered and endowed us. When fire desolated our village, and swept away the sacred house where in childhood he listened to those truths which have been the guide and solace of maturer years, he helped to rebuild the rafters and point again the spire to heaven. When a pious local pride would rear an enduring monument to the memory of our fathers who fell in the first fight of the Revolution, it was his bounty, although he lived beneath the very shadow of the crown from which that Revolution snatched its brightest jewel, that assisted in rearing the granite pile, and transmitting to future ages the names and heroic deeds of our venerated martyrs. So, when, advancing a new step in the cause of public education, this town established two high schools for the better culture of its youth, it was his untiring generosity that awoke new life, and kindled fresh desire for knowledge, by ordaining a system of prize-medals, carefully discriminating and judicious, and which will embalm his name in the affections of unborn generations of youthful scholars. And, lastly, when, four years ago, the town of Danvers celebrated the centenary of its municipal life, it was the same constant, faithful friend that sent to our festival that noble sentiment, 'Education, — a debt due from present to future generations;' and, in payment of his share of that debt, gave to the inhabitants of the town a munificent sum for the promotion of knowledge and morality among them.   Since that day, his bounty has not spared, but has flowed forth unceasingly, until the original endowment has been more than doubled, and until here, upon this spot, is founded an institution of vast immediate good, and whose benefits and blessings for future years, and upon the generations yet to come, no man can measure.   Such are some of the reasons why the news of Mr. Peabody's contemplated visit to this country was received with peculiar emotions here; why every heart was warmed; why all the people, with one accord, desired to see his face and hear his voice; and why the towns of Danvers and South Danvers, in their corporate capacities, and in obedience to the popular will, extended to him, on his arrival upon our shores, an invitation to visit their borders."

Hon. Robert S. Daniels also spoke of the early home of

the subject of this record, and of him, in fitting words, as follows : —

" It is now more than forty years since Mr. Peabody was a resident of this town ; and many and great are the changes which have taken place during that period. Many of them are of a pleasing character : some of them, however, which are the result of the universal law of Nature, will be remembered with sorrow. And I would ask with reference to these changes, in the language of Scripture, ' The fathers — where are they ? ' They are all gone. Their seats in our halls and in our churches are all vacant. The active business-men of that day have all passed from time to eternity.

" The population of Danvers, at that period, was about three thousand: now more than ten thousand. We then had but two churches: we now have nine. The salaries paid the ministers were about a thousand dollars, and now estimated at ten thousand dollars. We then had but two or three public schoolhouses: now some fifteen, and a number of them large and costly buildings, and thronged with hundreds of happy children. We then appropriated about two thousand dollars for their support: now about ten thousand dollars ; and are trying to pay the debt due from present to future generations. Our old public avenues are filled with dwellings and stores. Many new streets have been located, and built upon. The power of steam was then almost unknown. Railroads are now laid in all directions through our town, and almost thirty trains per day pass through this village. We then had no banks, and no post-offices: we now have three banks and four post-offices. And I feel warranted in stating that the business of the town would show a greater increase than any thing else.

"Mr. Peabody left this place with no capital but a good character and his inherent energy and firm resolve. He now returns to us under circumstances known to you all: his unparalleled success has not blotted from his memory his old home and his old friends."

It was Mr. Peabody's privilege, and he always felt it to be such, to minister to the comfort of his widowed mother; and the minds of his surviving relatives, who knew him in childhood and youth, are stored with precious memories of his noble deeds. It has been said that "Mr. Peabody did not bestow many gifts to relieve individual poverty or distress: he thought that much of the money thus contributed only tended to increase the evil it sought to alleviate." But it is certain that his immediate friends and relatives were never at a loss to know the character of his feelings toward them. He manifested his good will by word and deed, as freely, in proportion to his means, when he had but a few hundred dollars, as when he possessed millions.

From a child, George Peabody had to rely on his own exertions. At the early age of eleven, he was apprenticed to a Mr. Sylvester Proctor, who kept a "country store" of groceries, drugs, &c., in Danvers. Here, for four years, he was a faithful laborer, giving great satisfaction by his honesty, promptness, and fidelity. But, at the age of fifteen, he began to be discontented. He longed for a change, and for a larger field of action. He wanted to engage in business on a larger scale. Accordingly, after he had spent a year with his maternal grandfather in Vermont (of which year mention will be made in another chapter), he joined his elder brother, David Peabody, in a dry-goods or "draper's" shop, in Newburyport. This was in 1811. Here he was the same faithful young man, exact and prompt in business, and winning the respect of all who knew him. It is said that "the first money Mr. Peabody earned outside of the small pittance he received as a clerk was for writing ballots for the Federal party in Newburyport. This was before the day of printed votes." His penmanship was superior in beauty. His letters were usually brief, and very much to the point; but they were easily read, and specially enjoyable, because of his clear and nice chirography.

Among the incidents concerning Mr. Peabody's early life, "The Boston Transcript" is responsible for the following: —

"Two gentlemen are living, who were friends of Mr. Peabody in boyhood, and who willingly paid his share of the cost of sailing and fishing parties, tenpins, &c., during the war of 1812-14; his excellent company being considered more than an offset to his lack of funds.

"The late Rev. Daniel Dana, D.D., of Newburyport,

was the clergyman whose preaching first attracted Mr. Peabody's attention when a lad. Dr. Dana was uncle to Mr. Samuel T. Dana of this city, who has been Mr. Peabody's agent of late years."

During young Peabody's stay in Newburyport occurred a great fire, which destroyed a large amount of property, and, by the burning of his brother's store, was the means of causing him to leave that town. Mr. Peabody, in after-life, claimed to be the first to give the alarm. He was putting up the shutters at his brother's store, when he discovered the enemy. Shortly after, he went away. The years of his boyhood were fully past. He was a young man, and a promising merchant. He departed to new scenes and to new triumphs. But he never forgot that town ; and afterwards showed, by a munificent gift, his interest in it. " The Herald " of that place says, —

" The cause of Mr. George Peabody's interest in Newburyport was not alone that he had lived here for a brief period, or that his relatives had lived here ; but rather it was the warm friendship that had been shown him, which was, in fact, the basis of his subsequent prosperity. He left here in 1811, and returned here in 1857. The forty-six intervening years had borne to the grave most of the persons with whom he had formed acquaintance. Among those he recognized were several who were in business, or clerks, on State Street in 1811, — Messrs. John Porter, Moses Kimball, Prescott Spaulding, and a few others. Mr. Spaulding was fourteen years older than Mr. Peabody, and in business when the latter was a clerk with his uncle, Col. John Peabody. Mr. Peabody was here in 1857, on the day of the Agricultural Fair, and was walking in the procession with the late Mayor Davenport, when he saw Mr. Spaulding on the sidewalk, and at once left the procession to greet him.

" Mr. Spaulding had rendered him the greatest of services. When Mr. Peabody left Newburyport, he was under age, and not worth a dollar. Mr. Spaulding gave him letters of credit in Boston, through which he obtained two thousand dollars' worth of merchandise of Mr. James Reed; and Mr. Reed was so favorably impressed with his appearance, that he subsequently gave him credit for a larger amount. This was his start in life, as he afterwards acknowledged; for at a public entertainment in Boston, when his credit was good for any amount, and in any part of the world, Mr. Peabody laid his hand on Mr. Reed's shoulder, and said to those present, ' My friends, here is my first patron; and he is the man who sold me my first bill of goods.' After he was established in Georgetown, D.C., the first consignment made to him was by the late Francis Todd of Newburyport. It was from these facts that Newburyport was always pleasant in his memory; and the donation he made to the Public Library was on his own suggestion, that he desired to do something of a public nature for our town."

The fact was, George Peabody loved to give, and was a grateful, appreciative man; and this chapter concerning his early days cannot be better closed than by quoting one of the best things said by him, — spoken at the late re-union in his native town : —

"It is sometimes hard for one, who has devoted the best part of his life to the accumulation of money, to spend it for others; but practise it, and keep on practising it, and I assure you it comes to be a pleasure."

CHAPTER II.

OUT IN THE WORLD.

The Commercial Assistant. — Going South. — Business-Habits. — Love
Stories.

"A wit's a feather, and a chief a rod:
An honest man's the noblest work of God." — POPE.

"Provide things honest in the sight of all men." — ROM. xii. 17.

THE burning of his brother's store in Newburyport left George Peabody without employment.
But he was not one to eat the bread of idleness.
He sought for employment; and his uncle, John
Peabody, who had settled in Georgetown, adjoining the
Federal capital, invited young George to become his commercial assistant. To the South, for the first time, he
went; and there he tarried two years, managing with peculiar ability a large part of the business, though still in
his teens. His honesty was unquestionable, his tact unusual. Of course, he succeeded in winning friends and
securing trade.

No wonder that he always felt an interest in the South.
Thither he had gone when the avenue to business-success

seemed closed to him at the North by the misfortune of that great Newburyport fire; and, with his well-known gratitude, it is not strange, that, in after-years, to him the South was remembered more as the refuge of the young seeker after profitable employment than as the antipodes of the North.   In those days, there was no North or South mentioned in contrast: but to him the vicinity of the Federal capital was as much a part of his native land as any other portion; and he loved it all.   So the South became as a home to him; and he always looked back to Georgetown and its vicinity as a child looks back to the shelter and comfort of a father's roof.

Here the young merchant made many friends by his affability and consistent politeness.   According to testimony gathered from those who knew him personally, Dr. Hañaford states, that, —

" Unlike most persons in similar circumstances, — and, indeed, those possessing far less wealth and enjoying far less reputation, — he never seemed to assume unusual importance, or demanded special favors.   He was bland, social, and genial; indicating by his general manner a willingness to converse with those with whom he accidentally came in contact, yet never arrogating to himself the right to monopolize conversation.   It seemed to be his wish to travel like other men, mingle with his fellows as an equal; manifesting a commendable retiring and modest spirit.   At the station, if he wished attention, his baggage disposed of, he was willing to await his turn; manifesting no impatience, and then saying that he had 'baggage to put in the room, when you are at liberty,' &c.; never manifesting by his manner that he claimed any special attention or favors: while he never failed to express his gratitude and acknowledgments for favors and attentions extended to him. Politeness seemed a special and remarkably prominent characteristic, manifested on what would be ordinarily regarded as unimportant occasions; yet he seemed to regard all occasions, while mingling with his fellows, as of sufficient importance to justify respectful consideration, and the manifestation of a refined politeness commanding the respect of all who knew him. It is probable that his success in business was attributable, in part at least, to his respectful bearing, his affability, and his general correctness of deportment.

" In this connection, it is proper to say that Mr. Peabody was a remarkable man in his intercourse with his fellows. It was the remark of a station-agent, — one intimately acquainted with him, — that he was a ' comfortable man to have around; ' that he would be a ' popular man if he was not worth a dollar.' Though a man of large wealth, — one who was the object of general admiration, not for his money only, but for his own sake, on whom many and distinguished honors were bestowed with a lavish hand, — he was apparently unconscious of remarkable merit.

" Mr. Peabody was scrupulously exact and punctual in the discharge of his obligations; not only those relating to his financial transactions, but personal obligations, — those con nected with his intercourse with his fellows in the ordinary walks of life. The following incidents will well illustrate his characteristics in these relations. While spending a short time with his sister, Mrs. Daniels, at Georgetown, in 1857, he said to Mr. P., the conductor, 'Mr. P., I am considerably isolated, and do not see the papers as I would wish. Please bring me some of the Boston dailies.' When asked what ones he would prefer, he decided to see 'The Advertiser' as a commercial paper, and 'The Post,' that he might read both sides in politics. These were promptly delivered by the gentlemanly and accommodating conductor, who was very willing to indicate his respect for such a man by an act of kindness; never thinking that he should merit or receive any special notice from the financier.

" Some weeks after, while riding in the cars, as he frequently did, between Georgetown, Boston, Salem, &c., Mr. Peabody asked his indebtedness to the conductor for the papers, &c. He was assured that he was very welcome, and that he esteemed it a privilege to confer such favors upon one who was doing so much for humanity; and that it was a very trifling affair on his part. But little was said on the subject, and they parted at the station.

" Some months afterward, the conductor received by express a beautiful morocco case, which, when opened, was found to contain several photographs of Mr. Peabody, taken in different postures, &c., executed in different parts of Europe; an embossed silver vase, about eight inches in height, of exquisite workmanship, with the conductor's name engraved on it, and the name of the distinguished donor. It also contained an autograph-letter, in which he was requested to 'transmit these articles to his children as a memorial-gift,' indicating the esteem of the donor for the recipient. It is probable that the conductor's gentlemanly bearing toward the distinguished traveller, his politeness, and general accommodating spirit, may have suggested the honor conferred, since he had been heard to say that he always felt at home in his train; as other travellers will also testify."

" The Boston Post," shortly after the departure of Mr. Peabody, contained an article concerning his personal and business habits, from which the following extracts are taken : —

" Mr. Peabody, say his old friends and neighbors at Salem, was eminently a peculiar man. Possessing a strong will and firm determination in the carrying-out of his purposes, he obtained at once the respect and admiration of those with whom he came in contact. Although, like a genuine Yankee, Mr. Peabody was fond of a good bargain, his every action was beyond the breath of a suspicion of meanness. His desire was only to be treated as other men were. Several years ago, there lived in Salem a hackman named Davis, who was more remarkable for his independence and plain-speaking than for the quality of his accommodations. His prices, also, were below those of his competitors. Mr. Peabody rode with this hackman one day, and, on arriving at his destination, tendered the usual fee of fifty cents.

" ' Here's your change, sir,' said Davis, returning at the same time fifteen cents.

" ' Change ! ' exclaimed Mr. Peabody : ' why, I'm not entitled to any.'

" ' Yes, you are : I don't tax but thirty-five cents for a ride in my hack.'

" ' How do you live, then ? '

" ' By fair-dealing, sir. I don't believe in making a man pay more than a thing is worth just because I've got an opportunity.'

" Mr. Peabody was so pleased with this reply, that he ever after sought Davis out, and gave him the bulk of his patronage. This, however, was not very remunerative. Mr. Peabody cherished an inveterate dislike to parade, and carried this feeling sometimes to a ridiculous length. When at the zenith of his fortune, he has been known to stand out-doors for some minutes in a drenching storm because he preferred a horse-car to a hackney-coach. This feeling extended even to his dress. His plain and substantial garb exhibited no token of the wealth of its wearer, and was shaped in the plainest and most substantial manner. He very seldom wore an article of jewelry. His watch was attached to a plain, black-silk guard ; and pearl buttons only were visible in his shirt-bosom. Until his last visit to this country, Mr. Peabody refused, notwithstanding the repeated solicitations of his friends, to employ a valet ; preferring to discharge the duties of his own toilet. These duties, however, became irksome with declining years; and he finally consented to lay them off his shoulders. He therefore took with him to England a favorite and trusty servant who had been in the family of a relative for many years, and whose position was rather that of a confidential friend than a menial. This man was with Mr. Peabody from the time of his departure, last August, up to the hour of his death, and will accompany the remains to this country."

Newspaper reports are often unreliable, but yet full of interest; and when, among the questions asked concerning Mr. Peabody, came this, " Why was he never married? " " The Boston Transcript" made a partial attempt to solve it in these words: —

" " About a quarter of a century ago, Mr. Peabody was so much pleased with an American lady visiting London, that he offered her his hand and fortune, which were accepted. Learning, a short time afterwards, that she was already engaged, — a fact of which she had kept him in ignorance, — he rebuked her lack of sincerity, and broke off the engagement."

Another newspaper created a sensation with an article headed, " A Romantic Episode in the Life of George Peabody," and went on to state as follows: —

" The reason why George Peabody, the great philanthropist, remained a bachelor all his life, may be explained, perhaps, by the following chapter in his history: —

" When Mr. Peabody was just entering upon his career of success as a business-man, in Baltimore, he met by chance a poor girl, who was but a child, but whose face and gentle manner attracted his notice. Questioning her in regard to parentage and surroundings, he found her in every way worthy his regard, and a fit subject for his benefaction. He at once adopted her as his ward, and gave her an education. As she advanced in age, her charms of person, as well as brightness of intellect, won the affections of her benefactor. Through this relationship, he had an ample opportunity of watching her progress; and day by day her hold upon his affections grew stronger.

" At length, as the ward bloomed into womanhood, though much her senior in years, Mr. Peabody offered her his hand and fortune. Greatly appreciating his generosity, and acknowledging her attachment for him as a father, she, with great feeling, confessed that honor compelled her to decline the acceptance of this his greatest act of generosity; informing her suitor that her affections had been given to another, a clerk in the employ of her benefactor.

" Though disappointed and grievously shocked, the philanthropist sent for his clerk; and, learning from him that the engagement had been of long duration, Mr. Peabody at once established his successful rival in business, and soon after gave his benediction upon the marriage of his ward. This, it is said, was the first blow his heart received; and it is possible that from this episode came the inspiration that made the future of Mr. Peabody so universally distin-

guished, and has rendered his name famous as a remarkable public benefactor."

But " The Providence Journal " claims to be best informed of any, and publishes from an anonymous correspondent the following : —

" A story has been going the rounds of the newspapers,
giving as a reason why Mr. Peabody was never married,
that he adopted a young girl, whom, after she grew up, he
wished to make his wife ; but, finding that she preferred a
clerk in his establishment to the chief of the house, he
' never told his love,' but calmly gave her up, and saw
her married to a younger rival.   Of the truth of *that* story
I know nothing ; but I can vouch for *this* that I am now
going to relate : —

" More than thirty years ago, in the far-famed school of
that prince of teachers, John Kingsbury, was one of the
fairest of all the fair daughters of Providence, celebrated
far and near though that city has ever been for its lovely
girls.   Her school-education finished, she went with friends
to Europe ; not, however, before having given her youthful affections to a young man whom she had met in a sister-
city.   But, before marriage had consummated their happiness, adversity came upon him, and he found himself in no
situation to marry.   He was not willing she should waste
her youth and glorious beauty in waiting through long
years for the day to come when he could call her his own :
so he released her from her vows, and they parted ; she
going, as I said before, to Europe.

" There she met George Peabody, then, comparatively speaking, a young man, but one who was already making his mark, and whose wealth was beginning to pour in on every side.

" He saw her, and was struck (as who that ever saw her was not struck?) with her grace, her winning ways, her exceeding loveliness; and, after a while, he 'proposed.' Her heart still clung to her loved one across the wide Atlantic; but, after some time, she yielded perhaps to the wishes of her friends, perhaps to the promptings of worldly ambition: who can tell? Who can fathom the heart of a young and beautiful maiden? She became the affianced wife of Mr. Peabody. After a little interval, she came back to this country, and, soon after her arrival, met her first love, and, after-events justify me in saying, her 'only love.' At sight of him, all her former affection came back, — if, indeed, it had ever left her, — and Mr. Peabody, with his wealth and brilliant prospects, faded away; and she clung with fond affection to her American lover, and was willing to share a moderate income with the chosen of her heart. All was told to Mr. Peabody; and he, with that manliness that characterized his every action, gave her up, and in due time she was married, and settled in a city not more than three hundred miles from Providence. What she suffered in coming to a final conclusion was known to but few. Her fair cheeks lost their roundness, and grew wan and pale; her lovely eyes had a mournful wistfulness that touched every heart. Some

blamed her: others praised her. Those who were ambitious of worldly honors pronounced her ' mad,' ' foolish,'
to throw over a man like George Peabody, whose ever-in-
creasing wealth would bestow every luxury upon her, and
place her in a position in London that would make her lot
an envied one, to marry a man who might never have more
than a limited income to live upon. Others — and shall I
say the nobler part? — justified her in thinking that love,
true love, was more to be desired than wealth or earthly
fame.

" The painful conflict was at length ended. Her true
womanhood vindicated itself, and she wavered no more.

" I well remember, when in London, twenty-eight years
ago, hearing all this talked over in a chosen circle of American friends; and also, at a brilliant dinner-party given by
Gen. Cass in Versailles, it was thoroughly discussed in all
its length and breadth. Whether, in his visit to this country, Mr. Peabody ever met his once-affianced bride, I cannot say; neither do I know whether, when she heard of
his more than princely wealth, her heart ever gave a sigh
at the thought, ' All this might have been mine.'

" After several years of wedded bliss, death took her
husband from her side, when the glorious loveliness of
her youth had ripened into the full luxuriance of perfect
matronhood."

CHAPTER III.

PATRIOTISM.

The Citizen-Soldier. — The First Partnership. — The Travelling Member
of the Firm. — Life in Baltimore.

> " Breathes there the man with soul so dead
> Who never to himself hath said,
> ' This is my own, my native land ' ? " — SCOTT.
>
> " Every man to his own country." — 1 KINGS xxii. 36.

AMONG the peculiar characteristics which Americans have exhibited, or at least among the
virtues they have made prominent in their
national career, is love of country. Patriotism, from the hour when this land was declared free from
all other jurisdiction, has always been found in the American heart; and the dear old flag has ever had its faithful
followers. Some of George Peabody's ancestors were
among the Revolutionary heroes; and so it was not strange,
that in the war of 1812, which occurred when he was a
young man, and during the early part of the Georgetown
period of his life, he exhibited qualities which proved that
he was not unworthy of them. The war with the mother-

country, long threatened, appeared inevitable; for the British fleet had ascended the Potomac, and were menacing the capital. This roused the patriotism of the young merchant; and, though he had not yet reached the age when military service could be required of him, he joined a volunteer company of artillery, and soon found himself on duty at Fort Warburton, which commanded the river-approach to Washington. "Appletons' Journal" states, that "for this service, together with a previous short service at Newburyport, Mr. Peabody lately received one of the grants of one hundred acres of land, bestowed under certain conditions, by act of Congress, upon the defenders of the Republic at this perilous time;" and, to use the words of an American writer, "if he gained here no military honors, at least he showed that he had within him the soul of a patriot and the nerve of a soldier."

After spending two years in the employment of his uncle, he entered into partnership in a wholesale drapery business with Mr. Elisha Riggs; Mr. Riggs furnishing the capital for the concern, and young Peabody agreeing to transact the business. It is said, that, "when Mr. Riggs invited Mr. Peabody to be a partner, the latter said there was one insuperable objection, as he was only nineteen years of age. This was no objection in the mind of the shrewd merchant, who wanted a young and active assistant." His unfaltering perseverance and indomitable energy had full scope; and they who may be supposed to know of the matter, say, that, to all concerned, the partnership of Riggs & Peabody proved a most successful and satisfactory arrangement. In 1815, the house was removed to Baltimore; and, seven years later, its extended operations were such as to justify the establishing and opening of branches at Philadelphia and New York: and about the year 1830, by the retirement of Mr. Riggs, George Peabody found himself the senior partner and the virtual director of one of the largest of mercantile firms.

In one of the large, illustrated English papers, — "The London News," — a fair portrait of Mr. Peabody is given, and a brief sketch of his career, in which the writer, from his stand-point, thus describes the Baltimore partnership of which mention has been already made: "The short war being over, his proved skill and diligence in trade brought him the offer of a partnership in a new concern. It was that of Mr. Elisha Riggs, who was about to commence the sale of 'dry goods' — all sorts of clothing - stuffs, as distinguished from 'groceries' — throughout the Middle States of the Union. . . . Peabody acted as bagman, and often travelled alone on horseback through the western wilds of New York and Pennsylvania, or the plantations of Maryland and Virginia, if not farther; lodging with farmers or gentlemen slave-owners, and so becoming acquainted with every class of people and every way of living. . . . Mr. Peabody's character as a man of superior integrity, discretion, and public spirit, already distinguished him from others. He coveted no political office; he courted the votes of no party; he

waited upon no ' caucus ; ' put his foot down upon no
' platform ; ' went for no ' ticket ; ' but held aloof from the
hateful strife of rival American factions. He chose rather
to bestow on his native Commonwealth the most perfect
example of justice, honor, and liberality in social life,
with the quiet self-culture of individual manhood. A
republic composed of such persons would have small need
of political cunning. The honest man was so much
greater than the state or nation, that, while he sat at
home, they came to him for aid and counsel. His private
morality and prudence were invoked to redeem the disasters of public finance. So it has often happened in the
history of such affairs : the worth of one good citizen, as
it saved Maryland from bankruptcy, would save a whole
empire in many a similar case."

The allusions of the English writer will be more easily
comprehended by reading the subjoined extract from the
address of Gov. Swann of Maryland, when, on the
1st of November, 1866, Mr. Peabody was welcomed to
the State by the Trustees of the Peabody Institute, which
his liberality had established, and of which further mention will be made.

The governor said, "In the financial crisis of 1837,
which spread over this whole Union, affecting more or
less almost every State within our limits, when we required countenance and support abroad, you, sir, stood the
fast friend of the State of Maryland [applause] ; and by
your efforts, by the weight of your great name, pointed

us to that career of prosperity and success in the manage-ment of our financial affairs which has placed us to-day, I will not say in advance, but by the side, of the most prosperous of our sister States. For this, Mr. Peabody, the State of Maryland owes you a debt of gratitude. [Applause.] And I consider myself fortunate that this opportunity is afforded me, in the presence of this vast audience here assembled, to make this acknowledgment, due to the important services rendered to our State. . . . Your career has been one of uninterrupted prosperity. In all the business of life, you have adorned by your honesty and straight-forwardness every position in which you have been placed. And no man, Mr. Peabody, whether living or dead, in this country or any country, has attracted a larger share of the public attention by works of disinter-ested charity and benevolence. [Applause.] You have not lived for yourself alone. Two hemispheres attest your princely liberality. Returning to your native country after so many years' absence, crowned with all the honors that human applause can bestow upon a private citizen, not excepting the applause of royalty itself, I feel proud, standing within the walls of this noble institution, the work of your own hands, for which we are indebted to your unaided liberality, to say, sir, that I speak here to-day, not only the sentiments of the vast crowd before me, but of the whole State of Maryland, when I assure you, that, in honoring George Peabody, we honor ourselves." [Ap-plause.]

Mr. Peabody's response to these words of Gov. Swann have such reference to his life in Baltimore, that it is here inserted : —

"Your Excellency, Ladies and Gentlemen, — I thank you most kindly for the honor which the Governor of Maryland has done me in the sentiment which he has expressed; and I thank you, ladies and gentlemen, for the enthusiasm which you have been so kind as to manifest at the mention of my name. [Enthusiastic applause.] The Governor of Maryland has referred to the assistance which he gives me the credit of performing thirty years ago, or more, for the resuscitation, in some measure, of the credit of the State of Maryland. The same compliment was yesterday paid me by the Mayor and Council in reference to the same subject. I will, therefore, only say to you, that what I did at that time, any pledge that I ever made at that time, has been fully sustained by the State of Maryland throughout the duration of that time.

" It is upward of half a century since I came from Georgetown, in the District of Columbia, where I had for some time been in business, to reside in this city. I was then but twenty years of age, and commenced business in company with Mr. Elisha Riggs of Georgetown, at 215½ Market Street, then called ' Old Congress Hall; ' and there it was that I gained the first five thousand dollars of the fortune with which Providence has crowned my exertions. From that period, for twenty years of my life, though a New-England man, and though strong prejudices existed, even at that time, between the Northern and Southern States, I never experienced from the citizens of Baltimore any thing but kindness, hospitality, and confidence.

" It would, then, be strange indeed if I were not deeply attached to Baltimore; and from the time of which I have spoken, to the present moment, I have ever cherished the warmest and most grateful feelings towards the inhabitants of this beautiful city, where I entered upon a business-career which has been so prosperous.

" And although I have lived abroad for more than thirty years, under the government of a queen who is beloved not only in her own realm, but throughout all civilized countries, and who has bestowed upon me very high honor, yet my appreciation (warm though it is) of kindness and honor bestowed upon me in England has never effaced the grateful remembrance and warm interest which I must ever connect with the home of my early business and the scene of my youthful exertions.

" I am, therefore, glad to meet you here; to stand again where I can look upon the scenes which recall so many memories of my younger days; and still more glad to receive from you this warm greeting, the token that my course of life has met with your approbation.

" But yet I come to you now, in some degree, with a saddened heart, at finding that nearly all my early acquaintances in Baltimore have left the stage of life, and and *I* am left so nearly alone among them all; and, in lately looking over a list of the principal importing merchants of Baltimore (headed by Alexander Brown & Son, and George & John Hoffman), attached to a circular addressed to our shipping-merchants in Europe, dated fifty-one years ago, and containing ninety-three firms, composed of one hundred and forty-five names, I can now trace out, as living, but seven persons, of whom I am one. And, having but once before visited my native land in thirty years, I feel now as if addressing a community to whom I am personally almost wholly unknown; and as if I were standing here a relic of past years, and addressing a generation to which I do not myself belong.

" But my interest both in the present and in future generations is, I trust, not less than in that which has passed or is passing away. The fathers of many of you who hear my voice were among my intimate friends; and, thus situated, I hope I may not be presuming in what I shall have to say.

" Since my last visit, nearly ten years ago, many and great changes have taken place. I then had the pleasure of expressing my regard for this city, and my desire for the good of its future citizens, by the establishment of the institution in which I am now addressing you. I could then hardly expect to address you here at this time; but God has been pleased to prolong my years beyond the threescore years and ten allotted to man, and to enable me to carry out at this time the views I then entertained with regard to the operations and benefits of this institution.

" With the details of the scheme and organization of the Institute I do not propose to interfere. I am fully confident that I leave them in the hands of those who are devoted earnestly, and even enthusiastically, to devising and carrying out such plans as will, for all coming time, work for the highest good and culture of those for whom its benefits were intended. But I am sure you will pardon me, my fellow-citizens, if, on one point to which Gov. Swann has eloquently alluded, — the spirit of harmony in which all should be carried out, — I speak a few words, coming as they do from the very depths of my heart, and appealing to you, — *you*, the people of Baltimore, with whom rests the success or failure of this Institute. For as years advance, and what were forebodings for the future have become merged in the past, the earnest desire for unity and brotherly feelings which I cherished and expressed ten years ago, in the terms referred to by the Governor of Maryland, has become deeper and more intense. It is my hope and prayer that this Institute may not only have and fulfil a mission in the fields of science, of art, and of knowledge, but also one to the hearts of men, teaching always lessons of peace and good-will; and, especially, that now it may, in some humble degree, be instrumental in healing the wounds of our beloved and common country, and establishing again a happy and harmonious Union, — the only Union that can be preserved for coming ages, and the only one that is worth preserving. And here I may well refer to a subject, which, though of a personal nature, has its bearings on what I have said. I have been told several times that I have been accused of want of devotion to the Union: and I take this occasion to place myself right; for I have not a word of apology, not a word of retraction, to utter.

"Fellow-citizens, the Union of the States of America was one of the earliest objects of my childhood's reverence. For the independence of our country, my father bore arms in some of the darkest days of the Revolution; and from him, and from his example, I learned to love and honor that Union. Later in life, I learned more fully its inestimable worth; perhaps more fully than most have done: for, born and educated at the North, then living nearly twenty years at the South, and thus learning, in the best school, the character and life of her people; finally, in the course of a long residence abroad, being thrown in intimate contact with individuals of every section of our glorious land, — I came, as do most Americans who live long in foreign lands, to love our country as a whole; to know and take pride in all her sons, as equally countrymen; to know no North, no South, no East, no West. And so I wish publicly to avow, that, during the terrible contest through which the nation has passed, my sympathies were still and always will be with the Union; that my uniform course tended to assist, but never to injure, the credit of the government of the Union; and, at the close of the war, three-fourths of all the property I possessed had been invested in United-States Government and State securities. and remain so at this time.

" But none the less could I fail to feel charity for the South ; to remember that political opinion is far more a matter of birth and education than of calm and unbiassed reason and sober thought. Even you and I, my friends, had we been born in the South, — born to the feelings, beliefs, and perhaps prejudices of Southern men, — might have taken the same course which was adopted by the South, and have cast in our lot with those who fought, as all must admit, so bravely for what they believed to be their rights. Never, therefore, during the war or since, have I permitted the contest, or any passions engendered by it, to interfere with the social relations and warm friendships which I had formed for a very large number of the people of the South. I blamed, and shall always blame, the instigators of the strife, and sowers of dissension, both at the North and at the South. I believed, and do still believe, that bloodshed might have been avoided by mutual conciliation. But, after the great struggle had actually commenced, I could see no hope for the glorious future of America, save in the success of the armies of the Union ; and, in reviewing my whole course, there is nothing which I *could* change if I would, nor which I *would* change if I could. And now, after the lapse of these eventful years, I am more deeply, more earnestly, more painfully convinced than ever of our need of mutual

forbearance and conciliation, of Christian charity and for-
giveness, of united effort to bind up the fresh and broken
wounds of the nation.

" To you, therefore, citizens of Baltimore and of Maryland, I make my appeal; probably the last I shall ever
make to you. May not this Institute be a common
ground where all may meet, burying former differences
and animosities, forgetting past separations and estrange-
ments, weaving the bands of new attachments to the
city, to the state, and to the nation? May not Baltimore,
her name already honored in history as the birthplace of
religious toleration in America, now crown her past fame
by becoming the daystar of political tolerance and charity?
And will not Maryland, in place of a battle-ground for
opposing parties, become the field where milder counsels
and calm deliberations may prevail; where good men of
all sections may meet to devise and execute the wisest
plans for repairing the ravages of war, and for making the
future of our country alike common, prosperous, and glorious, from the Atlantic to the Pacific, and from our northern to our southern boundary? "

CHAPTER IV.

LONDON LIFE.

Removal to London. — Disinterestedness. — Kindness to Americans. — Saving the Credit of his Country at the Crystal Palace.

> " A smile for one of mean degree,
>   A courteous bow for one of high;
> So modulated both, that each
>   Saw friendship in his eye."—HIRST.

> " Be ye kind one to another."—Rom. xii. 10.

WITH characteristic manner, " The London News " adds to the statement before given, " But the time arrived, happily for this country, and well, perhaps, for the English race on both sides of the Atlantic, when Mr. Peabody came to London. His first visit to us was in 1827, while he was still chief partner of the Baltimore firm. From this he at length withdrew, and fixed himself here as merchant and money-broker, with others, by the style of 'George Peabody & Co. of Warnford Court, City.' He held deposits for customers, discounted bills, negotiated loans, and bought or sold stocks. As one of three commissioners appointed by the State of Maryland to obtain means for restoring its credit, he refused to be paid for his services. He received a special vote of thanks from the Legislature of that State. Americans in Europe were always glad to know Mr. Peabody, from whom they gained, if they deserved it, the most useful assistance, as well as the kindest welcome. His private hospitality — not less delicately than freely offered, though he was a bachelor, simply and cheaply living in chambers — was exerted without stint of cost for the pleasure of those who called on him with a letter of personal introduction. He used to give them pleasant little dinners at his club, or at Richmond, or Hampton Court, — places dear to the American visitor. The anniversary of American Independence — the 4th of July — he used to celebrate with a semi-public dinner at the Crystal Palace. Mr. Peabody, indeed, was, of all men, least like a hermit or ascetic ; but his taste was, to be social in the enjoyment of all good things. He would spend little for himself: his only solitary gratification, we believe, was the peaceful sport of the angler, in which, like Mr. Bright, he was quite an adept. These little personal habits of a man so much beloved are not unworthy of recollection."

A writer on this side the water says of Mr. Peabody, that, " without being in the slightest degree a gourmand, he prided himself very highly upon his table, and took especial pleasure in the selection of the viands. Mr. Peabody generally possessed a hearty appetite. His taste, however, was more for wholesome, well-cooked food than for luxuries. He seldom indulged in pastry or cake, but was passionately fond of fruit, which he kept upon his table at all seasons of the year." And yet it is declared that " Mr. Peabody's personal expenses never exceeded three thousand dollars during the last ten years of his life." Evidently Mr. Peabody thought of the tastes, comfort, and needs of others, more than of himself; and in this disinterestedness lies one of the chief glories of his character. He was just as well as generous. " The Boston Transcript " says, " Mr. Peabody was strongly opposed to fraud in little matters. The conductor on an English railway once overcharged him a shilling for fare. He made complaint to the directors, and had the man discharged. ' Not,' said he, ' that I could not afford to pay the shilling; but the man was cheating many travellers to whom the swindle would be oppressive.' "

It is said to have been " one of the peculiarities of Mr. Peabody, that he never would have a house of his own. He cared little for himself in all things. It was his habit, for instance, to dine off a mutton-chop at the grand dinners he used to give, where every luxury was spread upon the table. He used to live in London in the most retired manner; and his name did not appear in any directory or ' Court Guide.' "

He was a banker only in the American sense of the term; for while, like the Rothschilds and the Barings, he loaned money, changed drafts, bought stocks, and held deposits for customers, yet he did not pay out money, as English bankers do, and therefore was not deemed a banker in England. "The magnitude of his transactions in that capacity, perhaps, fell short of one or two great houses of the same class; but in honor, faith, punctuality, and public confidence, the firm of George Peabody & Co. of Warnford Court stood second to none." As already shown, Mr. Peabody had not been long across the waters, when those unfortunate failures occurred which shook American credit abroad, and brought so much reproach in certain business-circles upon the American name. "The default of some of the States, and the temporary inability of others to meet their obligations, and the failure of several of our moneyed institutions, threw doubt and distrust on all American securities. That great sympathetic nerve of the commercial world, — credit, — as far as the United States was concerned, was for the time paralyzed. At that moment, — and it was a trying one, — Mr. Peabody not only stood firm himself, but he was the cause of firmness in others. His judgment commanded respect; his integrity won back the reliance which men had been accustomed to place upon American securities." And a late writer has truly said, that "it is because Mr. Peabody at that trying time rose far above the mere financier, — coming to the rescue with his true American heart, as well as with his English purse and English credit, — that he rose at once into the rank of public benefactors."

" The Boston Advertiser " is responsible for the following anecdote, which illustrates the quick wit of the London banker, and, to the candid mind, does not compromise his loyalty : —

" The fame of Mr. George Peabody rests so exclusively upon the immense gifts of the last years of his life, that some peculiar incidents of his earlier career as an American merchant in London, illustrating other traits of character than splendid liberality, are apt to be overlooked. Mr: Peabody was never a commonplace man ; and, in many situations of life, he did things which brought him strong friends and made him bitter enemies, and caused controversies which would be now remembered, but for the great torrent of giving which has swept them out of the memories of most people. At the time of the Great Exhibition of 1851, Mr. Peabody earned the gratitude of Americans in London and at home, and became more widely known than his wealth, already great, had made him, by advancing a large sum, for which no provision had been made, to enable the products of American industry to be displayed in the Crystal Palace. In the same year, he gave his first great Fourth-of-July feast, at Willis's Rooms, to American citizens and the best society of London, headed by the Duke of Wellington. It was ' the affair of the season.' Mr. Peabody, after this, extended his hospitality to a larger extent than ever before ; established the unprecedented practice of inviting to dinner every person who brought a letter of credit on his house ; and celebrated every Independence Day by a special dinner to the Americans in London, inviting some distinguished English friends to meet them.

" At these banquets, it was the invariable custom of the host to have the first toast in honor of the Queen. After her, the President's health might be drunk. It was Mr. Peabody's own preference, and nobody had a right to object. But, in 1854, a number of Americans, led by Mr. Daniel E. Sickles, who was then secretary of legation at London, proposed a special subscription-dinner on the 4th of July, as a more purely national affair. During the preparations, Mr. Peabody expressed an acquiescence in the project, but asked to be allowed to provide the dinner, which might be managed, as to the matter of invitations and toasts, by a committee of arrangements. His proposal was gladly accepted ; and, as it was supposed that the great merchant had desired to imply a willingness to conform to the general preference in the matter of the sentiments, all was left in his hands, and no committee of arrangements was appointed. After the material portion of a luxurious repast was over, Mr. Peabody arose, and said, in deference to her sex, if not to her position, he would propose as the leading toast, ' The health of her Majesty, Queen Victoria.' The astonishment and wrath of some of the guests were very great. Not a few, headed by Mr. Sickles, left the room in ostentatious anger. Others, among whom was Mr. Buchanan, the American minister, refused to rise. There was an uproarious min-

gling of hisses with the cheers which followed the toast
The affair seems at this distance of time a small one, and
undoubtedly the result of a misunderstanding; but it
caused great bitterness of feeling in 1854, and gave rise
to enmities which only the death of Mr. Peabody has
terminated."

The testimony of the late President Felton of Harvard
College, given at the Danvers reception, is so much in
point, that it is here inserted : —

" I am one of that famous tribe of ' wandering Arabs '
who have crossed the ocean, and have shared in the hospitalities of your distinguished guest ; and I am indebted to
him, — it is not egotism that prompts me to say it, but a
desire to add my tribute to the chaplet of honor with
which you have crowned him to-day, — I am indebted to
him, I say, for much of my enjoyment in the Old World.
I reached London a stranger to him, having no letter of introduction to him, not even a letter of credit. [Laughter.]
He sought me out, and invited me to one of those almost
regal entertainments ; and the hours that I spent in the
society gathered by him on that delightful occasion are
among the most pleasant reminiscences of my foreign tour.
I well remember the society brought together on that
occasion. The noble sons and lovely daughters of England came, honoring by their presence your fellow-citizen,
who had honored them by his invitation ; and they felt it
so : and there I listened to words of friendship towards
the American nation which would make every heart in

this assembly throb with delight if they could hear them, as I heard them, spoken by the most eloquent lips of England.

" I think, Mr. President, if there is any Englishman here present, he must have felt that the sentiment of friendship for that great and illustrious nation — the foremost nation in modern civilization, the great bulwark of liberty, whose language, as has been well and truly said by one of their great writers, is the only language upon the face of the earth in which the accents of freedom can be uttered — is congenial to the American heart; he must have felt that the words of good will so often uttered on those festive occasions of which Mr. Peabody was the originator have found a ready response from the people of this country, as proved by this multitudinous assembly. And I must confess, republican as I am, ultra republican as I am [cheers], that my heart beat quicker when the mention of the royal lady of England was received with three hearty cheers from this republican assembly; for that sovereign lady illustrates, in her high position, all those domestic and household virtues, which, while they give dignity to the lowliest position, are the ornament and the pride of the most exalted. It is true, we owe her no political allegiance; but the virtues of the Queen of England, while they secure to her the love and loyalty of her subjects, entitle her to the willing fealty of every honorable man in republican America." [Loud cheers.]

" The Advertiser " also remarks that " it was in the

banking-business that the bulk of the huge fortune was made. Mr. Peabody had a strong faith in American securities. He dealt in them largely and confidently. That keen business-instinct, indescribable, unacquirable, inborn as much as the power of poetry or of art, secured for him the happy result of a wise selection among invest ments which certainly were not universally perfect. The result was, that his wealth, not previously remarkable, began to roll up rapidly and enormously. He remained a shrewd business-man to the end of his long life. Munificently as he gave away, he never, in the strict matter of making money, grew lax or unbusiness-like. Very properly, he kept the two functions entirely distinct, and did not confound liberal generosity with merchant-like dealing. In private life, his habits were little changed by the acquisition of riches. Frugal from necessity in early life, frugal he remained, so far as the gratification of his own tastes was concerned, to the end. But his hospitality was exceptionally wide-spread and sumptuous, and such as is always considered to be needful and becoming in the complete picture of the ideal 'merchant-prince.' Men who spent lavishly for luxuries and show often pointed with something like a sneer at his modest bachelor quarters. But while he was sheltering the poor of a great kingdom, and educating the ignorant in a mighty republic, he could afford to let the cavillers have their say. He was content to find his chief and quiet pleasure at his favorite game of whist, in congenial company. . . .

" Though the temptations of business, and perhaps of taste, induced Mr. Peabody to expatriate himself for so many years, it is needless to say that he never ceased to be at heart an American citizen. Unlike most men who belong to two countries, he slighted neither for the other, but distributed his affections and his money between them in a manner which left room for nothing but gratitude on the part of each. Americans will long remember and long miss his hearty friendship in a foreign land."

According to " The Boston Transcript," " When Mr. Peabody first resided in London, he lived very frugally ; taking breakfast at his lodgings, and dining at a club-house. His personal expenses for ten years did not average six hundred pounds per annum.

" He had a very retentive memory, particularly in regard to names and places. He would give the most minute particulars of events that occurred between fifty and sixty years ago.

" He first appeared in print as the champion of American credit in England at the time our State securities were depressed on account of the non-payment of interest by Pennsylvania.

" He was very fond of singing ; Scottish songs being his favorites.

" He was a good talker : at the table, few men were his equals. His idea of a pleasant dinner-party was where there was a great deal of talk, and he could take the lead in conversation.

" The favorite games of Mr. Peabody were backgammon after dinner, and whist in the evening. He was as fond of the latter, and as rigorous a player, as Charles Lamb's friend, Sarah Battle, who neither gave nor took quarter."

At the time of the Great Exhibition of 1851, in England, Mr. Peabody redeemed the good name of his countrymen by promptly supplying a sum of fifteen thousand dollars, which was greatly needed, in order to place in suitable array the contributions to the World's Fair from America, and to save his native country from appearing unworthy of its public and private enterprise. On the occasion of Mr. Peabody's public reception by his native town, in 1856, Hon. Edward Everett thus eloquently alluded to this generous deed of the London banker ; saying, " We are bound as Americans, on this occasion particularly, to remember the very important services rendered by your guest to his countrymen who went to England in 1851 with specimens of the products and arts of this country to be exhibited at the Crystal Palace. In most, perhaps in all other countries, this exhibition had been a government affair. Commissioners were appointed by authority to protect the interests of the exhibiters ; and, what was more important, appropriations of money were made to defray their expenses. No appropriations were made by Congress. Our exhibiters arrived friendless, some of them penniless, in the great commercial Babel of the world. They found the portion of the Crystal Palace assigned to our country unprepared for the specimens of art and industry which they had brought with them; naked and unadorned by the side of the neighboring arcades and galleries fitted up with elegance and splendor by the richest governments in Europe. The English press began to launch its too ready sarcasms at the sorry appearance which Brother Jonathan seemed likely to make; and all the exhibiters from this country, and all who felt an interest in their success, were disheartened. At this critical moment, our friend stepped forward. He did what Congress should have done. By liberal advances on his part, the American department was fitted up; and day after day, as some new product of American ingenuity and taste was added to the list, — McCormick's reaper, Colt's revolver, Powers's Greek slave, Hobbs's unpickable lock, Hoe's wonderful printing-presses, and Bond's more wonderful spring governor, — it began to be suspected that Brother Jonathan was not quite so much of a simpleton as had been thought. He had contributed his full share, if not to the splendor, at least to the utilities, of the exhibition. In fact, the leading journal at London, with a magnanimity which did it honor, admitted that England had derived more real benefit from the contributions of the United States than from those of any other country."

CHAPTER V.

GREAT AND GOOD GIFTS.

Help to find Sir John Franklin. — Donation to Danvers. — The Peabody
Institute in Peabody. — The Public Reception of the Benefactor.

> " For his bounty,
> There was no winter in't: an autumn 'twas,
> That grew the more by reaping."
>
> SHAKSPEARE: *Antony and Cleopatra.*

" He that giveth, let him do it with simplicity." — ROM. xii. 8.

IN 1852, Mr. Peabody again showed himself a generous giver to good and noble objects. That friend of humanity in America, Henry Grinnell, had generously offered a vessel owned by himself, — " The Advance," — for a second expedition, under the brave and dauntless Dr. Kane, to the Arctic seas, in search of poor lost Sir John Franklin. Sympathizing with the pluck and energy and perseverance of the American explorer, and also with the deep sorrow of the devoted Lady Franklin and other English friends, who mourned the unexplained delay of the intrepid adventurer, Mr. Peabody felt it to be his privilege to aid in the matter.

According to "The Boston Transcript," "a private individual offered a vessel for the purpose, on condition that Congress should make a grant of money in aid of the expedition; and when time ran on, and Congress seemed inclined to do nothing in the matter, Mr. Peabody provided the means of equipping 'The Advance.' By this timely aid, Dr. Kane was enabled to carry out his enterprise; and the name of 'Peabody Land' will be found marked upon part of the northern shores which that gallant discoverer then visited."

In the month of June, 1852, the town of Danvers held its centennial celebration, and Mr. Peabody was invited to be present.

.   .   .   .

"Although Mr. Peabody had long been absent, yet the many proofs by which he had, in previous instances, evinced his regard for the place of his birth, gave him peculiar claims to be included among the invited guests. Accordingly, an invitation was early forwarded to him, by the committee of the town, to be present at that festival, with a request, that, if unable to attend, he would signify by letter his interest in the occasion. In his reply, after stating that his engagements would allow him to comply only with the latter part of the request, he said, ' I enclose a sentiment, which I ask may remain sealed till this letter is read on the day of celebration, according to the direction on the envelope.'

" The indorsement on the envelope of the sealed packet was as follows : —

" ' The seal of this is not to be broken till the toasts are being proposed by the chairman, at the dinner, 16th June, at Danvers, in commemoration of the one hundredth year since its severance from Salem. It contains a sentiment for the occasion from George Peabody of London.'

" In obedience to the above direction, at the proper moment the reading of the communication was called for; and the following was received by the delighted audience with loud acclamations : —

" ' BY GEORGE PEABODY of London : —

" ' EDUCATION, — *A debt due from present to future generations.*'

" ' In acknowledgment of the payment of that debt by the generation which preceded me in my native town of Danvers, and to aid in its prompt future discharge, I give to the inhabitants of that town the sum of TWENTY THOUSAND DOLLARS for the promotion of knowledge and morality among them.

" ' I beg to remark, that the subject of making a gift to my native town has for some years occupied my mind; and I avail myself of your present interesting festival to make the communication, in the hope that it will add to the pleasures of the day.

" ' I annex to the gift such conditions only as I deem necessary for its preservation, and the accomplishment of the purposes before named. The conditions are, that the legal voters of the town, at a meeting to be held at a convenient time after the 16th June, shall accept the gift, and shall elect a committee of not less than twelve persons, to receive and have charge of the same, for the purpose of establishing a lyceum for the delivery of lectures upon such subjects as may be designated by a committee of the town, free to all the inhabitants, under such rules as said committee may from time to time enact; and that a library shall be obtained, which shall also be free to the inhabitants, under the direction of the committee.

" ' That a suitable building for the use of the lyceum shall be erected, at a cost, including the land, fixtures, furniture, &c., not exceeding seven thousand dollars; and shall be located within one-third of a mile of the Presbyterian Meeting-House, occupying the spot of that formerly under the pastoral care of the Rev. Mr. Walker, in the south parish of Danvers.

" ' That ten thousand dollars of this gift shall be invested by the town's committee in undoubted securities, as a permanent fund; the interest arising therefrom to be expended in support of the lyceum.

" ' In all other respects, I leave the disposition of the affairs of the lyceum to the inhabitants of Danvers, — merely suggesting that it might be advisable for them, by their own act, to exclude sectarian theology and political discussions forever from the walls of the institution.

" ' I will make one request of the committee; which is,

if they see no objection, and my venerable friend, Capt. Sylvester Proctor, should be living, that he be selected to lay the corner-stone of the lyceum building.

     " ' Respectfully yours,

          " ' GEORGE PEABODY.' "

The citizens of Danvers accepted the trust, in a proper manner expressing their gratitude for the gift.

" Mr. Peabody afterwards added TEN THOUSAND DOL-LARS to his first donation; the whole to be so expended, that seventeen thousand dollars should be appropriated for the land and building, three thousand to the-purchase of books as the foundation of a library, and ten thousand to remain as a permanent fund. Further donations have since been received, swelling the aggregate of Mr. Peabody's gifts to the Institute to an amount exceeding FIFTY THOUSAND DOLLARS."

This was the amount in 1856, when the memorial volume was written. Since then, the gifts to Danvers have increased, till now, it is said, the Peabody Institute has received nearly two hundred thousand dollars from its generous founder.

The memorial volume, printed to commemorate Mr. Peabody's reception in his native place, thus speaks of the edifice which bears the honored name of " Peabody Institute : " —

" The difficulty of procuring a suitable lot of land within the prescribed distance from the meeting-house

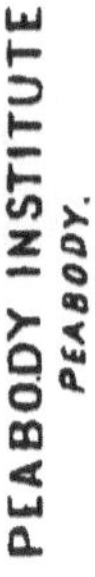

PEABODY INSTITUTE
PEABODY.

PEABODY INSTITUTE
DANVERS.

caused some delay in the erection of the building. But at length a site was selected on Main Street; and the corner-stone of the new structure was laid, with appropriate ceremonies, on the 20th of August, 1853; Hon. Abbott Lawrence, an intimate friend of Mr. Peabody, performing the part assigned to Capt. Sylvester Proctor, who had deceased. The building was finished in the course of the following year, and dedicated to its future uses on the 29th of September, 1854. Hon. Rufus Choate delivered an eloquent address on that occasion.

"It is a stately edifice, eighty-two feet in length by fifty in breadth, built of brick, and ornamented with brown Connecticut freestone. On its front, a slab of freestone bears the words, PEABODY INSTITUTE, in relief. The lecture-hall, occupying the whole of the upper story, is finished with neatness and simplicity, and is furnished with seats for about seven hundred and fifty persons. Over the rostrum hangs a full-length portrait of Mr. Peabody by Healy, which has been pronounced by *connoisseurs* to be a *chef d'œuvre* of that artist. It was sat for by him at the request of the citizens of the town; but, at its completion, was presented to them. The library-room, in the lower story, is commodiously arranged for the delivery of books. The shelves for books are placed around the walls of the room; but, by the addition of alcoves, its capacity can be greatly increased.

"Courses of lectures have been delivered in the lyceum-hall to large and attentive audiences. The situation of

Danvers — within an hour's ride, by railroad, of the metropolis — is highly favorable for availing herself of the best talent in this field of literary labor.'"

"In December, 1854, a donation of books was unexpectedly received from Mr. Peabody; affording a new proof of his generosity and his continuing interest in the institution that bears his name. These books, in all about two thousand five hundred volumes, were selected by his order, in London, by Mr. Henry Stevens, agent of the Smithsonian Institute. They comprise many valuable and even rare works; among which may be mentioned 'The Philosophical Transactions of the Royal Society,' and a complete set of 'The Gentleman's Magazine.'"

At the laying of the corner-stone of this noble edifice, which has since been enlarged and made more elegant in appearance, Hon. Alfred A. Abbott reminded the hearers, "how, at the early age of eleven years, in the humble capacity of a grocer's boy, in a shop hard by where we now stand, he commenced his life of earnest but successful toil; how, four years after, having sought promotion in another sphere, he found himself, by his father's death and his brother's misfortunes, an orphan, without means, without employment, without friends, and all in the most gloomy times; but how, buoyed up by firm resolve and a high endeavor, he turned his back upon the endeared but now desolate scenes of his boyhood, and sought under a southern sun those smiles of fortune denied him by the frowning skies of his northern home; how, there in Georgetown, in the District of Columbia, he became, while not yet nineteen years old, — such was his capacity and fidelity, — partner in a respectable firm, which afterwards removed to Baltimore, and had branches established in two or three of our principal cities; and how, at length become the head of his house, and having crossed and recrossed the ocean many times in the transaction of his foreign business, he at last, in 1847, established himself permanently in London, having now created an immense business, and amassed a princely fortune; how, through all this career from poverty to opulence, that simple heart and kindly nature, which in youth divided with his orphan brothers and sisters the scanty earnings of his toil, and in later and more prosperous days expanded in social amenities and timely charities to his countrymen in a strange land, — how this true nature remained ever the same, untainted by that proud success which too often corrupts, mellowed only by those growing years which seldom fail to blunt our finer sensibilities; and, lastly, how, while with a private life above reproach, and a professional character distinguished even among the merchant-princes of England, he had come to be pointed out, both at home and abroad, as the model of a man and a merchant; how, all this time, his heart fondly turned to his native country; and how, true to her interests and her honor, in the darkest hour of her adversity, he stood up manfully in her defence, and, throwing patriotism, energy, and capital into the breach, sustained her credit, vindicated her good name, and won the gratitude and received the thanks of sovereign States."

The Hon. Abbott Lawrence laid the corner-stone, previously saying, "I came here as the representative of Mr. George Peabody; and upon that it may generally be asked how Mr. Peabody achieved so much good for his country. I know him well. I have known him for many years. I have seen him day by day, month after month, and year after year; and, for the benefit of the younger portions of this audience, I will tell you how he has achieved all that has been so eloquently portrayed by the honorable gentleman who preceded me. In the first place, Nature gave him a good constitution and a sound mind; secondly, he is a man of indomitable moral courage; thirdly, he has patience, perseverance, industry, and, above all, the strictest integrity.

"Ladies and gentlemen, I know him well: and I can say here, in the face of this summer's sun and this audience, that I deem Mr. George Peabody the very soul of honor; and that is the foundation of his success. Those traits of character I have mentioned — this integrity of purpose and determination — have given him all the success he has achieved."

When the beautiful edifice was dedicated, the eloquent Rufus Choate, himself an Essex-County boy, delivered the address. After saying that the community was happy in such educational provisions, he went on to say, —

" Happy, almost above all, the noble giver whose heart

is large enough to pay of the abundance which crowns his life — to pay out of his single means — the whole debt this generation owes the future. I honor and love him: not merely that his energy, sense, and integrity have raised him from a poor boy, waiting in that shop yonder, to be a guest, as Curran gracefully expressed it, at the table of princes, to spread a table for the entertainment of princes; not merely because the brilliant professional career which has given him a position so commanding in the mercantile and social circles of the commercial capital of the world has left him as completely American, the heart as wholly untravelled, as when he first stepped on the shore of England to seek his fortune, sighing to think that the ocean rolled between him and home; jealous of our honor; wakeful to our interests; helping his country, not by swagger and vulgarity, but by recommending her credit; vindicating her title to be trusted on the exchange of nations; squandering himself in hospitalities to her citizens; a man of deeds, not of words, — not for these merely I love and honor him; but because his nature is affectionate and unsophisticated still; because his memory comes over so lovingly to this sweet Argos; to the schoolroom of his childhood; to the old shop and kind master, and the graves of his father and mother; and because he has had the sagacity and the character to indulge these unextinguished affections in a gift, not of vanity and ostentation, but of supreme and durable utility. With how true and rational a satisfaction might he permit one part of the charitable rich man's epitaph to be written on his grave-stone : ' What I spent, I had ; what I kept, I lost ; what I gave away remains with me ' ! "

On the ninth day of October, 1856, Mr. Peabody was publicly received in his native town. It was a grand ovation. Willing hearts, heads, and hands planned and executed the various details. It was no forced greeting in solemn mockery of the real public sentiment, but a genuine expression of gratitude and respect. There was a grand procession, in which the schools formed a prominent part ; an address of welcome in behalf of the citizens, by Hon. Alfred A. Abbott ; a public dinner and an evening levee, for the purpose of affording opportunity to many of a personal introduction to the man whom Danvers delighted to honor. The day was lovely, the route filled with interested spectators, the houses and streets finely decorated, and the welcome entire.

Mr. Peabody had been offered public honors by the citizens of other places, but would accept none save that invitation which came from his native town. His admirable reply to the New-York deputation is here inserted, that his own pen may tell with what spirit he came back to the land of his birth : —

"NEWPORT, Monday, Sept. 22, 1856.

" GENTLEMEN, — Your letter of the 16th inst. is before me. Allow me to say, without affectation, that no one can be more surprised than myself at the cordial welcome which you extend to me. Had my commercial and social life in London produced even half the results with which your kindness endows it, I should esteem myself more than repaid for all labors there by such a letter, subscribed as it is by many old and dear friends, by gentlemen whose names in letters are co-extensive with the knowledge of our own language, and by merchants whose enterprise has carried the flag of our country into every sea that commerce penetrates.

" If, during my long residence in London, the commercial character and honor of our countrymen have stood upon an elevated position, it has not been the result of my humble efforts. In common with many of you, I have tried to do my part in accomplishing these ends. That the American name now stands where it does in the commercial world, is mainly owing to her merchants at home, who have extended her commerce till its tonnage equals that of any other nation; who have drawn to her shores the wealth of other lands; under whose directions the fertile fields of the interior have been made accessible and peopled; and whose fidelity to their engagements has become proverbial throughout the world.

"It has been my pleasure, during a long residence in London, to renew many old friendships, and to form many new acquaintances, among my countrymen and countrywomen; and it has been my good fortune to be permitted to cultivate these in social life, where I have endeavored as much as possible to bring my British and American friends together. I believed, that, by so doing, I should, in my humble way, assist to remove any prejudices, to soften political asperities, and to promote feelings of good will and fraternity between the two countries. It gives me great pleasure to be assured that my countrymen at home have sympathized in these objects, and have believed that they are partially accomplished. The recent temporary estrange ment between the two governments served to demonstrate how deep and cordial is the alliance between the interests and the sympathies of the two peoples. By aiding to make individuals of the two nations known to each other, I supposed that I was contributing my mite towards the most solid and sure foundation of peace and good will between them ; and, while the power remains to me, I shall continue in a course which you approve.

"In returning to my native land, after an absence of twenty years, I had several objects in view. I wished once more to see the land of my birth and early youth, and the surviving members of my family ; once more to greet my friends in every part of the country ; and to see and know the new generations that have come up since I left, and who are to be their successors. I also desired to visit every section of the Union, and to witness with my own eyes the evidences at home of the prosperity of which I have seen abundant proofs abroad. The twenty years that have elapsed since my last visit are the most impor- tant twenty years in the commercial history of America. Like Rip Van Winkle, I am almost appalled at the won- derful changes that already meet my eyes. Although, as you well know, I have not slumbered meanwhile in a Sleepy Hollow, I stand amazed at the energy and activity which characterize your city. It is my wish and purpose to remain in the country long enough to understand these changes and their causes.

" On mature reflection, gentlemen, I think, that, if I accept the hospitalities which have been tendered to me by yourselves and by friends in Baltimore, Philadelphia, Boston, and other cities, I shall very seriously interfere with the objects of my visit. I have, therefore, been obliged to come to the conclusion to refuse all invitations to dinner, with the single exception of my native town of Danvers in Massachusetts. I assure you most sincerely that I regret very much that my plans thus compel me to decline the high honor which you propose to confer upon me, and to deny myself the pleasure of meeting so many personal friends.

" With great esteem and respect,

" I am, gentlemen, your faithful servant,

" GEORGE PEABODY.

" Messrs. Nathaniel L. & George Griswold; Brown Brothers & Co; Duncan, Sherman, & Co.; Grinnell, Minturn, & Co.; Goodhue & Co.; Wetmore, Cryder, & Co.; Spofford, Tileston, & Co.; A. & A. Lawrence & Co.; Washington Irving; William B. Astor; Daniel Lord; George Newbold; John J. Palmer; William J. Wetmore; Charles Augustus Davis; E. Cunard; and others.

To the eloquent address of welcome Mr. Peabody made the following response : —

" Mr. Abbott and Fellow-Townsmen, — I have listened to your eloquent words of welcome with the most intense emotions, and return you for them my warmest acknowledgments. My heart tells me that this is no common occasion. This vast gathering, comprising many old associates, their children and their grandchildren, to welcome me to the home of my childhood, almost unmans me. Though Providence has granted me an unvaried and unusual success in the pursuit of fortune in other lands, I am still in heart the humble boy who left yonder unpretending dwelling many, *very* many years ago.

"I have felt it necessary to decline many proffered hospitalities: but I could not resist the impulse which prompted me to accept yours, and to revisit the scenes once so familiar; to take you again by the hand, and to tell you how it rejoices my heart to see you.

" You can scarcely imagine how the changes to which you have referred impress me. You have yourselves grown up with them, and have gradually become familiarized with all; but to me, who have been so long away, the effect is almost astounding. It is gratifying to find, however, that these transformations have gone hand in hand with your prosperity and improvement.

" The solitary fields which were the scenes of my boyish sports now resound with the hum of busy labor; and the spirit of improvement, not content with triumph on land, has even converted Foster's mill-pond into solid ground, and made it the scene of active enterprise.

"But time has also wrought changes of a painful nature. Of those I left, the old are all gone. A few of the middle-aged remain, but old and infirm; while the active population consists almost entirely of a new generation.

" I now revert to a more pleasing theme, and call your attention to the brightest portion of the picture of the day.

"One of the most pleasing and touching incidents of this morning is the large number of scholars who have come forth to bid me welcome, and who now surround me. In addressing a few words to you, my dear young friends, I would bid you remember that but a few years will elapse before you will occupy the same position towards your own children which your parents now hold towards yourselves. The training you are now receiving is a precious talent, for the use or abuse of which each will, on a future day, be called upon to give a severe account. May you then be ready to render up that talent with ' usury ' ! There is not a youth within the sound of my voice whose early opportunities and advantages are not very much greater than were my own ; and I have since achieved nothing that is impossible to the most humble boy among you. I hope many a great and good man may arise from among the ranks of Danvers boys assembled here to-day. Bear in mind, however, that, to be truly great, it is not necessary that you should gain wealth and importance. Every boy may become a great man in whatever sphere Providence may call him to move.

"Steadfast and undeviating truth, fearless and straight-forward integrity, and an honor ever unsullied by an unworthy word or action, make their possessor greater than worldly success or prosperity. These qualities constitute greatness: without them you will never enjoy the good opinion of others, or the approbation of a good conscience.

"To my young female friends I would say, Remember that there have been and are great women as well as great men, — great in their domestic graces, as daughters, as wives, and as mothers; and I trust that future times may record many a name so distinguished, whose seeds of good were sown within this town. And allow me to hope that my eye now rests upon some of them.

"May the advice I have given you be impressed upon your young hearts! It is given with great sincerity by one who has had much experience in the world; and, although Providence has smiled upon all his labors, he has never ceased to feel and lament the want of that early education which is now so freely offered to each one of you. This is the first time we have met; it may prove the last: but, while I live, I shall ever feel a warm interest in your welfare. God bless you all!"

At the dinner, there were also addresses; among them, one by Henry J. Gardner, then Governor of Massachusetts. He said, —

" In response to a sentiment complimentary to Massachusetts, I am always proud to raise my voice; and, responsive to this allusion in honor of her institutions, I think to-day, in this presence, an answer may be peculiarly fitting. I have never before participated in an occasion of this kind. Where was there one? A young man, with no other capital, as you well said, but his hands and his integrity, going abroad across the waters unheralded and unknown; by his own industry and integrity distinguishing himself among his fellows, and, in the good gifts of Providence showered upon him every hour of every year, seeking how he might benefit his countrymen at home [cheers]; rendering his name illustrious, also, for his princely hospitality, and his commercial house, to which you refer, a proverb upon the marts and commercial highways of nations, — to see such a one return, so honored and so beloved, to the scene of his birth, is indeed a new and interesting event.

" But I cannot, I will not, detain you. I cannot, however, but refer to one circumstance in the career of your distinguished guest, which makes me peculiarly proud, and feel deeply honored now to address him. He is a merchant: he belongs to that fraternity to which my own humble life and services have been devoted. It has not the glittering attraction of the warrior, whose fame can be carved out by his sword upon the battle-field; it has not, ladies and gentlemen, that attraction which he who spreads abroad the glad tidings to all nations finds in his

profession; it has not the attraction of legal or of political excitement; it has not, necessarily, — though there
are many exceptions, — it has not, I say, necessarily, that
connection with the cultivation of the intellect, the
improvement of the mind, which the learned professions,
so called, always require: but, sir, you and I know it
has its pride and its value. There must be patient attention to petty details, to exacting, minute transactions;
there must be great and careful and prudent attention
paid to them all, hour after hour, and day after day: but,
when the successful result is reached, there is a compen-
sation in that very success itself, and high honor in the
means by which it has been attained.

" And, sir, in your career there is much that the young
merchants of Massachusetts can profit by. In the first
place, they can take a lesson from that integrity of purpose of which we all to-day have read upon banner, upon
house, upon staff, and upon the faces and in the words of
our citizens. We can see, too, in your career, — where
the siren Hope in early days beckoned you where deeper
waters ran, and pointed to the furled sail at the mast-
head, — how you stood resolutely on in your own path of
duty, and defied the siren-song. There is in that a lesson
for the young merchants of Massachusetts to remember.
[Cheers.]

" But further, beyond and above all this, when Providence in his mercy has filled your treasury to overflowing,
when you have reached the goal of all your anticipations,

—all you ever could have hoped or desired, — ay, there is a lesson, my friends, for the young and the old merchants all to bear in mind as to the manner in which those rich rewards have been distributed."   [Loud cheers.]

The Hon. Edward Everett also spoke eloquently, and, among other true words, said, —

" Mr. President, — I suppose you have called upon me to respond to this interesting toast chiefly because I filled, a few years ago, a place abroad which made me in some degree the associate of your distinguished guest in the kindly office of promoting good will between the two great branches of the Anglo-Saxon or Anglo-Norman race (for I do not think it matters much by which name you call it) — 'the fair mother and the fairer daughter' — to which the toast alludes.   At all events, I had much opportunity, during my residence in England, to witness the honorable position of Mr. Peabody in the commercial and social circles of London; his efforts to make the citizens of the two countries favorably known tc each other; and, generally, that course of life and conduct which has contributed to procure him the well-deserved honors of this day, and which shows that he fully enters into the spirit of the sentiment just propounded from the chair.

.   .   .   .

" Your quiet village, my friends, has not gone forth in eager throngs to meet the successful financier ; the youth ful voices to which we listened with such pleasure in the morning have not been attuned to sing the praises of the prosperous banker. No: it is the fellow-citizen, who, from the arcades of the London exchange, laid up treasure in the hearts of his countrymen; the true patriot, who, amidst the splendors of the Old World's capital, said in his heart, 'If I forget thee, O Jerusalem! let my right hand forget her cunning; if I do not remember thee, let my tongue cleave to the roof of my mouth.' It is the dutiful and grateful child and benefactor of old Danvers whom you welcome back to his home.

"Yes, sir; and the property you have invested in yonder simple edifice, and in providing the means of innocent occupation for hours of leisure, — of instructing the minds and forming the intellectual character, not merely of the generation now rising, but of that which shall take their places when the heads of those dear children who so lately passed in happy review before you shall be as gray as mine, and of others, still more distant, who shall plant kind flowers on our graves, — it is the property you have laid up in this investment which will embalm your name in the blessings of posterity, when granite and marble shall crumble to dust. Moth and rust shall not corrupt it: they might as easily corrupt the pure white portals of the heavenly city, where 'every several gate is of one pearl.' Thieves shall not break through and steal it: they might as easily break through the vaulted sky, and steal the brightest star in the firmament."

Mr. Everett concluded by playfully referring to the sentiment sent by Mr. Peabody to the centennial assembly, in these words: "Now, we all know, that, on an occasion of this kind, a loose slip of paper, such as a sentiment is apt to be written on, is in danger of being lost: a puff of air is enough to blow it away. Accordingly, just by way of paper-weight, — just to keep the toast safe on the table, and also to illustrate his view of this new way of paying old debts, — Mr. Peabody laid down twenty thousand dollars on the top of his sentiment; and, for the sake of still greater security, has since added about as much more. Hence it has come to pass that this excellent sentiment has sunk deep into the minds of our Danvers friends, and has, I suspect, mainly contributed to the honors and pleasures of this day.

"But I have occupied, Mr. President, much more than my share of your time; and, on taking my seat, I will only congratulate you on this joyful occasion, as I congratulate our friend and guest at having had it in his power to surround himself with so many smiling faces and warm hearts."

Other excellent speeches and many good letters also marked this pleasant occasion; but space forbids further reference to them. Are they not all chronicled finely in the memorial volume published by order of the committee of arrangements?

CHAPTER VI.

GOOD GIFTS CONTINUED.

The Donation to Thetford, Vt. — Grandfather Dodge. — The Wood-
Sawing Story.

> " What you desire of him, he partly begs
>   To be desired to give. It much would please him,
>   That of his fortunes you would make a staff
>   To lean upon." — SHAKSPEARE: *Antony and Cleopatra.*

> " Give, and it shall be given." — LUKE vi. 38.

TO a communication addressed to the trustees of the Peabody Library at Thetford, Vt., the Rev. A. T. Deming, Chairman of the Board, very kindly responded as follows : —

" We have, as yet, *no printed* account of Mr. Peabody's gift ; though we hope to have one soon in connection with the printed catalogue.

" The following embraces, I think, the material facts which you desire.

" During the fall of 1866, Mr. Peabody, while visiting friends here, expressed his desire to do something in be-

102

half of the place. The citizens assembled Aug. 6, 1866, and passed the following resolutions: —

" '*Resolved*, That we most gratefully appreciate the benevolence of Mr. George Peabody, and do extend to him our hearty thanks for the very generous and munificent gift which he proposes to make us for the purpose of a village library; and will most cheerfully carry out the plan he presents in establishing it; and, in accordance therewith, have elected Dr. H. H. Niles and Isaiah Coburn as trustees, to act with those already chosen by him.

" '*Resolved*, That the library shall take the name of its munificent founder, and be called " The Peabody Library."

" '*Resolved*, That Rev. Charles Scott be appointed a committee to present the above resolutions to the donor, and request him to make such conditions and regulations respecting said fund as he may deem proper.'

" The resolutions were accordingly forwarded, and the following response from Mr. Peabody received: —

" ' GEORGETOWN, September, 1866.

" 'To Rev. C. SCOTT, Chairman of Peabody-Library Committee, Post Mills, Vt.

" '*Dear Sir*, — I have to acknowledge the receipt from you of the resolutions of the citizens of Post Mills in regard to my proposed gift of a library to that village: and, in accordance with the desire therein expressed, I beg to state my wishes in regard to the management of the library.

" ' Of the $5,000 which I proposed giving for the purpose mentioned, I have placed $1,500 in the hands of Samuel T. Dana, Esq., of the firm of Dana & Co., South Market Street, Boston, subject to your order when money shall from time to time be required for building-purposes or for the purchase of books; he allowing you interest at the rate of five per cent per annum in account.

" ' For $1,500 of the remainder, I have employed Mr. H. G. Somerby of London (a friend who has bought largely for me for other libraries) to purchase standard and useful books as the foundation of your library; and I am sure they will prove cheaper and better than we could get them in this country. I think they will be here by the first of January next. You can, therefore, go on with your building accordingly.

" ' With the remaining $2,000 I have purchased two gold-bearing coupon-bonds of the United States, of the denomination of $1,000, numbers 33,194 and 60,182,— popularly called five-forties. These I bought for you on my return, and they are now worth nearly seventy dollars over cost; the two bonds being in the hands of S. T. Dana, who holds them for your account.

" ' It is my wish, and a condition of my gift, that this sum of $2,000 shall always remain and be kept permanently invested by the trustees or library committee in United-States bonds or other safe securities as a library-fund, the income of which shall be applied to the purchase of books or other wants of the library, as their discretion may determine.

" 'It is my wish that the privileges of the library shall be enjoyed (under such restrictions, as to suitable age or character, as may from time to time be made by the trustees, or committee having it in charge) by the inhabitants of the two school-districts in the town of Thetford, which are comprised in the village of Post Mills; and I would suggest that these privileges may be extended in particular cases, at the discretion of the library-officers, to others, who, though not within the above limits, may reside near them, and may be in the habit of doing business at the village of Post Mills.

" 'And wishing, as I have ever done, to encourage and cherish a spirit of harmony and good will among all, it is my desire that at no time shall any preference or distinction be made in the selection of books, or in any matter connected with the library, on account of any political party or religious sect; and it is my wish, that, whenever a minister or ministers of the gospel are or may be settled in Post Mills Village, he or they may be upon the library committee.

" ' The motive which has most strongly impelled me to make this gift is my sense of gratitude for kindness shown me in my early life by my late revered uncle, Eliphalet Dodge, and his excellent wife, who still lives in your village. It is therefore my desire that there shall always be three of their descendants, and bearing their name (so long as there shall remain so many of them inhabitants of Post Mills Village), among the trustees of the library, sanc tioned by yourself and others.

" ' I have selected as a site for the library-building a lot of land which has been given for the purpose by Harvey Dodge, Esq., and which appears to me to be central, and eminently suitable for the location.

" ' I will send you Mr. Dana's letter of acknowledgment for the two bonds, and the money, in a few days.

" ' I am, with great respect,

" ' Your obedient servant,

" ' GEORGE PEABODY.'

" Sept. 15, a meeting of the inhabitants of the village was held, the above letter of Mr. Peabody read, and a series of resolutions passed unanimously.

" The resolutions provided for the appointment of officers, and otherwise carrying out the wishes expressed in the preceding letter.

" March 1, 1867, Mr. Peabody penned the following: —

" ' 91 LAFAYETTE STREET, SALEM, MASS., March 1, 1867.

" ' *Dear Sir*, — Understanding from your letter to me, received to-day, that your library-building will require, to complete it, $500 in addition to the sum allowed for that purpose from the $5,000 already given, I enclose a check on New York for the same, payable to your order.

" ' Very respectfully yours,

" ' GEORGE PEABODY.

" ' Mr. WM. DODGE.'

" Aug. 17, 1869, a full-sized portrait of Mr. Peabody was received at the library. A series of resolutions passed by the trustees upon its reception was published in 'The Vermont Chronicle.' Possibly you have seen them.

"On receiving intelligence of Mr. Peabody's death, the trustees and friends of the library passed the following testimonial of respect to his memory:—

"'God, in his providence, having removed by death Mr. George Peabody, the founder of this library; and it being eminently fitting that some record should be made of our appreciation of his excellences, and our grateful sense of his benefactions: therefore

"'*Resolved*, That we bow in humble submission to the all-wise providence of God in the removal of this our friend and benefactor; remembering that to this same all-wise and gracious providence Mr. Peabody was accustomed to attribute all the honor of what he was enabled to become and to accomplish.

"'*Resolved*, That we record, with thankfulness to the Father of all mercies, our high appreciation of the character and life of Mr. Peabody, our high estimate of his pre-eminent financial abilities, of his sterling integrity, and of his republican simplicity, unshaken by the applause of the multitude or the attentions of the great.

"'*Resolved*, That, with a still deeper gratitude, we record our high sense of the value of his work as a philanthropist, in ministering with princely munificence to the education of the ignorant, and to the comfort and elevation of the poor; and this both in the land of his adoption and in his native land, elsewhere and in this community.

" 'Resolved, That, with equal gratitude, we record his earnest efforts to heal the wounds of war and spread the arts of peace in the two leading nations of the earth; and express the hope that his name, now received as a heritage by England and America, may form another strand in the cord binding these great powers together in amity.

" 'Resolved, That, as trustees and friends of this library, we pledge ourselves anew to carry out the wishes of the benevolent donor, and to hold up for imitation before us, and before the minds of the people of this community, his commendable traits of character and of life.' "

A writer in " The Boston Traveller " says, concerning the donation to Thetford, " All the newspaper biographies of the great philanthropist state, that, at the age of fifteen, he spent a year with his grandfather at Post Mills Village, Thetford, Vt.; and all lists of his benefactions mention his gift of some thousands of dollars for a library in that village. This gift was made while on a visit to his relatives there, during his last visit but one to his native country. Perhaps some things which I happen to know about the grandfather and family and residence may interest some of your readers.

" Post Mills is a little village in the north-west corner of. Thetford, containing, at the time of George's visit, a grist-mill and saw-mill, a schoolhouse, one or two variety-stores, a blacksmith's shop, a tavern, and probably a young phy-sician; though Dr. Niles may have settled there a year or two later. The rest of the people were farmers of mod-erate means: some of whom, however, occasionally made shoes or put up barns for their neighbors. The nearest house of worship was five miles south, on Thetford Hill, where lived the Rev. Asa Burton, D.D., well known throughout New England as a teacher in theology, and as the great promulgator and defender of the 'Taste Scheme.' Jeremiah Dodge, George's grandfather, lived in a small, neat, white, two-story house, a little out of the village, on the north side of the road leading east to the Connec-ticut River, and Oxford, N.H. His son Eliphalet lived a few rods farther east, on the south side of the road, in a one-story farmhouse, unpainted, unless it had once been slightly tinged with Spanish brown. Their farm was almost wholly on the south side of the road. I do not know its exact size; probably one hundred acres or more: much of it, around the houses, beautifully level, and rea-sonably fertile. He had a large family of boys and girls, by whose help the labor of the farm was done.

"Another son, Daniel, was a 'master mariner,' and lived with his father when at home. He commanded a ship which sailed from New York for Canton, with orders to trade between Canton and Acheen in Sumatra three years, and then load at Canton and return. Before the three years had quite expired, he inferred from the news-papers that war was imminent between the United States and England, — the war of 1812. He therefore loaded and returned to New York as quickly as possible; arriving just in season to escape capture by the first British squadron sent to blockade the coast. As his trips to Acheen had been successful, and as the price of China goods had risen, and continued to rise, on account of the war, the voyage proved very profitable to the owners.

"Jeremiah Dodge, when I first knew him, some ten years afterwards, was a white-headed old man, too feeble, from age, for the severe labor of the farm, but still erect in his posture, and commonly busy about such light work as he needed to keep him from the tedium of idleness. He was a very quiet man; never obtrusive, but always affable; never excited, never talkative; but showing, when occasion called for it, — which was not often, — a keen, quiet wit, which raised a smile among the hearers, and commonly closed an argument to which he had been listening. His wife was several years younger, more active, and, though not a talkative woman, was more ready to engage in conversation than her husband. They were both members of the church in Thetford: but, about the time last mentioned, a house of worship was erected at Post Mills; and they, with the other Congregationalists at that place, transferred their membership to the church in West Fairlee, worshipping there and at Post Mills on alternate sabbaths. As church-members, they were too old to be very active; but nobody ever accused them of any thing, either in the way of omission or commission, inconsistent with their profession.

"With such grandparents and such surroundings, George Peabody's year at Post Mills must have been a year of intense quiet, with good examples always before him, and good advice whenever occasion called for it; for Mr. Dodge and his wife were both too shrewd to bore him with it needlessly. It was on his return from this visit that he spent a night at a tavern in Concord, N.H., and paid for his entertainment by sawing wood the next morning. That, however, must have been a piece of George's own voluntary economy: for Jeremiah Dodge would never have sent his grandson home to Danvers without the means of procuring the necessaries of life on the way; and still less, if possible, would Mrs. Dodge. Perhaps he told them that he did not need any help, relying on his own ability to make his way home, without burdening them with the expense; but, more probably, he just saw a chance for an hour or two of profitable labor, and took advantage of it to save money for other uses.

"The interest with which Mr. Peabody remembered this visit to Post Mills is shown by his second visit so late in life, and his gift of a library, — as large a library as that place needs. Of its influence on his character and subsequent career, of course, there is no record. Perhaps it was not much. But, at least, it gave him a good chance for quiet thinking, at an age when he needed it; and the labors of the farm may have been useful both to mind and body.

"It has been reported that he wished his relatives at

Post Mills to give a lot for the library-building; but they declined. It may be that he mentioned such a thing; but I cannot believe that he urged it. The people of that village are better able to buy a suitable building-lot than they are to give it; and the building is placed in a better location than could be found for it anywhere on their farm. From the well-known character of the family, it may be fairly presumed that they contributed their just proportion for the purchase of the lot."

Dr. Hanaford furnishes the following explanation for this chapter: —

"In this connection," he says, "it is proper to refer to at least one of the many erroneous statements that have appeared in the public prints, and, of course, gained some credence, in reference to the early history of Mr. Peabody. I refer to the statement, that, in his poverty, he was obliged to walk from Georgetown to Thetford, and that he sawed wood for his lodging while spending the night at Concord, N.H. Perhaps there was more foundation for this report than for some others; though his father was in humble circumstances, yet not so much so as to demand such fatigues and privations of the lad. The foundation for some of the items of the report were the following: While Mr. Peabody, in the latter part of his life, was spending a short time in that place, on one occasion, while in the company of Judge Upham and others, one of the company asked him if he had ever visited Concord before. He replied that he had in his early life, and that he sawed wood for his lodging at the hotel. At that moment something occurred to divert his attention, and he failed to explain the circumstances. In his boyhood, when about to visit friends at Thetford, a marketman who had been to the city, and was on his return, stopped at his father's house, and a passage for the lad was engaged. In accordance with the custom of the times, the food was probably taken (sometimes, in winter, 'bean-porridge,' frozen, with a cord in it, and hung upon the load), demanding only lodging for the driver, &c. The night was spent at Concord. The marketman arrived before night: but, as there was no convenient place to stop north of Concord, where the night would overtake him if he drove on, he decided to spend the night there; which gave the young Peabody some little time to look about. He soon made the acquaintance of a boy of about his own age; and, being passionately fond of fishing, he asked his new friend to go with him. But the boy, who was connected with the hotel, informed him that he had a stint, or ' stent ' as it was generally pronounced, and that he could not go until his task was performed. Accordingly, the two finished the labor, and then enjoyed their recreation.

" When the man called for his bill the next morning, he declined to ' take any thing for that boy, as he helped my boy saw wood.' These circumstances, probably, gave rise to the whole statement; the principal foundation being that he did pay for his lodging in that manner, though the sawing of the wood was not intended for that purpose.

It is highly probable, however, that he would not have declined any honest employment if necessary, even in after-life, if the circumstances had demanded such service; since he was a man who would prefer menial service to a dishonorable act, while he was remarkable for his industry, and strict and methodical attention to business."

CHAPTER VII.

STILL GIVING.

Peabody Institute at Baltimore. — Letter of Mr. Peabody. — Proceedings in Regard to the Donation. — Mr. Peabody's Remarks.

> " The classic days, those mothers of romance,
> That roused a nation for a woman's glance;
> The age of mystery, with its hoarded power,
> That girt the tyrant in his storied tower, —
> Have passed and faded like a dream of youth;
> And riper eras ask for history's truth." — BRYANT: *The Ages.*

"Every man also to whom God hath given riches and wealth, and hath given him power to eat thereof, and to take his portion, and to rejoice in his labor, — this is the gift of God." — ECCLES. v. 19.

AMONG the gifts of the man whom God greatly prospered after he removed to England was one of great value to the city of his early business success. After an absence of twenty years from his native land, Mr. Peabody fulfilled his intention, long before formed, of founding in the city of Baltimore an Institute comprising a large free library, the periodical delivery of lectures by eminent literary and scientific men, an academy of music, a gallery of art, and kindred purposes.

A trustee of that Institute says, " The annals of Baltimore, ever since Baltimore could boast the honors of a city, exhibit no act of private munificence, no act of associated philanthropy, nor, perhaps, even of public official benefaction, which, in the scope of its design of usefulness to the community, or in the prodigal generosity of the means contributed to its accomplishment, may claim the admiration and gratitude of our citizens by a merit so clear and unquestionable as the Institute which George Peabody this day offers to the city. An endowment amounting to a million of dollars has been appropriated to the establishment and completion of a broad and permanent structure of public education, which, when brought to its full development, is destined to become the well-spring of perennial and profuse bounty to many generations of the people of Baltimore and Maryland."

These words of the trustee were spoken on the day when the Institute was inaugurated in 1866; and he further said, —

" The stately edifice in which we are now assembled is but the first flower of this noble design. A great part of the work is not yet even begun. When the whole is finished, the Institute will stand in this apex of the city, the fairest of the buildings that adorn its triple hills. Here, in the centre of the most beautiful city-landscapes, its majestic figure reposing at the foot of the matchless column which symbolizes the immortality of the Father of our Union, it will be the second object to challenge the admiration of the passing stranger; whilst it will ever attract the veneration and gratitude of our own people, and the thousands of their descendants, who, through the lapse of years, shall be privileged to frequent its halls, and draw from its wells of living water exhaustless draughts of wisdom and virtue. Still more distinctly will it stand a cherished monument to perpetuate in the affection of our posterity the enviable memory of a patriot who served his country with imperial munificence. Let us add, it will stand for ages as the memorial of a good man whom Providence had blessed with a prosperity almost as lavish as his virtue, with a renown almost as rare as his wise appreciation of the true use of riches."

In his first letter, referring to his benefaction, dated Feb. 12, 1857, Mr. Peabody, after expressing his wishes in reference to the scope and character of the Institute, closed with the following excellent suggestions: —

" I must not omit to impress upon you a suggestion for the government of the Institute, which I deem to be of the highest moment, and which I desire shall be ever present to the view of the board of trustees. My earnest wish to promote at all times a spirit of harmony and good will in society, my aversion to intolerance, bigotry, and party rancor, and my enduring respect and love for the happy institutions of our prosperous republic, impel me to express the wish that the Institute I have proposed to you shall always be strictly guarded against the possibility of being made a theatre for the dissemination or discussion of sectarian theology or party politics; that it shall never minister, in any manner whatever, to political dissension, to infidelity, to visionary theories of a pretended philosophy, which may be aimed at the subversion of the approved morals of society; that it shall never lend its aid or influence to the propagation of opinions tending to create or encourage sectional jealousies in our happy country, or which may lead to the alienation of the people of one State or section of the Union from those of another: but that it shall be so conducted, throughout its whole career, as to teach political and religious charity, toleration, and beneficence, and prove itself to be, in all contingencies and conditions, the true friend of our inestimable Union, of the salutary institutions of free government, and of liberty regulated by law. I enjoin these precepts upon the board of trustees, and their successors forever, for their invariable observance and enforcement in the administration of the duties I have confided to them.

"And now, in conclusion, I have only to express my wish, that, in providing for the building you are to erect, you will allow space for future additions, in case they may be found necessary; and that, in its plan, style of architecture, and adaptation to its various uses, it may be worthy of the purpose to which it is dedicated, and may serve to embellish a city whose prosperity, I trust, will ever be distinguished by an equal growth in knowledge and virtue.

"I am, with great respect,

"Your friend,

"GEORGE PEABODY."

The munificent donation of Mr. Peabody was partially expended in the erection of a white-marble edifice, which was completed in 1861. The sad years of civil war forbade its formal dedication till Oct. 25, 1866, when Mr. Peabody was able to be present. Rev. Dr. Backus, pastor of the First Presbyterian Church, offered prayer, in which he said, "We thank Thee that Thou hast put it into the mind and heart of Thy servant, whom Thou hast so highly blessed and prospered, to employ so large a portion of the talents intrusted to him in securing the well-being and happiness of this community; that, allured from grosser pleasures and inferior pursuits, they may seek that intellectual and moral improvement which may tend to their true elevation, refinement, usefulness, and pleasure,— binding them together in social harmony and unity; making this city a centre of increasing light and purity, and exerting a happy influence throughout the land.

"May he be spared to see the ripe fruits of his noble and generous benefactions, experience the satisfaction of having been in Thy hands the instrument of lasting good to his race, and receive not only the gratitude of those who shall enjoy the benefits of this Institute through coming ages, but also be replenished with the richest blessings of Thy providence and grace, so that his declining years may be full of peace and hope and joy! and, when he has accomplished his work on earth, may he be gathered to his fathers, full of honors, enjoying the respect of mankind, peace of conscience, and an abundant entrance into the kingdom of our Lord and Saviour Jesus Christ! and may numbers rise up, not only to call him blessed, but also to imitate his example!"

After this, the Governor of Maryland addressed Mr. Peabody in language appropriate to the occasion; and Mr. Peabody responded. A portion of the governor's speech, and the whole of Mr. Peabody's reply, are already given in a previous chapter.

On the Friday after the dedication of the Institute, the school-children, some twenty thousand in number, greeted Mr. Peabody; and from the steps of the Institute he addressed them in the following excellent words: —

" When I arrived in Baltimore on Wednesday, my dear young friends, I did not expect to meet you thus; but finding, by a visit from your School-Commissioners' Board, that such was your desire, I concluded to meet you, even should it be necessary to postpone my departure from Baltimore beyond the time originally fixed. And I take to myself no credit for doing so: for I assure you that my desire to see you is as strong as yours can possibly be to see me; and never have I seen a more beautiful sight than this vast collection of interesting children. The review of the finest army, with soldiers clothed in brilliant uniforms, and attended by the most delightful strains of martial music, could never give me half the pleasure that it does to look upon you here with your bright and happy faces. For the sight of such an army as I have spoken of would be associated with thoughts of bloodshed and human suffering, of strife and violence: but I may well compare you, on the other hand, to an army of peace ; and your mission on earth is not to destroy your fellow-creatures, but to be a blessing to them; and your path, when you go out from these public schools, is to be marked, not by ravages and desolation, but, I trust, by kindly words and actions, and by good will to all you meet.

" With such an assemblage as this, therefore, I am glad to have my name associated, as I see that it is by the badges worn by many of you: and I shall feel it to be a very great honor if the medals thus bearing my name shall continue, as I am informed they have heretofore done, to prove incentives to application, diligence, and good conduct; and I shall ever take a sincere interest in those to whom they are awarded.

" There is another relation in which I look upon you; and that is, the future guardians of the Institute from which I speak to you. For, in a few short years, you will have left the places you now occupy, and, taking the positions of those now in active life, will have the care and enjoy the privileges of this institution. And I hope most earnestly that it may be the means of all the good to you that was contemplated in its foundation ; and that you, on your part, may see that it is carried on always with kind feeling and harmony. And so I trust, my dear young friends, that in passing by this edifice, young though you are now, you will feel, in looking upon it, not that it is one for grown-up

men and women, and with which you have no concern,
but that it is yours also; that you will at no distant day have
a right in it as your heritage; and so will even now, in
your tender years, take an interest in it and all things connected with it.

" I have now but little advice to give you; for I am sure
that your parents and teachers have bestowed, and always
will bestow, upon you the kindest and most earnest counsel: but I would say, Attend closely to your studies, and
remember that your close attention to them is a thousand
times more important to you than to your teachers. Bear
in mind, that the time of your studies, though it may now
appear long to you, is, in reality, very brief; and at a future
day, when it is, perhaps, too late, you yourselves will feel
that it is so. Do not be ashamed to ask advice and take
counsel from those older than yourselves: the time will
come when you, in your turn, may advise those younger
than you, and who will follow in your footsteps. Strive
always to imitate the good example of others. I am glad
that your assemblage is in this most interesting place: for
I hope that your future recollections of this occasion may
be connected with the thought of him whose statue crowns
yonder beautiful monument, — the illustrious father of
his country, — and that you may be induced to take him
more and more for your model; for he, pre-eminently
great among men, was also great and good in his boyhood
and youth. As time has passed, it has rendered eulogy of
him as superfluous as if it were to praise the sun for its

brightness; and it is as the most perfect example for imitation the world has ever seen that we must look upon the character of Washington. Remember, then, his youthful life ; the instances, too familiar to need repeating by me, of his truthfulness, his self-denial, his integrity, his perseverance, his reverence for age, his affection for his parents, and his fear of God. Finally, strive always to act as if the eye of your heavenly Father were upon you; and, if you do this, his countenance will always smile upon you.

" I fear, my young friends, this · is the last time I shall ever speak to you. I therefore bid you farewell. God bless you all !"

From the report of the treasurer, it may be seen, that, in all, George Peabody gave to the Peabody Institute in Baltimore the sum of one million dollars. A princely benefaction for a desirable end !

CHAPTER VIII.

GREATER BENEFACTIONS.

Amelioration of the Condition of the Poor in London. — Magnificent Bequest of Mr. Peabody. — Description of the Buildings.

> "O ye who bask in Fortune's sun,
> And Hope's bright garlands wear!
> Your blessings from the God of love
> Let his poor children share." — MRS. HALE.

"He that hath pity upon the poor, lendeth to the Lord; and that which he hath given will he pay him again." — PROV. xix, 17.

WHEN, in 1859, Mr. Peabody returned to England from a visit to his native land, he set about giving effect to his long-cherished intentions of doing something for the laboring poor of London.   For this purpose, he donated $1,750,000 between March 1, 1862, and Dec. 5, 1868.   It is said that Mr. Peabody did not bestow many gifts to relieve individual poverty or distress.   He thought that much of the money thus contributed only tended to increase the evil it sought to alleviate.   "The Philadelphia Press" contrasts the wisdom of George Peabody, who was the executor of his own liberal schemes, with the folly of Dr. Rush of that city, who left a million-dollars' bequest in such a shape that no one is satisfied.

Col. J. W. Forney, in his interesting "Letters from Europe," speaks of the magnificent bequest of Mr. Peabody, and describes his visit to Peabody Square; previously mentioning Mr. Peabody as he saw him on board "The Scotia" when he was returning to England. His glowing sentences are cheerfully inserted here. Says the colonel, "A more congenial company never sailed from the New World to the Old; and, when we separate, the regret at parting will be increased by the recollection that our intercourse might have been profitably prolonged. Of course, George Peabody is the central figure of our circle. As I studied the venerable philanthropist, yesterday, as he lay dozing on one of the sofas in the forward saloon, I confessed I had never seen a nobler or more imposing figure. Never has human face spoken more humane emotions. The good man's soul seems to shine out of every feature and lineament. His fine head, rivalling the best of the old aristocracy, and blending the ideals of benevolence and integrity, his tranquil and pleasing countenance, and his silver hair, crown a lofty form of unusual dignity and grace. The work of this one plain American citizen silences hypercriticism, and challenges gratitude. He has completed it without leaving an excuse for ridicule or censure. He has given millions to deserving charity, without pretence or partiality. The wealth gathered by more than a generation of honest enterprise and business sagacity he distributes among the poor of the two nations in which he accumulated it, first liberally providing for his own blood and kindred. If this is not an honorable close of a well-spent life, what is? That the example of George Peabody will awaken imitation in England, I do not know. Unhappily for the British aristocracy, they do not respond to the call of a genial philanthropy; and it may be claimed that none but an American can truly feel for the sufferings of the unfriended poor. Therefore I am not surprised, that, before Mr. Peabody left the United States, he was satisfied that what he has done for London will be surpassed by two of his opulent friends for the city of New York. . . . Mr. Peabody leaves 'The Scotia' at Queenstown, Ireland, where he will stay for some time to enjoy the salmon-fishing, in company with his old friend, Sir Curtis Lampson, an American, recently made a baronet for his services in connection with the Atlantic Telegraph. As showing the difference between the great landholders of Great Britain and the sturdy farmers of the United States, it deserves to be recorded, that, for the privilege of catching trout and salmon for six months, Mr. Peabody pays the neat sum of $2,500 in gold to the nobleman who owns the stream in which he intends to angle. These preserves of game and fish are, therefore, not only a source of pleasure, but of large profit, to their titled proprietors. Mr. Peabody has offered me letters to his agents in London, which I will not fail to use, for the purpose of personally inspecting the commencement of the great work in that city, which will associate his name with all that is noble and generous, as long as the genius of Shakspeare and Milton is remembered and cherished among the sons of men."

A few days later, Col. Forney wrote, —

" LIVERPOOL, ENGLAND, May 13, 1867.

"Mr. Peabody and over sixty of the passengers of ' The Scotia ' took leave of us about midnight of Friday in an open tug and in the midst of a smart shower, which, before they reached the shore, increased to a heavy storm of rain. . . . On the day he bade us farewell, a characteristic incident took place between Mr. Peabody and the committee appointed by the Americans on board, when they tendered him their resolutions of grateful respect for his many friendly acts of benevolence. One of the resolutions referred to the fact, that, whereas Smithson and Girard had bequeathed their benefactions to the care of posterity, Mr. Peabody had enhanced the value of his example by courageously becoming his own executor, and by giving his personal care to the execution of his splendid trust. When this resolution was read to him, he asked that it might be read a second time ; after which, with a winning courtesy I shall not soon forget, he said that he would be greatly obliged if the whole passage could be stricken out of the proceedings. ' Whatever may be said of me,' he added, ' and however just your abstract view may be, yet even the shadow of a contrast that might be construed into a criticism upon these two illustrious men should be carefully avoided. They did their best, and they did nobly, and, if they had thought of it, would probably have taken exactly my course.' The suggestion was instantly complied with."

.   .   .   .

"MAY 25, 1867.

" This morning, in company with Sir Curtis M. Lampson, one of the trustees of the Peabody Fund for the benefit of the poor of London, and Mr. Somerby, the secretary of the board (both born in the United States), I made my promised visit to Peabody Square, Islington, one of the five structures already in use, or soon to be devoted to the noble objects of the generous founder. Mr. Lampson, a native of New England, was, in October, 1866, created a baronet by Queen Victoria, in token of his numerous public services, but particularly for his connection with the successful enterprise, — the Atlantic Telegraph Cable. I found him, like Mr. Somerby, nevertheless, a devoted admirer of America and her institutions, and a genuine sympathizer in her progress and her principles. The management of the trust has been properly confided to gentlemen of known American proclivities. Lord Stanley is president, assisted by Sir Curtis Lampson, Sir Emerson Tennett, Mr. J. L. Morgan the eminent banker, and Mr. Somerby as secretary; and the manner in which they have so far discharged their duty is proved by the singular success that has crowned their labors. With the

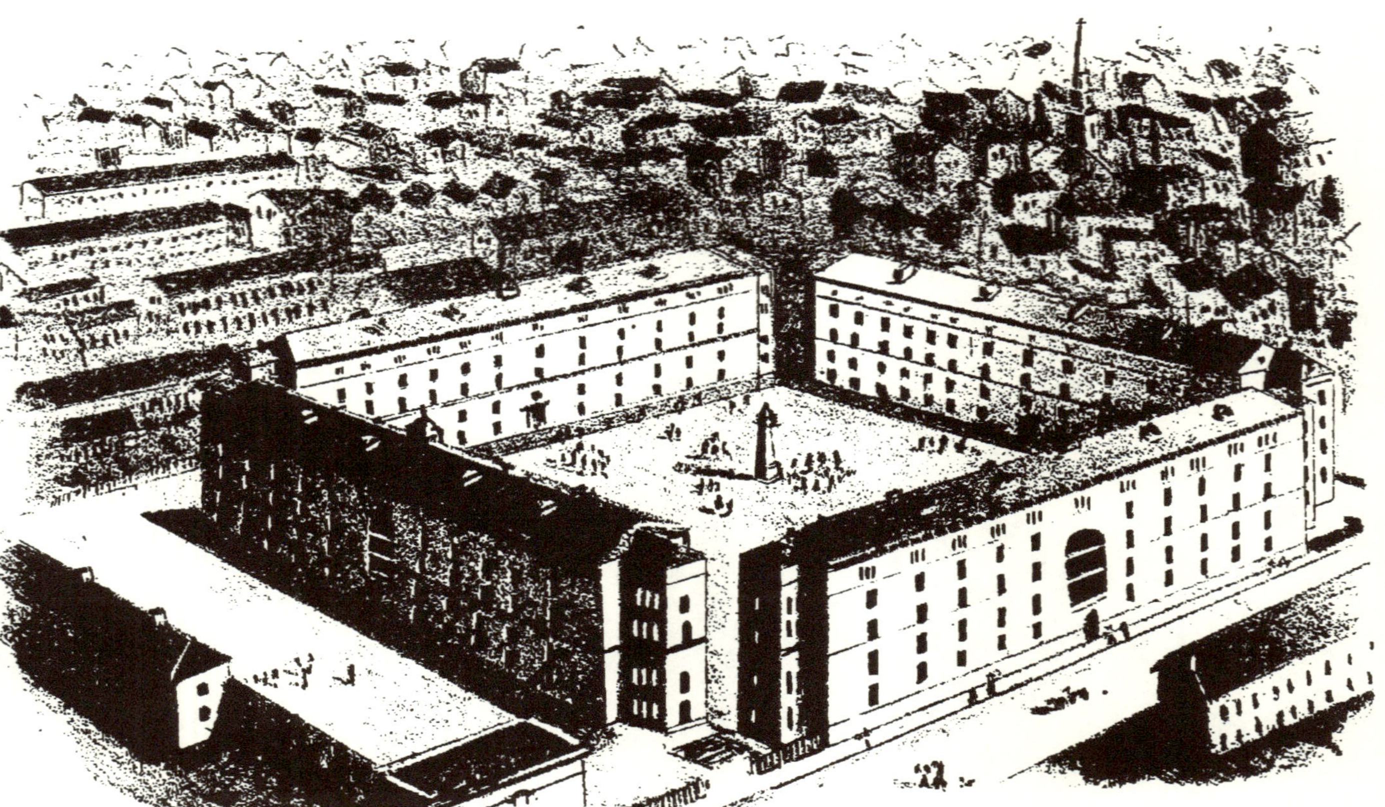

PEABODY SQUARE, ISLINGTON, LONDON

exception of the secretary, they all serve without remuneration. The first difficulty they met was how to define the phrase 'the poor,' and decide in what shape (after that problem was solved) the money should be distributed. After careful reflection, they resolved to confine their attention, in the first instance, to that section of the laborious poor who occupy a position above the pauper; and to assist these by furnishing to them comfortable tenements at reasonable rates, in healthy locations. It will be seen at a glance that more good can be effected by this course than by attempting to alleviate the condition of those who are thrown upon the public charge, and are necessarily objects for the care of merely charitable institutions, such as almshouses, hospitals, dispensaries, &c. The working-classes of London, more than the working-classes of any other city in the world, need exactly such benefactors as Mr. Peabody; and the plan thus agreed upon benefits them directly, without impairing their self-respect. The honest laborer always shrinks from becoming an object of charity, and thousands prefer the pangs of want to the pangs of dependence; and the effort of the trustees to prevent the tenements from becoming merely establishments for the abject poor is obvious in all their arrangements. The impossibility of obtaining good tenements at a reasonable rent, in this swarm of humanity, has thrown the laboring-classes into the vilest haunts of vice, disease, and filth; and the sure effect has been to pollute their children in mind and body. The Peabody benevolence meets at least one part of this demand; with the double advantage of providing good tenements for the industrious poor, and of adding the small rents they pay to the general fund, so as to perpetuate the good work, and to increase the number of tenements with increasing years. Sir Curtis Lampson estimates, that, if the money thus accumulated is honestly administered for two hundred years, it will have accumulated enough to provide for three-fourths of all the industrious poor of London. That this is not an extravagant expectation can be shown by a simple calculation of the annual interest of the nearly million of dollars donated, with the regular accretions from the moderate funds. There are many interesting incidents on record of the growth of small bequests, in the course of time, into enormous charities.

" The premises at Islington consist of four blocks of buildings; comprising, in all, one hundred and fifty-five tenements, accommodating six hundred and fifty persons, or nearly two hundred families. The whole cost of these buildings, exclusive of the sum paid for the land, amounted to £31,690. The principle and organization in each of these extensive structures are the same. Drainage and ventilation have been insured with the utmost possible care; the instant removal of dust and refuse is effected by means of shafts, which descend from every corridor to cellars in the basement, where it is carted away; the passages are all kept clean, and lighted with gas, without any cost to the tenants; water, from cisterns in the roof, is distributed by pipes into every tenement; and there are baths free for all who desire to use them. Laundries, with wringing-machines and drying-lofts, are at the service of all the inmates, who are thus relieved from the inconvenience of damp vapors in their apartments, and the consequent damage to their furniture and bedding.

"Every living-room, or kitchen, is abundantly provided with cupboards, shelving, and other conveniences; and each fireplace includes a boiler and an oven. But what gratify the tenants, perhaps, more than any other part of the arrangements, are the ample and airy spaces which serve as playgrounds for their children, where they are always under their mothers' eyes, and safe from the risk of passing carriages and laden carts.

"In fixing the rent for all this accommodation, the trustees were influenced by two considerations. In the first place, they felt it incumbent on them, conformably with the intention of rendering the Peabody Fund reproductive, to charge for each room such a moderate percentage on the actual cost of the houses as would bring in a reasonable actual income to the general fund. In the second place, they were desirous, without coming into undue competition with the owners of house-property less favorably circumstanced, to demonstrate to their proprietors the practicability of rendering the dwellings of the laboring poor healthful, cheerful, and attractive; and, at the same time, securing to the landlords a fair return for their investments.

" At the present moment, owing to the vast changes in the metropolis, by which the houses of the laboring poor have been demolished to so great an extent, the cost of accommodation for them has been greatly increased. It, of course, varies in different localities; but, on an average, the weekly charge for a single room of a very poor description is from two shillings and sixpence to three shillings,—about seventy-five cents American money; for two rooms, five shillings, or five shillings and sixpence; and for three, from six shillings and sixpence to seven shillings. But the mere test of rent affords no adequate standard by which to contrast the squalor and discomfort of one of these tenements with the light and airy and agreeable apartments in the Peabody buildings: and, for one room there, the charge per week is two shillings and sixpence; for two rooms, four shillings; and for three rooms, five shillings.

" As Mr. Peabody had directed by his letter that the sole qualification to be required in a tenant was to be in 'an ascertained condition, of life such as brings the individual within the description of the poor of London, combined with moral character and good conduct as a member of society,' it became the duty of the trustees to ascertain by actual inquiry, — first, that the circumstances of the person proposing himself as a tenant were such as to entitle him to admission; and secondly, that, in the opinion of his employers, there was nothing in his conduct or moral character to disqualify him from partaking in the benefits of the fund.

"These two conditions once established, the tenant, on taking possession of his new residence, finds himself as free in action, and as exempt from intrusive restraint or officious interference, as if he occupied a house in one of the adjacent streets. His sense of independence is preserved by the consciousness that he pays for what he enjoys; and by this payment he provides himself with a dwelling so much superior to that which he had formerly been accustomed to, that the approach to his home is no longer accompanied by a feeling of humiliation. As the result of the above inquiries, several applications for admission were declined, on the grounds either of a condition in life too easy to entitle the individual to be classed with the laboring poor, or of a moral character which could not bear investigation, because of habitual drunkenness, or conviction before a legal tribunal. In some instances, too, the families of persons desirous to become tenants were found to be too numerous for the accommodation available; and these, to avoid unwholesome crowding, were unavoidably excluded.

"The number of persons who took possession of their new homes in Spitalfields was upwards of two hundred; including such classes as char-women, monthly nurses, basket-makers, butchers, carpenters, firemen, laborers, porters, omnibus-drivers, seamstresses, shoemakers, tailors, waiters, &c.

"In the buildings at Islington, which were opened in September, 1865, the inmates are of the same class, with the addition of persons employed in other trades, — watch-finishers, turners, stay-makers, smiths, printers, painters, laundresses, letter-carriers, artificial-flower makers, dress-makers, and others. The entire community there now consists of six hundred and seventy-four individuals; of whom nineteen are widows, the rest married persons and children.

" In evidence of the improved salubrity of the buildings, the superintendents report that ill health is rare ; and that the number of deaths since the first buildings were opened, nearly three years ago, have been one man aged thirty, who died of a chronic complaint, and four children, one of whom was under five, and two under two years old. The social contentment of the tenants is freely expressed. No complaints have been made of any of the arrangements provided for their comfort; and they all speak approvingly of the unaccustomed advantages they enjoy. Amongst these, they particularize the security of their furniture and effects, which are no longer liable, as they formerly were, to be taken in distress, should the landlord become a de-faulter.

" As regards the moral conduct of the tenantry, the superintendent reports that habitual drunkenness is un-known, and intoxication infrequent; and where the latter does occur, to the annoyance of others, it is judiciously dealt with by giving notice to the offender, that, in the event of its recurrence, he must prepare to leave. There has been but one person removed for quarrelling and dis-

turbing the peace, and one expelled for non-payment of
rent. These exceptions, out of a community of eight
hundred and eighty persons, speak strongly for the self-
respect and moral principles by which they are influenced.

"There are four other squares, two of which have
already received occupants; and the others will soon be
completed. The main buildings are of stone, five stories
high; four being occupied by the families, and the last, or
upper range, used for the purpose of a laundry for drying
clothes, where fine baths are provided for general use. I
conversed with many of the inmates: they were all clean,
healthy, and happy. The men were off at work, and the
women seemed to be industrious and tidy. The contrast
between their condition and that of the poor in the misera-
ble houses around us was painful in the extreme. In some
of the rooms of the latter, as many as seven people were
crowded. In other sections, the difference was even more
saddening. The airy and comfortable quarters of Mr.
Peabody's tenants, with the neat kitchens and comfortable
bedrooms, and the fine playground for the children, the
garden for common cultivation and use, and the work-
shops for such of the men as might prefer working on the
premises, proved that the architect had given a conscien-
tious study to his work.

"Mr. Peabody's example will be followed, now that its
complete success is established, in both hemispheres. Mr.
A. T. Stewart of New York has already procured copies
of the plans, and photographs of the buildings, I have

attempted to describe. Parliament has repeatedly noticed the work itself; and the owners of the colossal fortunes — the Plutocracy of England — cannot resist the eloquent invocation to their consciences and pockets. They cannot afford the reproach that they have been indifferent while England's honest poor have been relieved by an American. Indeed, the trustees have already received a bequest of thirty thousand pounds sterling from a worthy gentleman. The romantic stories founded upon wills and legacies in this country, taken, in most cases, from the facts, may well lead to the hope that other rich men, to prevent their falling to the crown, will throw their estates into this noble fund. There is hardly a great city in America in which Mr. Peabody's liberality should not be followed up; and there is not one in which infinite good cannot be wrought. 'The poor ye have always;' and as I saw these happy children enjoying their spacious playground this morning, and talked with their gratified parents, and heard the report of the superintendent, I felt proud that the author of all this splendid benevolence was an American, and predicted that his royal generosity would find many imitators in his own and other countries."

A recent writer in " The Boston Journal " thus tells of a visit to Peabody Square : —

" I must tell you of my visit to Mr. Peabody's model buildings near Islington ; or, rather, the buildings which the trustees of his fund built according to their own ideas.

Told that Peabody Square was the most favorable speci-
men of these groups of workmen's homes, I drove down
there on a recent Sunday and a foggy one. My route
lay through Islington; and, long before coming there, we
drove through one of those interminable streets called
roads in London, where one sees only immense museums
of trade and horrible poverty. . . . But the neighborhood
was more respectable towards Peabody Square. The fog,
however, was of the consistency of cream, and seemed to
strike us in the face as we cut through it. At last, cabby
showed me up a narrow and dark alley, which finally
opened on a square, around which were ranged four fine
five-story stone blocks, each exactly like the other. Here
were no quarrelling or fighting children, no drunken women,
no discouraged-looking men. There were flowers in the
windows, and bright, happy faces looked out from among
them; but the blocks had a prison-like appearance, nevertheless. There was not a blade of grass, or a twig, to be
seen in the stone-paved yard; and the fog settled down into
the area worse than outside. The outer doors were open;
and I soon made the acquaintance of a brawny English-
woman in the porter's lodge of one of the blocks. How
many families were there in each building?

"'Forty-two; and p'raps six in a family, sir.'

"So I began to question her on the internal arrangements of this London Sybaris; because you often hear it
said that Mr. Peabody's money has been misused, and
that the workmen pay too highly for their tenements.

" ' Me'n my husban' has been porter (*sic*) here for more'n two year; an' my man was here from the beginnin', sir. We likes it ever so much. We pays four shillin' a week for these two rooms; and most o' them generally pays the same. 'Tisn't dear, — oh, no! but it's about all most o' them can pay. Still ' —

" We looked into some of the rooms. It depended on the taste, more than the resources, of the individual tenant, how comfortable he made himself. There were neatly tiled floors, whitewashed walls. The rooms were small, but planned as economically, as to space, as a travelling-jacket. I noticed, especially, that each room was well lighted and ventilated. Some families had three rooms, so planned as to avoid any of the lamentable lack of decency which large families crowded into small tenements sometimes exhibit in London and New York and Boston. Each floor is divided into lettered sections, which are traversed by spacious corridors. Each tenement, or suite of rooms, has one door, numbered, opening on these corridors: There are iron traps in the halls in each story, into which the dirt and rubbish from each tenement is swept; so that there is no chance for an accumulation of filth. In the upper story of each building is a co-operative laundry, which the women also consider as their exchange, and where they get acquainted over their work.

" ' Most all on us knows every other one, on us here,' said the portress. Pity Mr. Peabody didn't specify that all the tenants under his fund should be taught grammar!

There was gas in many of the rooms; but that was paid for as an extra. ' Are these workmen, living here, of what you would call the better class?' I asked.

" 'I rather think not, sir,' was the answer. ' Most o' them does common sort o' work; 'n sometimes they hasn't any in the dull season: but they manages to stick by the square, in any case. Me'n my man does all the hirin' rooms; and we never has any disputes. All pays, allers.'

" Which rather proves that the workmen find it cheap and advantageous to live there; because collecting rents elsewhere, in the dens which are made to serve the poor as houses, is sometimes even dangerous. But you have only to put a man in a den to make him a beast.

" So, in this square, here are one hundred and sixty-eight families, averaging six members each, renting comfortable rooms, in a clean, airy, and respectable quarter of the city, for about five dollars per month, per tenement. Their condition is much improved by the arrangements made for them; and any drunkenness or fighting in the building is never known. I saw, in many of the rooms, the men at home, evidently enjoying the society of their families, instead of swilling beer at the public-house. I should give my testimony in favor of the success of Mr. Peabody's money as a most practical beneficence."

" The London Illustrated News " thus refers to the benefaction of Mr Peabody : —

" On March 12, 1862, Mr. Peabody addressed a letter

to Mr. C. F. Adams, American minister, the Right Hon. Lord Stanley, Sir J. E. Tennet, Mr. (now Sir) Curtis M. Lampson, Bart., and Mr. J. S. Morgan, his own partner in business, informing them that a sum of £150,000 stood in the books of Messrs. George Peabody and Co., to be applied by them for the amelioration of the condition of the poor of London.

"The gentlemen above named duly entered on their trust, which has been applied in the mode indicated by the donor; namely, in the erection of model dwellings for working-men. In January, 1866, Mr. Peabody added another £100,000 to the fund; and, on Dec. 5 last, he made a further donation of about fifteen acres of land at Brixton, 5,642 shares in the Hudson's Bay Company, and £5,405 in cash, — making a total of £100,000; thus raising the amount of his gift to London to £350,000. This gift is held by the trustees under two deeds, the first having reference to the £150,000 first given, and the second including the remaining £200,000; which latter was not to be put in operation until July, 1869, and has, therefore, but now begun to be dealt with. It appears, by the statement of the trustees for the year 1868, that they now hold property under the first deed valued at £173,-313; the increase being the produce of rents on the buildings, added to the interest on unexpended capital. Four ranges of buildings have been already erected, which house a population of 1,971 individuals, composed of the families of working-men earning wages, on the average, under twenty-one shillings a week. The trustees have acquired other sites, on which they are about to complete further blocks of houses for similar purposes.

"By the last will and testament of Mr. Peabody, opened on the day of his funeral, his executors, Sir Curtis Lampson, and Mr. Charles Reed, M.P., are directed to apply a further sum of £150,000 to the Peabody Fund in London. This makes half a million sterling bestowed by Mr. Peabody for that single object."

CHAPTER IX.

APPRECIATION.

Visit to his Native Land. — The Freedom of the City of London. — The Queen's Letter. — The Queen's Portrait. — The Peabody Statue.

> " Praise is but virtue's shadow."
> HEATH'S *Clarastella*.
>
> " Honor to whom honor."— ROM. xiii. 7.

HE munificence of the man who remembered the poor of London was appreciated by the people of England. The merchants and capitalists of London showed their appreciation of the noble deed by causing a costly statue of Mr. Peabody to be placed in one of the squares of that city; and, shortly before he left England for a visit to his native land, he received other tokens of appreciation from the people of his adopted home, and from the sovereign lady of the realm. But his characteristic modesty made it difficult for a grateful and admiring people to express their appreciation in a tangible form. The same feelings that led Mr. Peabody to decline the public acknowledgments of the cities of his native land in 1857 prevented him from accepting the honors which Englishmen were ready to shower upon him. The freedom of the city was bestowed upon him by the corporation of London, and acknowledgments from many other public bodies were freely offered. Arrangements were also entered into for the erection of his statue. The only occasion on which he appeared in public was at the close of the Working-Classes' Exhibition in the Guildhall in 1866, when he received an enthusiastic welcome which even royalty itself might envy.

A short time before his sailing for America in 1866, a proposal was made to confer on Mr. Peabody either a baronetcy or the Grand Cross of the Order of the Bath ; but he declined them both. When asked *what* gift, if any, he would accept, he replied, " A letter from the Queen of England, which I may carry across the Atlantic, and deposit as a memorial of one of her most faithful sons." To this modest request a ready response was given by the following letter : —

"WINDSOR CASTLE, March 28, 1866.

" The Queen hears that Mr. Peabody intends shortly to return to America; and she would be sorry that he should leave England without being assured by herself how deeply she appreciates the noble act, of more than princely munificence, by which he has sought to relieve the wants of her poorer subjects residing in London. It is an act, as the Queen believes, wholly without parallel ; and which will carry its best reward in the consciousness of having contributed so largely to the assistance of those who can little help themselves.

" The Queen would not, however, have been satisfied without giving Mr. Peabody some public mark of her sense of his munificence ; and she would gladly have conferred upon him either a baronetcy or the Grand Cross of the Order of the Bath, but that she understands Mr. Peabody to feel himself debarred from accepting such distinctions.

" It only remains, therefore, for the Queen to give Mr. Peabody this assurance of her personal feelings; which she would further wish to mark by asking him to accept a miniature portrait of herself, which she will desire to have painted for him, and which, when finished, can either be sent to him in America, or given to him on the return which she rejoices to hear he meditates to the country that owes him so much."

To this letter Mr. Peabody replied : —

"THE PALACE HOTEL, BUCKINGHAM GATE,
LONDON, April 3, 1866.

" MADAM, — I feel sensibly my inability to express in adequate terms the gratification with which I have read the letter which your Majesty has done me the high honor of transmitting by the hands of Earl Russell.

" On the occasion which has attracted your Majesty's attention, of setting apart a portion of my property to ameliorate the condition and augment the comforts of the poor of London, I have been actuated by a deep sense of gratitude to God, who has blessed me with prosperity, and of attachment to this great country, where, under your Majesty's benign rule, I have received so much personal kindness, and enjoyed so many years of happiness. Next to the approval of my own conscience, I shall always prize the assurance which your Majesty's letter conveys to me of the approbation of the Queen of England, whose whole life has attested that her exalted station has in no degree diminished her sympathy with the humblest of her subjects. The portrait which your Majesty is graciously pleased to bestow on me I shall value as the most gracious heirloom that I can leave in the land of my birth ; where, together with the letter which your Majesty has addressed to me, it will ever be regarded as an evidence of the kindly feeling of the Queen of the United Kingdom toward a citizen of the United States.

"I have the honor to be

"Your Majesty's most obedient servant,

"GEORGE PEABODY."

A writer in a Boston paper states, that, —

"After the completion of the Institute at Peabody in 1854, its founder made it the depository of all those appreciative personal testimonials which are commonly the heirlooms of families, and which, in America, constitute the only substitutes for the decorations, arms, and insignia of rank. It is well known that the intimation that Mr. Peabody would decline a baronetcy, or any other title or decoration with which England usually recognizes and rewards merit, induced the queen to offer her miniature as a substitute for the honors he declined, and a testimonial of her appreciation of his benevolence to the poor of London. On the occasion of Mr. Peabody's visit to this country in 1866, he informed the trustees of the Institute that the miniature would be confided to their 'personal charge and custody;' and a share of the large additional sum which he then gave for the enlargement of the Institute building, and the increase of its funds, was expended in the construction of a vault in which to preserve the valuable gifts which he had received as an acknowledgment of his various charities.

" Among the gifts deposited in the vault are the gold box containing the freedom of the city of London ; a gold box from the Fishmongers' Association of London; a book of autographs which Mr. Peabody collected himself, and which he highly prized, as a memorial of his wide acquaintance, and of a more general appreciation of his character than gifts alone could supply; a presentation-copy of the Queen's first published book, with her autograph in the usual form; a cane which belonged to Benjamin Franklin, and which, given to one of Franklin's London friends in the last century, can be traced from one donee to another, until it became the property of Mr. Peabody; the Congressional medal which was presented in token of that magnificent educational gift to the South, which, in its all-embracing charity, makes no distinctions of race or color; and the miniature of the Queen, and her autograph-letter in which the gift is suggested. The great pecuniary value of the portrait, the unusual and generous character of the gift, and its inestimable value as an international courtesy, rendered it desirable, that, as far as human means permitted, it should be placed beyond the reach of accident.

"This picture is mounted in an elaborate and massive chased frame of gold. On the frame, above the miniature, is the royal crown. The miniature is a half-length, fourteen inches long, and ten wide. When the Queen sat for the picture, she was attired in such demi-robes of state as she has worn on a few public occasions since the decease of Prince Albert. Her dress was of black silk, with a dark-velvet train, both of which were trimmed with ermine. Her head-dress was the favorite Mary-Stuart cap, surmounted with a demi-crown. The Koh-i-noor and a jewelled cross were her principal ornaments. The portrait is in enamel, by Tilb, a London artist. It is the largest miniature of the kind ever attempted in England; and a furnace was specially built for the execution of the work. Its cost has been estimated at from thirty thousand to fifty thousand dollars in gold; but it is not known that any one in this country has information of the exact sum.

The likeness, though a good deal idealized, like the beautiful but too flattering portrait on porcelain, is said to be remarkably good; and a near inspection of the work shows that the artist has not been so supple a courtier as to neglect the impress which time and care, motherhood and widowhood, have left on that once handsome and joyous face. Such is the situation of the vault, the arrangement of the light, and the facilities for moving the picture, that it is conveniently and advantageously exhibited without removal.

"The library contains about thirteen thousand volumes; among which are many rare books and rarer serial publications, either collected by Mr. Peabody, or purchased and presented by him, from time to time, for the use and endowment of the Institute. The collection is particularly rich in reviews and magazines, and includes one of the very few sets in the country of 'The London Times.' The library-room also contains busts of Shakspeare, Milton, Webster, Hawthorne, and the founder of the Institute.

" The splendid full-length portrait of Peabody by Healy — ordered by the citizens of Danvers soon after the announcement of the original gift, and placed over the rostrum in the lecture-hall a few days before the dedicatory-exercises in 1854 — represents Mr. Peabody as many will recall him, and as he appeared on the occasion of his visit in 1856, — full of life, vigor, and health, his manly form unshrunken by age and disease, and his fine face retaining a larger share of the cheerfulness of youth than usually survives the vexations and cares of sixty years. A fine picture of Rufus Choate, who began his wonderful

PEABODY STATUE
LONDON.

PEABODY INSTITUTE
BALTIMORE

professional career in Danvers, and who always recalled those early associations with pleasure, also adorns the hall. The portrait of Edward Everett, a warm friend and admirer of Mr. Peabody, and the most eloquent of his eulogists, as those who recall his speech at the Peabody banquet in 1856 will readily admit, is also in the place of honor over the rostrum. Both of these pictures are by Ames, the American artist."

" The Christian Leader " thus refers to the inauguration of the Peabody statue : —

" George Peabody gave the poor of England a princely sum ; *so* gave it, that it will prove a stream of beneficence so long as London shall have the poor with it. The good Queen honors him, and presents him with her portrait, paying therefor the sum of seventy thousand dollars. The people of London honor him, and, by subscription, raise a fund to procure his statue, to be placed conspicuously in a city square. Mr. Story, the American sculptor, had the honor of executing the work. The Prince of Wales presided at the ceremony of ' unveiling.' It was not looked forward to as a 'sensation.' The depth of London's love for the philanthropist was not at all comprehended. Where hundreds were expected, the people came by thousands. ' The popular excitement,' says ' The Tribune's ' correspondent, ' surpassed expectation, and made the matter loom larger than the proceedings would have done without the huge crowd as a background. Mr. Peabody has, of course, a great popularity in London ; but no effort seems to have been made to bring it forward. People came spontaneously; and as they could not be admitted into the enclosure, nor get within sight or sound of what was going on, they filled all the open spaces about the band and in front of the Royal Exchange. Threadneedle Street was crammed; and Cornhill overflowed into all the cross-streets. There were more thousands of men than could be counted; and they occupied the leisure half-hour, before the speeches began, in the true British pastimes of cheering and chaffing the successive arrivals of the lucky few who had tickets to the enclosure. It looked, at one time, as if the police had more than they could do to keep a passage open. With the help of a troop of the Honorable Artillery Company, they did well. The Lord Mayor, Mr. Motley, and Mr. Story the artist, were present. It is with uncommon satisfaction we put into conspicuous type the Prince's brief address, at the same time calling special attention to the closing sentences. He said, —

" ' The name of George Peabody is so well known to all of you, that, really, I feel some difficulty in recounting any thing new. But, at the same time, it affords me the deepest gratification in paying a mark of tribute and of respect to the name of the great American citizen, the great philanthropist, — I may say, the citizen of the world. England can never adequately pay the debt of gratitude which she owes to that man ; London especially, to which his wonderful charity has been so liberally distributed. For a man not born in this country to give a sum of, I believe, more than a quarter of a million of pounds sterling towards benevolent objects is a fact which is unequalled. His name will go down to posterity as one who has, as Sir Benjamin Phillips so justly remarked, tried to ameliorate the condition of his fellow-citizens and especially to benefit their moral and social character. I have not yet had the opportunity of seeing the statue which is shortly to be unveiled; but, from having the privilege of knowing the sculptor (Mr. Story) for a space of now about ten years, I feel sure it will be one which is worthy of being placed here, and worthy of the man to whom it is dedicated. Before concluding the few imperfect remarks which I have ventured to address to you, let me thank Mr. Motley, the American minister, for his presence on this occasion, and assure him what pleasure it gives me to take part in this great, and, I might almost say, national ceremonial of paying tribute to the name of his great and distinguished countryman. Be assured that the feelings which I personally entertain towards America are the same as they ever were. I can never forget the reception which I had there nine years ago; and my earnest hope and wish is that England and America may go hand in hand in peace and prosperity.' "

" The Tribune " correspondent tells us that Mr. Motley stood by the side of the Prince, and bowed his response to these sentences, which were spoken with much more emphasis than the Prince commonly puts into his words,

and with evidently genuine feeling. Mr. Motley's reply
is as durable a monument to Mr. Peabody's memory as
the marble itself.   He said, —

"May it please your Royal Highness, my Lord Mayor,
ladies and gentlemen: I thank you sincerely for the very
cordial reception you have given me, and his Royal Highness for the kind and courteous words he has spoken.   I
should be glad, as an American citizen, to pronounce a fit
eulogy on our great philanthropist; but the brief and
rapidly-fleeting moments allotted on this occasion will
not permit such eulogy.   Nor is it necessary.   His name
alone is eulogy enough.   Most fortunate and most generous of men, he has discovered a secret for which misers
might sigh in vain, — the art of keeping a great fortune
to himself so long as time shall be.   In this connection, I
have often thought of a famous epitaph inscribed on the
monument of an old Earl of Devon, — one who was commonly called 'the good Earl of Devon.'   No doubt, the
inscription is familiar to many who now hear me: 'What
I spent, that I had; what I saved, that I lost; that
which I gave away remains with me.'   And what a magnificent treasure, according to these noble and touching
words, has our friend and the poor man's friend preserved for himself till time and he shall be no more!

'And tongues to be his bounty shall rehearse
When all the breathers of this world are dead.'

"Of all men in the world, he least needs a monument;

but, as it was to be erected, I am glad that the task has been committed to the great American sculptor whom I have had the honor and happiness of calling my intimate friend for many years. And, during a recent residence in Rome, I had the good fortune of seeing this statue, which has just been unveiled in this busy heart of England's great metropolis by the royal hand of England's Prince. I saw it grow, day by day, beneath the plastic fingers of the artist; and it was my privilege on one occasion — a privilege I shall never forget — of seeing Mr. Peabody and his statue seated side by side, and of debating within myself, without coming to a satisfactory conclusion, whether, on the whole, if I may be allowed so confused an expression, — whether the statue was more like Mr. Peabody, or Mr. Peabody more like the statue. It is a delightful, it always will be a delightful thought, that the thousands and tens of thousands who daily throng this crowded mart will see him almost as accurately as in the flesh. And the future generations — generations after generations, the long, yet unborn, but, I fear, never-ending procession of London's poor — will be almost as familiar with the form and the features of their great benefactor as are those of us who have the privilege and the happiness of knowing him in the flesh. Your Royal Highness and my Lord Mayor, I beg to thank you for your courtesy."

CHAPTER X.

MR. PEABODY IN AMERICA.

The Flood of Letters. — The Gift for Education in the South. — Mr.
Peabody's Letter. — His Gift seconded by Publishers.

<blockquote>
" 'Tis education forms the common mind:
Just as the twig is bent, the tree's inclined." — POPE.
</blockquote>

"To do good and to communicate, forget not; for with such sacrifices God is well
pleased." — HEB. xiii. 16.

IT is said that Mr. Peabody "was of course very much annoyed, during his last visits, by appeals to his purse, as well as by impertinent intrusions upon his privacy. To individual appeals for assistance he never listened. All his letters were opened and read by his sister; and she exercised her judgment about letting him see them, or throwing them into the fire. Begging-letters of any sort he never wished to read. Even deserving charitable institutions got nothing from him if they asked for it. He gave only as the mood took him; and it may be safely said, that all his benefactions were the spontaneous outgrowth of his own ideas of what the world needed, and what could be most easily and efficiently put into practical operation. He was, in

short, a philanthropist without sentiment; a man of ten
der heart and generous impulses, who believed that the
highest duty of the rich was, not to dole out small sums
for the relief of the improvident, but to put the commonwealth in the way of diminishing improvidence by general
education, and helping the poor to live in decency and
virtue. There was no imaginable reason why he should
not rigorously carry out his principle, that, while the public
had claims upon him, individuals had none. It will be a
part of his panegyric, in time to come, that he took this
plain, sensible view of his duties; that he saw so clearly
how he could make his money go farthest."

A perfect flood of letters poured upon him when last
in America; they were to be numbered by hundreds,
every day, it is said: but he rarely read one of them.
The sound of his munificence had gone abroad; and, very
naturally, there were needy ones who desired to share his
bounty, and felt at liberty to ask it. He felt at liberty to
refuse, so long as he gave so liberally in other directions.

His crowning donation was that of nearly two million
dollars to build up the cause of education in the South.
This last fund was placed in the hands of trustees of the
highest character for integrity and zealous interest in the
cause of education; and was to be applied to assist schools,
and to promote the education of the people, without distinction of race or color, in the Southern States.

An appropriate acknowledgment of this last generous
gift was made by the Government of the United States.

A costly and elegant gold medal was presented to him in pursuance of an act of Congress, bearing on one side a fine profile portrait of the recipient, and on the other the inscription, " The people of the United States to George Peabody, in acknowledgment of his beneficent promotion of universal education."

The following is a copy of the letter of Mr. Peabody to the trustees of the Southern Educational Fund: —

" To Hon. Robert C. Winthrop of Massachusetts; Hon. Hamilton Fish of New York; Right Rev. Charles P. McIlvaine of Ohio; Gen. U. S. Grant of the United-States Army; Hon. William C. Rives of Virginia; Hon. John H. Clifford of Massachusetts; Hon. William Aiken of South Carolina; William M. Evarts, Esq., of New York; Hon. William A. Graham of North Carolina; Charles McAllister of Pennsylvania; George N. Riggs, Esq., of Washington; Samuel Wetmore, Esq., of New York; Edward A. Bradford, Esq., of Louisiana; George N. Eaton, Esq., of Maryland; and George Peabody Russell, Esq., of Massachusetts.

" *Gentlemen*, — I beg to address you on a subject which occupied my mind long before I left England; and in regard to which, one at least of you (the Hon. Mr. Winthrop, the distinguished and valued friend to whom I am so much indebted for cordial sympathy, careful consideration, and wise counsel in this matter) will remember that I consulted him immediately upon my arrival in May last.

" I refer to the educational needs of those portions of our beloved and common country which have suffered from the destructive ravages and the not less disastrous consequences of civil war.

"With my advancing years, my attachment to my native land has but become more devoted. My hope and faith in its successful and glorious future have grown brighter and stronger; and now, looking forward beyond my stay on earth, as may be permitted to one who has passed the limit of threescore and ten years, I see our country, united and prosperous, emerging from the clouds which still surround her, taking a higher rank among the nations, and becoming richer and more powerful than ever before.

"But, to make her prosperity more than superficial, her moral and intellectual development should keep pace with her material growth; and, in those portions of our nation to which I have referred, the urgent and pressing physical needs of an almost impoverished people must, for some years, preclude them from making, by unaided effort, such advances in education, and such progress in the diffusion of knowledge among all classes, as every lover of his country must earnestly desire.

"I feel most deeply, therefore, that it is the duty and privilege of the more favored and wealthy portions of our nation to assist those who are less fortunate; and with the wish to discharge, so far as I may be able, my own responsibility in this matter, as well as to gratify my desire to aid those to whom I am bound by so many ties of attachment and regard, I give to you, gentlemen, most of whom have been my personal and especial friends, the sum of one million dollars, to be by you and your successors held in trust, and the income thereof used and applied in your discretion for the promotion and encouragement of intellectual, moral, or industrial education among the young of the more destitute portions of the Southern and South-Western States of the Union ; my purpose being, that the benefits intended shall be distributed among the entire population, without other distinction than their needs and the opportunities of usefulness to them.

" Besides the income thus derived, I give to you permission to use from the principal sum, within the next two years, an amount not exceeding forty per cent.

" In addition to this gift, I place in your hands bonds of the State of Mississippi, issued to the Planters' Bank, and commonly known as Planters' Bank Bonds, amounting, with interest, to about eleven hundred thousand; the amount realized by you from which is to be added to and used for the purposes of this trust.

" These bonds were originally issued in payment for stock in that bank held by the State, and amounted, in all, to only two million dollars. For many years, the State paid the interest, without interruption, till 1840 ; since which no interest has been paid, except a payment of about a hundred thousand dollars, which was found in the treasury applicable to the payment of the coupons, and paid by a *mandamus* of the Supreme Court. The validity of these bonds has never been questioned ; and they must not be confounded with another issue of bonds made by the State to the Union Bank, the recognition of which has been a subject of controversy with a portion of the population of Mississippi.

" Various acts of the Legislature, viz. of Feb. 28, 1842, Feb. 23, 1844, Feb. 16, 1846, Feb. 28, 1846, March 4, 1848, and the highest judicial tribunal of the State, have confirmed their validity; and I have no doubt, that, at an early day, such legislation will be had as to make these bonds available in increasing the usefulness of the present trust.

" Mississippi, though now depressed, is rich in agricultural resources, and cannot long disregard the moral obligation resting upon her to make provision for their payment. In confirmation of what I have said in regard to the legislative and judicial action concerning the State bonds issued to the Planters' Bank, I)herewith place in your hands the documents marked ' A.'

" The details and organization of the trust I leave with you; only requesting that Mr. Winthrop may be chairman, and Gov. Fish and Bishop McIlvaine vice-chairmen, of your body: and I give to you power to make all necessary by-laws and regulations; to obtain an act of incorporation, if any shall be found expedient; to provide for the expenses of the trustees, and of any agents appointed by them; and, generally, to do all such acts as may be necessary for carrying out the provisions of this trust.

" All vacancies occurring in your number by death, resignation, or otherwise, shall be filled by your election, as soon as conveniently may be, and having in view an equality of representation so far as regards the Northern and Southern States.

"I furthermore give to you the power, in case two-thirds of the trustees shall, at any time after the lapse of thirty years, deem it expedient to close this trust, and of the funds which at that time shall be in the hands of yourselves and your successors, to distribute not less than two-thirds among such educational or literary institutions, or for such educational purposes, as they may determine, in the States for whose benefit the income is now appointed to be used. The remainder may be distributed by the trustees. for educational or literary purposes, wherever they may deem it expedient.

"In making this gift, I am aware that the fund derived from it can but aid the States which I wish to benefit in their own exertions to diffuse the blessings of education and morality; but if this endowment should encourage those now anxious for the light of knowledge, and stimulate to new efforts the many good and noble men who cherish the high purpose of placing our great country foremost, not only in power, but in the intelligence and virtue of her citizens, it will have accomplished all that I can hope.

"With reverent recognition of the need of the blessing of Almighty God upon this gift, and with the fervent prayer that, under his guidance, your counsels may be directed for the highest good of present and future generations in our beloved country, I am, gentlemen, with great respect,

"Your humble servant,

"GEORGE PEABODY."

"The Boston Journal" states, that at the annual meeting of the trustees of this fund, held in Washington on the 15th of February, 1870, Hon. Robert C. Winthrop opened the meeting by an address, in which he made appropriate mention of the great loss they had sustained by the death of the founder of the fund. He also paid a high compliment to Dr. Sears, the general agent of the board, and stated that the work which Dr. Sears had performed met with the cordial approbation of Mr. Peabody. Mr. Winthrop made the following interesting remarks:—

"You all remember, that, on the first day of July last, our board held a special meeting at Newport, R.I., at the immediate request of Mr. Peabody. He had informed me confidentially, before I took leave of him in London in the previous summer, that he intended to visit his native country again, God willing, during the present year; and that he should then make a considerable addition to our fund. He was then strong and hopeful, and had great confidence that he might live at least ten years longer. But his health soon afterwards began to decline; and, as the next spring opened, he was led to entertain serious apprehensions that he might not live even until another year. After a careful consultation with his medical advisers, he

11

suddenly resolved to come over at once and complete his designs.

" On the very day of his arrival in Boston, he informed Dr. Sears, Gov. Clifford, and myself, who had met him at the station, and accompanied him to the hospitable home of his friend Mr. Dana, that the first desire of his heart, and that which he had crossed the Atlantic especially to gratify, was to meet our board once more, and to increase our means for carrying on the great work in which we were engaged. He met us, accordingly, at Newport, and added a second million of dollars to our cash capital, besides adding largely to the deferred securities which he had included in the original donation; all of which he had the fullest faith would, at no very distant day, become productive.

" In the letter addressed to us, communicating this second princely gift, he used the following language : —

" ' I have constantly watched, with great interest and careful attention, the proceedings of your board; and it is most gratifying to me now to be able to express my warmest thanks for the interest and zeal you have manifested in maturing and carrying out the designs of my letter of trust, and to assure you of my cordial concurrence in all the steps you have taken.

" ' At the same time, I must not omit to congratulate you, and all who have at heart the best interests of this educational enterprise, upon your obtaining the highly valuable services of Dr. Sears as your general agent, —

services valuabl.., not merely in the organization of schools and of a system of public education, but in the good effect which his conciliatory and sympathizing course has had, wherever he has met or become associated with the communities of the South in social or business relations.

" ' And I beg to take this opportunity of thanking, with all my heart, the people of the South themselves, for the cordial spirit with which they have received the trust, and for the energetic efforts which they have made, in co-operation with yourselves and Dr. Sears, for carrying out the plans which have been proposed and matured for the diffusion of the blessings of education in their respective States.'

" This letter of Mr. Peabody concluded as follows : —

" ' I do this with the earnest hope, and in the sincere trust, that with God's blessing upon the gift, and upon the deliberations and future action of yourselves and your general agent, it may enlarge the sphere of usefulness already entered upon, and prove a permanent and lasting boon, not only to the Southern States, but to the whole of our dear country, which I have ever loved so well, but never so much as now in my declining years, and at this time (probably the last occasion I shall ever have to address you), as I look back over the changes and the progress of nearly three-quarters of a century; and I pray that Almighty God will grant to it a future as happy and noble, in the intelligence and virtues of its citizens, as it will be glorious in unexampled power and prosperity.'   This sec-

ond letter has, indeed, proved to be, as he himself antici-
pated, his last letter to this board."

The publishing-houses of D. Appleton & Co. and of
A. S. Barnes & Co. evinced their appreciation of Mr.
Peabody's gift to the South, — the former by a donation
of a hundred thousand volumes of school-books, and the
latter by a gift of five thousand volumes of " The Teachers' Library " and twenty-five thousand school-books.

The Rev. Dr. Barnas Sears, late President of Brown
University, has accepted the post of general agent; and
the generous gift of Mr. Peabody, under his judicious
administration, will doubtless prove a great benefit to the
South.

CHAPTER XI.

MORE GIFTS FOR SCIENCE.

Money for Museums at Yale and Harvard. — Correspondence in Reference
to these Donations. — The Value of the Gift.

> " Walk
> Boldly and wisely in that light thou hast:
> There is a Hand above will help thee on." — BAILEY'S *Festus.*
>
> " The lips of knowledge are a precious jewel." — PROV. xx. 15.

WHILE Mr. Peabody founded institutions bearing his name in his native town and in the cities of his adoption, he was not unwilling to add to the influence of institutions already established in the land of his birth. Gratitude and courtesy sometimes led those ancient institutions to compliment the donor by calling some branch of their organization after his name. In that way Yale College honored him, and showed its gratitude by giving his name to a museum.

The second annual report of the Sheffield Scientific School of that college, in 1866–67, contains the following statements in regard to the generous gift: —

" It is already well known that George Peabody, Esq.,

of London, in October last, made the generous donation of
a hundred and fifty thousand dollars, to found, 'in connection with Yale College,' a museum of natural history.
Although this munificent gift is designed to benefit all departments of the university, it will obviously and necessarily be of more immediate advantage to the students of
natural science connected with this school; and hence the
donor's letter to his trustees, and the accompanying instrument of gift, may be fitly given here.

MR. PEABODY'S LETTER.

"'NEW YORK, Oct. 22, 1866.

"'To Prof. James D. Dana, Hon. James Dixon, Hon. Robert C. Winthrop, Prof. Benjamin Silliman, Prof. George J. Brush, Prof. Othniel C. Marsh, and George Peabody Wetmore, Esq.

"'*Gentlemen*,—With this letter I enclose an instrument giving to you one hundred and fifty thousand dollars
($150,000), in trust, for the foundation and maintenance
of a museum of natural history, especially of the departments of zoölogy, geology, and mineralogy, in connection
with Yale College.

"'I some years ago expressed my intention of making
a donation to this distinguished institution; and convinced
as I am of the importance of the natural sciences, and of
the increasing interest taken in their study, it now affords
me great pleasure to aid in advancing these departments
of knowledge.

"'The rapid advance which natural science is now

making renders it necessary to provide for the future requirements of such a museum, as well as its present wants; and I trust that the portion of the fund designed for this purpose will be found sufficient.

"'On learning of your acceptance of this trust, and of the assent of the President and Fellows of Yale College to its conditions, I shall be prepared to pay over to you the sum I have named; and I may then have some additional suggestions to make in regard to the general management of the trust. Confident that under your direction this trust will be faithfully and successfully administered,

"'I am, with great respect, your obedient servant,

"'GEORGE PEABODY.'"

THE INSTRUMENT OF GIFT.

"'I hereby give to James Dwight Dana of New Haven, Conn., James Dixon ·of Hartford, Conn., Robert C. Winthrop of Boston, Mass., Benjamin Silliman of New Haven, Conn., George Jarvis Brush of New Haven, Conn., Othniel Charles Marsh of New Haven, Conn., and George Peabody Wetmore of Newport, R.I., on his attaining his majority, the sum of one hundred and fifty thousand dollars, to be by them or their successors held in trust, to found and maintain a museum of natural history, especially of the departments of zoölogy, geology, and mineralogy, in connection with Yale College, in the city of New Haven, State of Connecticut.

"'Of this sum, I direct that my said trustees devote a part—not to exceed one hundred thousand dollars—to the erection, upon land to be given for that purpose, free of cost or rental, by the President and Fellows of Yale College, in New Haven, of a fire-proof museum-building, adapted to the present requirements of these three departments of science, but planned with especial reference to its subsequent enlargement; the building, when completed, to become the property of said college for the uses of this trust, and none other.

"'I further direct that the sum of twenty thousand dollars be invested, and accumulate as a building-fund, until it shall amount to at least one hundred thousand dollars, when it may be employed by my said trustees, or their successors, in the erection of one or more additions to the museum-building, or in its final completion; the land for the same also to be provided, free of cost or rental, by the President and Fellows of Yale College, in New Haven; and the entire structure, when completed, to be the property of Yale College, for the uses of this trust, and none other.

"'I further direct that thirty thousand dollars, the remaining portion of this donation, be invested, and the income from it be expended by my said trustees, or their successors, for the care of the museum, increase of its collections, and general interests of the departments of science already named; the part of the income remaining, after providing for the general care of the museum, to be apportioned in the following manner,—three-sevenths to zoölogy, three-sevenths to geology, and one-seventh to mineralogy ; the said collections, as well as the museum-building, to be exclusively for the benefit of the various departments of said college.

" ' The board of trustees I have thus constituted shall always be composed of seven persons, of whom not more than four shall at any one time be members of the Faculty of Yale College. They shall have the general management of the museum, keep a record of their doings, and annually prepare a report setting forth the condition of the trust and funds, and the amount of income received and paid out by them during the previous year. This report, signed by the trustees, shall be presented to the President and Fellows of Yale College, in New Haven, at their annual summer session, and be by them filed in the archives of said college.

" ' In the event of the death or resignation of either of my said trustees, I direct that his successor be the Governor of Connecticut, who, *ex officio*, shall forever afterward be a member of the board. Any other vacancy that may occur in the board of trustees, either by resignation or by death, shall be filled by the remaining trustees within a reasonable time after such vacancy shall have occurred.

" ' I give to my said trustees and their successors the liberty to appoint a treasurer, and to enter into any agreements with the President and Fellows of Yale College, not inconsistent with the terms of this trust, which may in their opinion be expedient.   . " ' GEORGE PEABODY.

" ' NEW YORK, Oct. 22, 1866.'

" This generous donation provides for one great and pressing want of the university, — a fire-proof museum-building for preserving the extensive and valuable collections which have been accumulating during the last half-century, and are now rapidly increasing. It is understood to be the intention of the trustees to commence the erection of the first wing of the museum at an early day. When completed, this part will, it is thought, be amply sufficient for the requirements of the immediate future, or until the reserved building-fund shall have increased sufficiently to provide for the erection of the main or central building; and this, in turn, will serve until the completion of the whole structure.

" Students of natural history in all departments of Yale College, and in all time to come, will be grateful to Mr. Peabody for thus rendering secure the collection and preservation of such a museum as the institution has long been in need of."

In October, 1866, Mr. Peabody testified his regard for the oldest college in his native land by giving Harvard a sum of money for a museum, which is now known by his name.   His letter and instrument of gift are as follows: —

" Georgetown, Oct. 8, 1866.

" To the Hon. Robert C. Winthrop, His Excellency Charles Francis Adams, Francis Peabody, Stephen Salisbury, Asa Gray, Jeffries Wyman, and George Peabody Russell, Esquires.

" *Gentlemen,* — Accompanying this letter, I enclose an

instrument giving to you one hundred and fifty thousand dollars ($150,000), in trust, for the foundation and maintenance of a museum and professorship of American archæology and ethnology in connection with Harvard University.

"I have for some years had the purpose of contributing, as I might find opportunity, to extend the usefulness of the honored and ancient university of our Commonwealth ; and I trust, that in view of the importance and national character of the proposed department, and its interesting relations to kindred investigations in other countries, the means I have chosen may prove acceptable.

"On learning of your acceptance of the trust, and of the assent of the President and Fellows of Harvard College to its terms, I shall be prepared to pay over to you the sum I have named.

"Aside from the provisions of the instrument of gift, I leave in your hands the details and management of the trust ; only suggesting, that, in view of the gradual obliteration or destruction of the works and remains of the ancient races of this continent, the labor of exploration and collection be commenced at as early a day as practicable ; and also, that, in the event of the discovery in America of human remains or implements of an earlier geological period than the present, especial attention be given to their study, and their comparison with those found in other countries.

"With the hope that the museum, as thus established

and maintained, may be instrumental in promoting and extending its department of science, and with fullest confidence, that, under your care, the best means will be adopted to secure the end desired,

"I am, with great respect, your humble servant,

"GEORGE PEABODY."

"I do hereby give to Robert C. Winthrop of Boston, Charles Francis Adams of Quincy, Francis Peabody of Salem, Stephen Salisbury of Worcester, Asa Gray of Cambridge, Jeffries Wyman of Cambridge, and George Peabody Russell of Salem, all of Massachusetts, the sum of one hundred and fifty thousand dollars, to be by them and their successors held in trust, to found and maintain a museum of American archæology and ethnology in connection with Harvard University, in the city of Cambridge, and Commonwealth of Massachusetts.

"Of this sum I direct that my said trustees shall invest forty-five thousand dollars as a fund, the income of which shall be applied to forming and preserving collections of antiquities, and objects relating to the early races of the American continent, or such (including such books and works as may form a good working library for the departments of science indicated) as shall be requisite for the investigation and illustration of archæology and ethnology in general, in main and special reference, however, to the aboriginal American races.

"I direct that the income of the further sum of forty-

five thousand dollars shall be applied by my said trustees
to the establishment and maintenance of a professorship of
American archæology and ethnology in Harvard University. The professor shall be appointed by the President
and Fellows of Harvard College, with the concurrence of
the overseers, in the same manner as other professors are
appointed, but upon the nomination of the founder or the
board of trustees. He shall have charge of the above-
mentioned collections, and shall deliver one or more courses
of lectures annually, under the direction of the government of the university, on subjects connected with said
departments of science.

" Until this professorship is filled, or during the time it
may be vacant, the income from the fund appropriated to
it shall be devoted to the care and increase of the collections.

" I further direct that the remaining sum of sixty
thousand dollars be invested and accumulated as a building-fund until it shall amount to at least one hundred
thousand dollars, when it may be employed in the erection
of a suitable fire-proof museum-building, upon land to be
given for that purpose, free of cost or rental, by the President and Fellows of Harvard College; the building, when
completed, to become the property of the college, for the
uses of this trust, and none other.

" The board of trustees I have thus constituted shall
always be composed of seven persons: and it is my wish
that the office of chairman be filled by Mr. Winthrop; in

the event of his death or resignation, by Mr. Adams; and so successively in the order I have named above. The trustees shall keep a record of their doings, and shall annually prepare a report, setting forth the condition of the trust and funds, and the amount of income received and paid out by them during the previous year. This report, signed by the trustees, shall be presented to the President and Fellows of the college.

"In the event of the death or resignation of Mr. Winthrop, I direct that the vacancy in the number of the board be filled by the President of the Massachusetts Historical Society, who, *ex officio*, shall forever after be a member of the board. In the event of the death or resignation of Mr. Peabody, the vacancy to be filled by the President of the scientific body now established in the city of Salem, under the name of the Essex Institute; of Mr. Salisbury, by the President of the American Antiquarian Society; of Prof. Gray, by the President of the American Academy of Arts and Sciences; and of Prof. Wyman, by the President of the Boston Society of Natural History, — all of whom shall forever after be, *ex officio*, members of the board.

"Should the president of either of the societies I have named decline to act as a trustee, such vacancy, and all other vacancies that may occur in the number of the trustees, shall be filled by the remaining trustees, who shall, within a reasonable time, make the appointment or appointments.

" I give to my said trustees the liberty to obtain from the Legislature an act of incorporation, if they deem it desirable; to make all necessary by-laws; to appoint a treasurer; and to enter into any arrangements and agreements with the government of Harvard College, not inconsistent with the terms of this trust, which may, in their opinion, be expedient.

(Signed)   " GEORGE PEABODY.

" GEORGETOWN, Oct. 8, 1866."

Rev. Dr. Walker, in referring to this munificence of Mr. Peabody, and the fact that officers of Harvard College and officers of the Massachusetts Historical Society were to be also trustees of the Peabody Museum, said, " Mr. Peabody, as it seems to me, has shown great wisdom by connecting his new institution, to some extent, with two of the oldest of these societies; so that, hereafter, we may have the benefit of both agencies, acting with more effect because more likely to act in harmony and together for a common object."

Rev. E. E. Hale then remarked, —

" I should not venture to add any thing, Mr. President, to what has been so fitly said, but that you have asked me to say something in acknowledgment of so great a gift to science, because, in some sort, I represent here the government of the American Antiquarian Society. In the establishment of the proposed museum, and of the professorship connected with it, under Mr. Peabody's munificent endowment, the Antiquarian Society saw the fulfilment of a cherished wish which it had entertained for half a century; and its government is confident, that, in the administration of this endowment, the studies of the American antiquary would be redeemed from any unfair suspicion which has considered them petty, or unworthy of profound scientific attention.

"Have we not been somewhat disposed to think that these arrow-points and pestles and stone axe-heads, such as I have brought down stairs from our own collection, were hardly worth a place in our museum ? Or, if any explorer southward or westward brought us his contributions of the work of our own native tribes, have we not been apt to think that they were mere curiosities, with little value for science ? Now, in the recent study of the antiquity of the human race, these very illustrations of what has been called the Stone Age are claiming a place of the very first importance in the study of the real primeval history of the world.

"And, Mr. President, so far as I am aware, Mr. Peabody, in his letter of gift, is the first person who has publicly called attention to the invaluable illustration which the antiquarian study of this country will thus give to this new science, which seeks to set in order the social progress of the world, — its moral palæontology, if I may hazard the expression, — of which we here can illustrate some of the steps far better than they can be illustrated in Europe. The little specimens which I have placed on the table — some of them the work of Nature, and some, to appearance much less carefully wrought, the undoubted work of man — will show how difficult it is for an untrained observer to say with certainty, in a given instance, whether a relic from another age is or is not a memorial of human art. In point of fact, the tools from the alluvium of the·Somme, figured by M. Boucher de Perthès in his ' Antiquités Celtiques,' were so rudely shaped, that many persons supposed they were stones which owed their peculiar forms to accidental fracture in a river's bed. In such ways the whole series of questions connected with the memorials of the stone age discovered in Europe have been embarrassed, from the fact that the scientific men of Europe, in studying that age, with them so distant, have been obliged to construct their theories simply from the handful of specimens preserved through so many intervening ages, — materials which were themselves the material under discussion. We here, however, have the stone age at hand : we can match these arrow-points and axe-heads from our own collections of thousands of such articles, — the work of a race not yet passed away. If we wish, we can question the men who have used them ; nay, can see them as they make them. And here is one more instance to be added to so many which are successively forced upon us, which show that our antiquarian studies are, in fact, not the baby-talk of the infants of a new world, but are

12

studies relating to the very oldest world, and, indeed, to the very foundation of social order.

"You remember, Mr. President, how often Mr. Agassiz dwells upon the fact, that, when it pleased God to divide the land from the water, — when 'fields grew green,' where for thousands of years 'oceans only had gathered,' — the first beach which rose above the icy waves was the strip of land which Mr. Agassiz calls ' the Laurentian Hills.' It is the strip which we have all heard described so many times — and in the language of geology also — as ' the highlands dividing the waters of the St. Lawrence from the waters of the Atlantic.' That was the phrase used by Adams and Franklin in our first treaty with England; and the commissioners chose that oldest ridge of land to be the eternal division between the two countries which were just then parted. All of us have noticed the curious revelation of recent science, which has pointed out the fact, that this region, made so familiar to us in the struggles of diplomacy, should prove to be really a landmark so ancient. Now, with every fresh revelation of science, sir, we are seeing more distinctly that the studies of this older continent are in every way essential to the studies of our younger sister continent on the other side of the ocean.

"It seems to me a very striking illustration of the comprehensive views of Mr. Peabody, that, while he was engaged in that work for the world to which a great merchant is called, he should have perceived the intimacy of the connection between the antiquarian study of this country and what I have a right to call the newly-created antiquarian science of Europe. These views of the antiquity of man, in which Professor Lyell has excited such wide popular interest, are but just now announced to the European world. Mr. Peabody has instantly seized on the fact, that, in this older world, we have peculiar advantages for illustrating them. Deeply interested himself in the new studies by which the geologists of Europe are illustrating the antiquity of the race, he has seen that we have here peculiar opportunity for contributing to those studies facts of great interest, and observations impossible excepting where the forms of the oldest social order may be studied while still alive. Observing this, with the most liberal endowment he creates the new institution which is to preserve the memorials and give persistency to the studies which are necessary in the illustration.

"I hold in my hand, and should gladly read here if I had not occupied so much of the society's time, a letter from Mr. Abbott Lawrence, written when he was our minister in England, acknowledging in the most cordial way the important services which Mr. Peabody again and again rendered in preserving a kindly feeling between America and England. He seems to have consecrated the immense influence which he has so worthily acquired to those friendly offices which best unite two lands that should be parted only by the ocean. The last great service we acknowledge to-day, in which Mr. Peabody shows us how the antiquarian science of each continent may contribute to that of the other; how essential, indeed, for the deepest research of each continent, is the kindred research, which, at the same moment, presses its inquiries in the other, — this last great service fitly illustrates that work of mediation and good feeling to which this distinguished man has so successfully devoted the efforts of his life."

The value of Mr. Peabody's gift will be best appreciated by those interested in the objects of the museum; and, that these may be better understood, the circular stating their wants and wishes is here given : —

" PEABODY MUSEUM OF AMERICAN ARCHÆOLOGY AND
ETHNOLOGY.

" Through the munificence of Mr. George Peabody of London, a museum of American archæology and ethnology has been established in connection with Harvard College. In carrying out the wishes of the founder, it is intended to bring together all objects illustrative of or bearing upon the origin, early history, manners and customs, and progress towards civilization, of the aboriginal races of North and South America. In furthering the objects of the above foundation, the undersigned, the executive committee, in behalf of the board of trustees, are desirous of obtaining any of the following articles : —

" 1. Implements of stone, such as axes, gouges, chisels, clubs, pestles, sinkers, tomahawks, mortars, arrow-heads, spear-heads, &c.

" 2. Articles of earthenware, such as vases, pots, pipes, bowls, or images of any kind.

" 3. Bows, arrows, quivers, spears, rattles, drums, shields, snow-shoes, knives, lodges, medicine-bags, tobacco-pouches, cooking-utensils, articles of dress, either of purely aboriginal make, or such as show the gradual contact of the savage and European races.

" 4. Mummies, skeletons, or parts of skeletons, of any of the North or South American races. Of the parts of skeletons, the skulls are always of great importance; and the long bones of the limbs, and the hip-bones, are of much value.

" 5. Antiquities, in the form of images or other sculptures, or the casts of them, from Peru, Mexico, Chili, or Central America.

" 6. Any articles made by or relating to the Esquimaux, and the Fuegians, or the Patagonians.

" It is within the plan of the founder to make collections relating to the archæology and ethnology of other aboriginal races, especially of such articles as have a bearing upon, or help to illustrate the history of, the American races. The trustees are, therefore, desirous of obtaining crania, skeletons or parts of skeletons, weapons and implements of all kinds, pottery, or any other articles of aboriginal make, from any portion of the world; also drawings or casts of them which may serve to show the differences or resemblances between the various human races in their earliest stages of existence.

"ROBERT C. WINTHROP,
ASA GRAY,
JEFFRIES WYMAN,   } *Executive Committee.*"

CHAPTER XII.

STILL HELPING EDUCATORS.

Peabody Academy of Science in Salem. — Essex Institute. — Mr. Peabody's Letter. — His Love for his native County of Essex.

> " Some there are
> By their good deeds exalted, lofty minds,
> And meditative authors of delight
> And happiness, which, to the end of time,
> Will live and spread and flourish." — WORDSWORTH.

" Receive my instruction, and not silver; and knowledge rather than choice gold. For wisdom is better than rubies; and all the things that may be desired are not to be compared to it." — PROV. viii. 10, 11.

AS intimated in the Preface, George Peabody was not forgetful of the Essex Institute in Salem. With his usual liberality, he bestowed a large sum upon those banded together in Essex County for historical and scientific purposes, and founded, in connection with the Essex Institute, whose library, museum, and officers were in Salem, an Academy of Science, so called, to be known henceforth by his name. The following characteristic letter accompanied his gift : —

"SALEM, MASS., Feb. 26, 1867.

"To Francis Peabody, Esq., Prof. Asa Gray, William C. Endicott, Esq., George Peabody Russell, Esq., Prof. Othniel C. Marsh, Dr. Henry Wheatland, Abner C. Goodell, jun., Esq., Dr. James R. Nichols, and Dr. Henry C. Perkins.

"*Gentlemen*, — As you will perceive by the enclosed instrument of trust, I wish to place in the hands of yourselves and your successors the sum of one hundred and forty thousand dollars for the promotion of science and useful knowledge in the county of Essex.

"Of this, my native county, I have always been justly proud, in common with all her sons; remembering her ancient reputation, her many illustrious statesmen, jurists, and men of science, her distinguished record from the earliest days of our country's history, and the distinction so long retained by her, as eminent in the education and morality of her citizens.

"I am desirous of assisting to perpetuate her good name through future generations, and of aiding, through her means, in the diffusion of science and knowledge; and after consultation with some of her most eminent and worthy citizens, and encouraged by the success which has already attended the efforts and researches of the distinguished scientific association of which your chairman is president, and with which most of you are connected, I am led to hope that this gift may be instrumental in attaining the desired end.

"I therefore transmit to you the enclosed instrument,

and a check for the amount therein named ($140,000), with the hope that this trust, as administered by you and your successors, may tend to advancement in intelligence and virtue, not only in our good old county of Essex, but in our commonwealth and in our common country.

" I am, with great respect,

" Your humble servant,

" GEORGE PEABODY."

During the session of the American Association for the Advancement of Science, which was held in Salem, Mass., in the summer of 1869, the dedicatory services of the Peabody Academy of Science were held in the Tabernacle Church; the building owned by the academy being too small for the audience.

According to " The Salem Observer " of Aug. 14, 1869, " The exercises were opened at three o'clock with prayer by the Rev. C. R. Palmer, pastor of the church; which was followed by the singing of a hymn written for the occasion by Rev. Jones Very, and which was well rendered by a select choir from the Salem Oratorio Class. The dedicatory address was then delivered by Mr. Endicott; and it was universally regarded as a very appropriate, excellent, and eloquent discourse. Remarks were afterwards made by Ex-Gov. Clifford, Mayor Coggswell, B. H. Silsbee, Esq., of the Marine Society, Dr. Wheatland, and Pres. Foster. Benediction by Rev. Mr. Willson."

The address of the mayor, Gen. William Coggswell, as reported in the same excellent newspaper, was as follows : —

"Mr. President and Gentlemen,—I know that I speak the sentiments of the people of this city when I congratulate you, sir, and your associate trustees, upon the successful establishment in our midst of the Academy of Science, under the wise and beneficent trust of that world-wide benefactor whose name stands at the head of your institution.

"Though your labors were at the outset clouded and increased by the great loss which we all felt here in the death of the first president of your board, yet the citizens of this place, which has been honored by the location of this Academy, though its purposes are to be devoted to the broader field of the whole county of Essex, have witnessed with pleasure the great and rapid progress which has been made in the discharge of the duties of your important trust. They are aware of the vast amount of labor, under the careful and able supervision of yourself and associates, which has wrought out all this. They are sensible of the good results which must inevitably flow therefrom ; and therefore it is, that, with honor and with pride, they feel they can join you this day in the dedication of the Peabody Academy of Science, and bid it, as they do now bid it, All hail, welcome, and God speed !

" Dedicated to the cause of science, — that cause to which all look for truth, instruction, and the explanation of the hidden mysteries of life ; through which we learn to understand the ways of Nature, and to make useful all the powers which God has given ; from which we learn to read aright the lessons of experience, and to make more perfect the labors of mankind ; science, which leads, not from, but to, a better, higher, nobler appreciation of God and his infinity, — dedicated to this great study, and in this presence of the eminent scholars of science of our land, who shall attempt to set forth its useful results, its perfect work, its future, or its effect upon the important study to which it is now dedicated and set apart?   Who will follow out its influences, unbounded and without a limit as they will be, as from father to son, from generation to generation, it shall send forth the influence and energy of developed truth into the great struggle of life and into the current of the great river of knowledge ?

" When we reflect upon the immense scope of its study, — touching every interest and inquiry of life ; sifting and exposing error ; underlying the superstructure of government, of life, of health, of knowledge, and of wisdom ; opening to us the secrets of Nature ; bringing us all, whether we will or not, up to a higher, broader, better plane of existence ; leading us to discard error and prejudice, and to adopt the truth ; training the lightning to do its bidding ; exchanging, as it does this day exchange, the thoughts and wishes of continents, and publishing the edicts of Nature in " the twinkling of an eye ; " — when we call to mind that all things yield up their secrets to the all-searching, never-tiring eye of the man of science ; when we consider more particularly its relation to the body politic, — that upon it government must depend alike for its implements of war and its arts of peace, — railroads, canals, surveys, harbor - improvements, the census, the levying of tax, finance, the waging of war, the commerce of the seas, the products of the soil; that ' the end of the institution, maintenance, and administration of government is to secure the existence of the body politic, to protect it, and to furnish the individuals who compose it with the power of enjoying in safety and tranquillity their natural rights and the blessings of life ; ' — when we consider all this, and that government, in all its branches and departments, in all the intricate machinery of administration, must follow the laws of science, or follow not at all, who but will welcome every aid in its behalf? who but will give thanks and praise at the founding of each and every academy devoted to its great and ennobling labors ? and who but will love and revere the man whose never-failing spring of love to his fellow-man has builded in our midst this temple in its honor ?   And most especially does it become the municipality which has been made the favored recipient of such a trust to take a deep and abiding interest in all that appertains to its welfare and success.

" I feel, gentlemen, the difficulty under which I labor

in speaking to the cause of science in this presence; for I am as a stranger in its fields: but I can bear my willing testimony to the vast amount of good it has already accomplished. I feel that to it all things are possible; and I know that I reflect the feelings of the citizens of Salem when I greet this as the dawning of better and more glorious days in the history of this our city, so full now of its proud memories which we all delight to honor, and in whose welfare we all take a loving and an earnest part.

" I shall fail, however, in my duty here, if I omit to pay my tribute of respect to the genius, the skill, the industry, and the devotion of those gentlemen, who, if life is spared to them, and they are spared to you, are destined to make your trust a perfect and a famed success. I refer to the present professors of your Academy. It is a delicate matter to speak of them in their presence; yet I cannot help saying, what everybody knows, that fortunate indeed is the institution which can claim them as its own.

" But, sir, I shall turn away from any attempt to speak the feelings of those I have the honor to represent, or of myself, — the feelings of admiration and gratitude and respect towards him whose bounty, reaching from continent to continent, has fallen upon our heads; for I feel that all words of praise would be commonplace, that all expressions of gratitude would be trite, and that all words of compliment would be empty, when brought by me and laid at the feet of so great a doer of good.

" And now allow me to say, that with the Essex Institute, so favorably known, under its wise and active management; with our Peabody Academy of Science, so
recently inaugurated; with the far-famed East-India Museum, brought now to a more public use; and with the
eminent men connected with them, —fortunate and happy
indeed must be the city which holds them all within its
limits; and I feel that I can pledge you at all times the
hearty and unbounded support and co-operation of the
citizens of Salem."

The Essex Institute of Salem, which was the institution
from which the Peabody Academy of Science is but an
outgrowth, is greatly indebted to one man especially for
its success. His untiring zeal, energy, and perseverance,
and his acknowledged ability as secretary and librarian
and manager-in-general of the affairs of the Essex Institute, have, in a large measure, been the source of its success. That man is Dr. Henry Wheatland of Salem, whose
silver hairs are a crown of glory, and whose afternoon of
life is so radiant, that it seems as if his sun stood still, as
in the days of Gideon, while he battles on the fields of
historic and scientific research.

He said, on the occasion of the dedication of the Peabody Academy of Science, and in response to a deserved
tribute paid the Essex Institute, —

" I thank you, Mr. President, in behalf of the Essex
Institute, for your kind notice on this occasion.

" The Institute has only to say, that it has been humbly following out the plan handed down by past generations for the promotion of education and general culture, modified in some degree to meet the wants of the community and the requirements of the age. What little success may have attended its efforts is mainly due to the examples and precepts of those who have preceded. These early pioneers in the cause of science have borne the heat and burden of the day, and have prepared the way, thus leaving it comparatively easy to follow.

"We have an honorable record. Each successive period in our history, from the landing of Conant, of Endicott, and Higginson, from the time of Roger Williams and Hugh Peters, to the present, has enrolled many names illustrious for professional attainments, mechanical industries, and commercial enterprises.

" These materials did not crystallize into any permanent form until about the middle of the last century, when it assumed that of a social club, composed of the leading spirits of the day, and holding weekly meetings; where the principal topics of the day were discussed, especially those of a literary and scientific character. One was the suggestion for the formation of a library similar in its character to that which Franklin had established in Philadelphia some twenty-five or thirty years previous, and that at Newport by Redwood a few years afterwards. This movement resulted in the formation of the Social Library in 1761. These meetings were held at Pratt's Tavern, located on the north-east corner of Essex and Washington Streets. At that time, the tavern was the great place of resort for the people; and meetings of the various clubs, committees, &c., were always held there.

"Some twenty years roll away, and we behold the privateer ship 'Pilgrim,' Hugh Hill, commander, owned by the Messrs. Cabot, bringing into the neighboring port of Beverly a collection of books, being a part of the library of the celebrated Irish chemist, Dr. Richard Kirwan, which was taken from a schooner captured during the early part of the year 1781 in the English Channel. These books, comprising the 'Philosophical Transactions of the Royal Society of London,' 'Mémoires de l'Académie Royale des Sciences,' Paris, 'Miscellanea Berolinensa,' Boyle's 'Works,' 'Bernouilli Opera,' 'Wolfii Elementa Matheseos,' and others, were purchased by a company of gentlemen; and thus was constituted the Philosophical Library. This addition gave a new impulse to scientific investigation, and aided many in their researches. The late Dr. Nathaniel Bowditch, when a young man, had access to these works, and thus was enabled to develop more fully that genius which enabled him to be the expounder of La Place, and to take a leading position among the mathematicians of his age. In his will, Dr. Bowditch makes honorable mention of his indebtedness to this library in his early studies. Among the proprietors of this library may be mentioned Rev. Joseph Willard, afterwards President of Harvard College; Rev. Dr.

Manasseh Cutler of the Hamlet in Ipswich, one of our earliest botanists, and the originator and conductor of a company who emigrated from this county in 1786 to the West, and thus founded the settlement at Marietta, on the banks of the Ohio; Drs. E. A. Holyoke and Orne of Salem; and others.

" Another score of years pass, and we behold in a small room, in the third story of a brick building erected on the site of the old tavern previously mentioned, and now occupied as a part of the printing-office of ' The Salem Observer,' the nucleus of a museum originated by several of our citizens engaged in the East-India trade, then the leading business in Salem, and around which, by gradual accretions, has grown the famous East-India Museum, the re-arrangement of which with the scientific collections of the Essex Institute the trustees of the Peabody Academy of Science this day dedicate to the public.

" It is perhaps needless to trace further in detail the growth of our institutions : the principal facts in their history have appeared in the printed publications of the Institute. Suffice it to mention that the Salem Athenæum was incorporated in 1810 : the Essex Historical Society, organized in 1821, and the Essex-County Natural History Society in 1833, were united and incorporated in 1848 under the name of the Essex Institute.

" The building of Plummer Hall in 1856, from funds bequeathed by the late Miss Caroline Plummer of Salem, and in which are deposited the principal libraries, constitute an important era in our history. It is a singular coincidence, that this building is erected on the site of the house in which Prescott the historian first saw the light of day.

" The donation of Mr. Peabody in 1867, and the consequent formation of the Trustees of the Peabody Academy of Science, — a full account of which has been so ably and so eloquently presented by you, Mr. President, on this occasion, — has relieved the Institute of a portion of its duties, some of which have already been transferred to the Academy, — the care and maintenance of its museum, and the publication of scientific papers, especially those that illustrate the natural history of the county. This forms another very important epoch in our history.

" This donation of Mr. Peabody came very opportunely, at a time when the materials were at hand to organize an institution on a good basis, with large and valuable museums and a corps of able workers. The Museum of the East-India Marine Society had been accumulating for many years, and had acquired a well-merited reputation. The Essex Institute had, within the past few years, gathered together a corps of active young naturalists and of historical students, and had awakened a deep interest in scientific studies and historic research by its field and other meetings, its lectures and publications ; at the same time, added largely to its library and its various collections; awaiting, as it were, for some such endowment as that of Mr. Peabody to galvanize them into a more active sphere of usefulness.

" The Institute has cause for great congratulation that one of its cherished departments is so well cared for; and that, under the auspices of the Academy, an accurate survey of the natural resources of the county will be made, that the same may be developed to the fullest extent; and that a knowledge of the sciences, especially their application to the arts, be diffused among the people, so that, by the aid of skilled labor, the greatest practical results can be obtained with the least expenditure of time and capital.

" The Essex Institute in its organization recognizes three departments, — those of natural history, history, and horticulture.

" The first, as has been before mentioned, is in good hands. It is immaterial who does the work, or who has the credit for doing the same, provided that it is well done. The second and third have received no special endowment; and what little provision they obtain must come from the ordinary income, or from future acts of munificence.

" The horticultural department has taken, in years past, a prominent position in the doings of the society. The exhibitions of fruits and flowers have been considered as ranking favorably with those of similar institutions. This city and the vicinity have always had a goodly array of enthusiastic and successful cultivators of the choicest productions of Flora and Pomona. Among those of the past, the name of Robert Manning the elder stands prominent as a pioneer in the cultivation of fruit, especially of the pear.

" The garden of J. F. Allen exhibited for several seasons a fine display of that gorgeous lily, the Victoria Regia; and his excellent treatise on this flower, with superb illustrations, finds a place in every public library. Yet later, Allen's Hybrids and Rogers's Hybrid Seedling Grapes are attracting the attention of all the cultivators of this choice and delicious fruit.

" Essex County is one of the oldest in New England. Her records date back to an early period. Its children have been and are now among the prominent in all the greatest enterprises of their respective periods, and have received their merited reward. Let us cherish their memories with strict fidelity, and transmit the same, unimpaired, to the latest posterity.

" To this end it is necessary to preserve with the greatest care all papers, loose manuscript-leaves, interleaved almanacs with inserted notes, old records, diaries, &c., that are scattered through our county. They are found in the archives of our towns, in the various parishes, and in almost every hamlet.

" The county commissioners have, with a wise forethought, done a good work in having the papers belonging to the old quarterly courts properly arranged and placed into volumes, the whole carefully indexed under the superintendence of W. P. Upham, one of our most careful and zealous antiquarian scholars. Thanks to the commissioners for what has thus far been done. May they be induced to extend the same protecting care to all the other records that are deposited in the various county offices!

" It is very desirable that the Essex Institute should be placed in a condition to collect and arrange in a similar manner all the scattered materials that will elucidate our history. If the originals cannot be obtained, exact copies of the same should be carefully made. Many of these papers will undoubtedly be found worthy of being printed; and, if no provision should be made that the same be done, an opportunity is here offered for some liberal-minded son or sons of Essex to contribute to this worthy object. In no better and more enduring way can one be remembered in the future than by cherishing a due regard for the memory of those who have contributed so much for the comfort and happiness of the present generation."

The whole of the above address is given, because it concerns the county which was nearest Mr. Peabody's heart, because it was his native county. It will be seen by the address that the Peabody Academy of Science does not take the place of the Essex Institute, nor is it overshadowed by the latter. They work together. According to the reliable statements of Dr. Wheatland, —

" The real status of the Essex Institute is nearly this: An institution with several hundred members resident in all the towns of Essex County, its headquarters in Salem, its rooms in Plummer Hall, where is deposited its library of some twenty-five thousand volumes, and a large collection of historical matter. It owns a fine collection of specimens of natural history, deposited with the Peabody Academy. It holds, in the summer-season, some half-dozen assemblies in fit localities, occupying a whole day at each: the forenoon is spent in explorations and research, and the afternoon given to discussions and reports. These occasions, called 'field-meetings,' are open to every one, and are always highly diversified and agreeable, combining the ease of the picnic with the profit of the lecture-room. In the winter-season, evening meetings are held on the first and third Mondays of each month; and, occasionally, courses of historical and scientific lectures are given. The publications consist of a volume of historical collections annually, of some three hundred pages, and the 'Bulletin,' a record of meetings, short communications on subjects of which the Institute takes cognizance, donations, correspondence, &c. Papers of a strictly scientific character, requiring illustrations, may probably be printed by the Peabody Academy, or arrangements to that effect will probably be made; otherwise by the Institute, under the appellation of ' Memoirs.'

" Thus we have in Salem two institutions, working in a common cause, having organizations entirely different in character,—the Academy, a close corporation of nine members, holding funds for specific purposes, and employing agents to perform duties not inconsistent with the instrument of trust; the other a popular institution of some hundreds of members, including a large portion of those citizens of the county who are interested in the promotion of general culture and refinement. The one supplements the other; and there is no reason why the two may not continue, as now, to co-operate harmoniously in the performance of the important duties committed to their care, and thus build up an institution, or a series of institutions, which will shed a brilliant lustre for a long term of years thoughout our land, and be a beacon-light to the investigation in history, science, art, and literature.

"In conclusion, it may be mentioned that Mr. Peabody, in his instrument of trust, empowers his trustees to make such arrangements and agreements with the Essex Institute as may be necessary or expedient for carrying into effect the provisions of his instrument; also that all the trustees, the director, the curators, and assistants, are members of the Institute; and those who reside within the limits of the county hold either an office or a place on some important standing-committee, as president, vice-president, superintendent, corresponding secretary, and curators.

"Though entirely distinct in their organization, these two institutions may, in part, be considered as one; many of the offices in both being held by the same persons. Thus linked together in a common bond of union, no diversity of interest can exist; each having its respective field of operations, and line of duty."

After a membership of nearly ten years, commencing while a resident of Essex County, and never relinquished, because so highly valued, the writer of this memorial volume can only add to Dr. Wheatland's remarks an emphatic "Amen."

CHAPTER XIII.

YET GIVING CHEERFULLY.

Massachusetts Historical Society. — Kenyon College, and Mr. Peabody's Donation to it. — Documents in Regard to the Acceptable Gifts.

> " And while ' Lord, Lord ! ' the pious tyrants cried,
>   Who in the poor their Master crucified,
>   *His* daily prayer, far better understood
>   In acts than words, was simply DOING GOOD." — WHITTIER.

"Through wisdom is a house builded; and by understanding it is established; and by knowledge shall the chambers be filled with all precious and pleasant riches." — PROV. xxiv. 3, 4.

AMONG the excellent institutions of Massachusetts is its Historical Society, which elected Mr. Peabody an honorary member on the 12th of July, 1866; and, at the society-meeting in September following, the corresponding secretary read a letter from Mr. Peabody, stating his acceptance of the honor. At the November meeting of the same year, the president of the society (Hon. R. C. Winthrop) laid before the society a copy of the letter and trust-instrument, whereby Mr. Peabody established a museum and professorship of American archæology and ethnology in connection with Harvard University, in which he named the

President of the Massachusetts Historical Society, *ex officio*, forever one of the trustees : whereupon the following resolution was submitted : —

" *Resolved*, That Mr. Peabody's letter, and instrument of trust, be entered in full on the records of this society ; and that the president be instructed to communicate to Mr. Peabody the deep and grateful sense which is entertained by us all of the interest and importance of the institution which he has thus founded, and of the munificence and wisdom with which he has provided for its management and support."

The remarks which followed the reading of this resolution are already mentioned in a previous chapter.

In January of the following year, the Massachusetts Historical Society was called on to be grateful in its own behalf particularly.   At the meeting in January, the president said that he had received a communication from our distinguished honorary member, Mr. George Peabody, which he was sure would be listened to with high gratification and with deep gratitude by every member present. He then proceeded to read the following letter : —

" Boston, Jan. 1, 1867.

" To the Hon. ROBERT C. WINTHROP, President of the Massachu-
.   setts Historical Society.

" *My dear Sir*, — I have for some time desired to gratify a wish which I once expressed to you, and while I should, at the same time, mark my strong personal esteem and regard for yourself, and my appreciation of the past labors and researches of the venerable and distinguished society of which you are president, to contribute, in some degree, to extend its future usefulness, and preserve its valued memorials.

" With these objects in view, therefore, I beg to present, through you, to the Massachusetts Historical Society, the sum of twenty thousand dollars in the five-per-cent ten-forty coupon-bonds of the United States, bearing accrued interest from the 1st of September last; which bonds, or their proceeds, shall be held by them as a permanent trust-fund, of which the income shall be appropriated to the publication and illustration of their proceedings and memoirs, and to the preservation of their historical portraits.

" I will thank you to do me the favor to communicate this to the society at their next meeting, to be held on the 10th inst.

" I am, with great respect, your humble servant,

" GEORGE PEABODY."

Dr. Ellis then offered the following resolutions: —

" *Resolved*, That the members of the Massachusetts Historical Society have listened with profound gratification to the reading, by their president, of the letter of Mr. George Peabody, accompanying his gift to the society of twenty thousand dollars; and that it is with the sincerest gratitude to the munificent donor that we thus find ourselves sharers in the comprehensive generosity which has been exercised in England and in the United States with such varied, discriminating, and admirable adaptation to so many noble interests of humanity, science, and liberal culture.

"*Resolved*, That we recognize this noble gift as especially opportune in time and occasion, and as peculiarly adapted, in the purposes which its donor assigns for it, to what have recently been felt to be the most pressing wants of the society. We, therefore, hereby pledge ourselves, and would bind our successors, to a faithful keeping and improvement of the fund, to be called henceforward 'The Peabody Fund,' of which we are thus put in possession; having regard alike to the conditions so intelligently set forth by Mr. Peabody, and to the importance of the special objects he has aimed to serve.

"*Resolved*, That our best appreciation of this gift, and the most fitting return which we can make to its donor, will be in our finding in it, individually and as a society, a new and continued incentive to industry, earnestness, and fidelity in pursuing the investigations and labors for which we are here associated.

"*Resolved*, That the president be requested to communicate to Mr. Peabody a copy of these resolutions, and to assure him that his gift is gratefully received, and shall be faithfully used."

Dr. Ellis then spoke as follows:—

"While we are content to repeat much the same familiar words and forms of speech in asking for favors, we often wish that we had new and fresh terms for acknowledging them. We should be glad to have a more ample range, and a fuller variety of expressions of recognition and gratitude. We feel that we might then adapt our acknowledgments of obligation for a favor received to the special occasion, to the opportuneness, and to the present and prospective value, of the benefit conferred, and thus avoid the generalities and commonplaces of thankful acknowledgment.

"So, at least, I felt, Mr. President, when, at your request, I set myself to draw up the formal resolutions of gratitude to our new benefactor, that should, at the same time, convey a personal tribute which we might hope would be acceptable to him, and express our high estimate of the opportuneness and value of his gift. There is something about the personality and the individuality of that honored and munificent man; something in the nature and method of his wide liberality; something in the concise forms and in the dignified simplicity of the writings which accompany his trust-funds, defining their conditions and uses; there is something in the style in which he thus confers great favors, — which would naturally prompt the recipients of them to make a careful choice of their words of thankfulness and appreciation. For if, of any one benefactor of his own and of coming generations, a wide notoriety for the multiplicity and variety and amount of his gifts might prompt a reiteration of the same epithets and praises, it will be difficult for writers in newspapers, and drawers-up of resolutions, to vary their eulogiums of him who now stands before the world as the example of a more than princely munificence, distributed in his native and in his adopted country to the most wisely-chosen and the best-discriminated objects. We can well imagine that all fulsome and extravagant terms would fail to find in him the weak spot of vanity or susceptibility; while still his modesty is conjoined with so true a discernment, and so practical a good sense, that he will not be indifferent to the fitness of the responses made to him by those whom he favors. He will expect to be assured of their purposes of fidelity in holding and using the trust-funds which he commits to them. Indeed, it has seemed to me that the more ambitious of our rising young business-men, who are eager for great acquisitions, may find Mr. Peabody betraying to them, in some sort, the secret of the method of his vast gathering of wealth, in the method of his distribution of it. Those accumulations of his, we know, with whatever felicities of good fortune he had to help him, must have engaged the patient, steady, and persistent exercise of an inquisitive and discreet mind given to practical dealing with the complicated affairs of business. He devotes much careful thought and scrutiny to informing himself about the enterprises and institutions to be benefited by his generosity. Putting himself into relations of confidence with their official representatives, he learns their actual purposes and wants. The impulse or the aid which he gives to any object that commends itself to him is accompanied, in its announcement or direction, by some sagacious counsel, readily inferred, if not distinctly expressed. I suppose, Mr. President, though you have been silent on the point, that we are at liberty to imagine some friendly offices of your own in behalf of the society, through your confidential relations with Mr. Peabody. He has certainly become well acquainted with our wants, and has met them when and where we have most sensibly felt them."

Remarks were also made, in grateful acknowledgment of Mr. Peabody's benefaction, by Col. Aspinwall, Judge Savage, and Leverett Saltonstall, Esq. On motion of Hon. Stephen Salisbury, it was voted to place a bust or portrait of Mr. Peabody in one of the rooms of the society. It was afterwards voted to allow Prof. Wyman to select aboriginal relics from the collection belonging to the Massachusetts Historical Society, and remove them to the Peabody Museum at Cambridge, with the idea, that, by connecting them with a large collection of other archæological objects, they will be made better to accomplish the purpose of the original donors.

Mr. Peabody also donated the sum of twenty-five thousand dollars to Kenyon College, Gambier, O., of which his friend, Bishop McIlvaine, was then president. Want of space forbids the insertion of the documents, which indicated the purpose of the donor, and the gratitude of those who were benefited by his gift.

CHAPTER XIV.

FILIAL DEVOTION.

Memorial Church at Georgetown. — Mr. Peabody's Love for his Mother. — Hymn for the Dedication, by John G. Whittier. — Gifts to his Family and Friends.

> "My mother! at that holy name,
> Within my bosom there's a gush
> Of feeling which no time can tame;
> A feeling, which for years of fame
> I would not, could not, crush." — GEO. P. MORRIS.

> "Forsake not the law of thy mother." — PROV. i. 8.

IN 1839, the town which was the birthplace of George Peabody's mother, and is now the residence of his sister, Mrs. Daniels, had its name changed from New Rowley to Georgetown, in honor of Mr. Peabody. The special correspondent of " The Washington Chronicle " says that " it has always been one of his favorite retreats when in this country. The people respected his wish for retirement; and this tact on their part was fully appreciated by Mr. Peabody, who said, when he was making arrangements in regard to a farewell reception, previous to his departure for England in 1867, that he 'should like to take each resident by the hand; for he had never, in any visit in Georgetown, been annoyed by calls or letters, and that not one of the citizens had ever in any way solicited help from him.' This fact he considered very remarkable, and with reason; for among the begging-letters which he constantly received, and which were never answered, but quietly turned over to his sister, was one from Georgia containing *forty closely-written pages.*

"Here Mr. Peabody erected a church to the memory of his mother, to whom, in death as in life, he was devoted; giving her the first dollar he earned in boyhood, and bestowing the last thoughts of his honored old age upon a memorial of her Christian character. . . . Mr. Peabody's devotion to his mother and family was as thoughtful as that of a woman; and, after he became very wealthy, the old townspeople used to revive reminiscences in that direction concerning him. I recollect hearing my mother say, that, as soon as he was established in Baltimore, he wrote to his mother that 'he should be able, for the future, to supply the family with flour;' and Mrs. Peabody remarked, as she mentioned the circumstance to a friend, that 'it was a great comfort to have George prosperous enough to bear the expenses.' And, from that day to her last, George never allowed his mother to want any thing that filial love could bestow.

"Mr. Peabody, as everybody knows, was a great lover of peace and concord. Nothing would disturb him more than the thought that any act of his might create strife.

14

This tendency was strikingly manifested at his farewell reception in Georgetown, when, referring to the Memorial Church, he distinctly stated that it was created solely as a tribute to his mother, and was given to *her* denomination, — Orthodox Congregational, — from reverence for her memory; and that it would have been given with equal satisfaction had she belonged to any other persuasion: thus showing his intention to deprive the gift of any sectarian bias which might cause bitterness.

"I used, as a child, to study the portrait of Mr. Peabody which hung in his sister's parlor. It represented a singularly handsome middle-aged man. I was always greatly impressed by the tone of mingled pride and affection with which his sister spoke of him; and I remember hearing a gentleman, in some discussion with this lady, ask her if she ever saw a person who had never told a lie: to which she promptly replied, ' Yes: I am sure that my brother George *never* told a lie.' I used to connect this statement, as children will, with the kind blue eyes and bright brown hair of the portrait; and occasionally, as I saw ' G. P.' in our Sunday-school books, indicating that Mr. Peabody had given them to us, I thought of him as the man who had never told a lie. I do not remember, however, that I ever saw him till 1866; when I was glad to recognize in the aged but still majestic man a striking likeness to the picture which had won my childish admiration. During this visit in 1866, he gave the town a public library, — a gift by which all the inhabitants could be benefited; and here, on the afternoon of his farewell reception, he reviewed the children of the public schools, standing with uncovered head on the steps of his sister's house as they filed past, bearing tiny flags of our national red, white, and blue. It was a pleasant sight; and many a teacher preached a sermon to her little flock from the text, — 'Seest thou a man diligent in business? he shall stand before kings; he shall not stand before mean men,' — with the courtly yet genial man, who had smiled and spoken so kindly to them, as a living illustration. . . .

"Here, during his last visit, he added a lecture-room to his previous gift of a library, and made arrangements for free lectures, and a fund for the support of the library. And, having completed every thing to his mind, he said smilingly to Mr. R. S. Tenney, the gentleman with whom he and his sister made their home, 'Well, I believe I have paid all my debts to this town: I believe I do not owe it any thing.' To which Mr. Tenney very happily replied, 'We cannot say the same of you, Mr. Peabody: we shall always owe you.' And Mr. Peabody responded with great feeling, 'If it has been as pleasant to you to receive as it has been to me to bestow, you have enjoyed a great deal.' "

The above paragraphs from the letter of Mrs. A. W. H. Howard to a Washington paper are of special interest. The story of the long letter from Georgia suggests addition of the statement of some paper, that " Mr. Peabody

received one letter of thirty-six foolscap pages from a
decayed English gentleman, who solicited a loan of a few
thousand pounds to establish the claims of his family to an
estate. Mr. Peabody wrote in reply substantially this :
' That you should have written such a letter would surprise your friends : that I should have read it would
indeed surprise mine.' "

But it is of the Georgetown church mention should
here be made. According to " The Newburyport Herald " of Jan. 10, 1868, " The church is a substantial and
elegant brick structure, in the English style, one hundred
and twelve feet long, sixty-eight feet wide, and one hundred and twelve feet high to the top of the tower. It is
finished in chestnut, with black-walnut mouldings ; the
interior harmonizing in all its details with the general
architectural plan. It contains one hundred pews, capable
of seating seven hundred persons. It is lighted by gas ;
the chandelier and sidelights numbering forty double burn-
ers. The bell, which is of twenty-eight hundred pounds
weight, and the clock, a fine piece of mechanism, were
sent by Mr. Peabody from London. The organ is one of
Hook's best instruments, built at a cost of four thousand
dollars. . . . At the end of the church, opposite the
entrance, are three marble tablets with dedicatory inscrip-
tions. Over the pulpit the legend is, ' Dedicated to the
service of Almighty God. Holiness becometh thine
house, O Lord ! forever.' The one on the right of
the pulpit has the following : ' This house, erected in

1866-7 for the use of the Orthodox Congregational Church and Society, is affectionately consecrated by her children, George and Judith, to the memory of Mrs. Judith Peabody, who was born in this parish July 25, 1770, and who died June 22, 1830.'

" The surroundings of the church are in perfect keeping with the edifice. . . . There is a massive iron fence in front, a commodious range of sheds in the rear ; while the vacant space between the church and the library-building is being graded and laid out, preparatory to the planting of trees and flowers. . . . The cost of the house is estimated at one hundred thousand dollars. It has been about a year and a half in building ; and the result is the finest place of worship in this section, a grand monument of Mr. Peabody's liberality, and an honor to all concerned in its erection."

At the dedication, a letter was read from Mr. Peabody. The sermon was preached by Rev. Dr. M. P. Braman of Danvers, and the consecration-prayer offered by Rev. John Pike of Rowley. The following touching memorial-hymn by John G. Whittier was sung : —

> Thou dwellest not, O Lord of all !
> In temples which thy children raise :
> Our work to thine is mean and small,
> And brief to thy eternal days.
>
> Forgive the weakness and the pride,
> If marred thereby our gift may be ;
> For love, at least, has sanctified
> The altar which we rear to thee.

The heart, and not the hand, has wrought,
    From sunken base to tower above,
The image of a tender thought,
    The memory of a deathless love.·

Though here should never sound of speech
    Or organ-anthem rise or fall,
Its stones would pious lessons teach,
    Its shade in benedictions fall.

Here should the dove of peace be found,
    And blessings free as dew-fall given;
Nor strife profane, nor hatred, wound
    The mingled loves of earth and heaven.

Thou who didst soothe with dying breath
    The dear one watching by thy cross,
Forgetful of the pains of death
    In sorrow for her mighty loss, —

In memory of her sacred claim,
    O Mary's Son! our offering take,
And make it worthy of thy name,
    And bless it for a mother's sake.

An editor says, —

"We recently had the pleasure of seeing, at the house of Mr. George J. Tenney, one of the last presents bestowed by Mr. Peabody before his final departure from this country. It consists of a heavy pitcher and goblet of solid silver (the latter lined with gold), enclosed in a handsome case; and the following inscription upon the pitcher tells the story of the gift: 'George Peabody and his sister Judith to Charles Carleton, in appreciation of his skill and fidelity as superintendent in the erection of the Memorial Church at Georgetown.'"

Mr. Peabody's benefactions to his family and immediate personal friends were worthy of mention; but it is not the purpose of this volume to record many beside his public benefactions. To the city of Newburyport, Mr. Peabody gave the sum of fifteen thousand dollars, in 1867, for the enlargement of the Public Library; saying, in his letter, that he wished to mark his memory of that portion of his youth that was passed in that town, and his grateful appreciation of the kindness there shown to him. About a year ago, he manifested a continued interest in that city by sending the following letter, addressed to E. S. Moseley, Esq. : —

"64 QUEEN STREET, CHEAPSIDE, LONDON, E.C.,
April 3, 1869.

"*Dear Sir*, — Some time last spring, I had an intimation, as coming from you as chairman of the Peabody Trust Fund, that a portrait from me, for their library, would be highly appreciated.

"I therefore employed one of the best of the Queen's portrait-painters, and gave him the last sitting a few days ago. The portrait is pronounced excellent. I shall ship it by an early steamer to Boston, and send you a bill of lading, with freight and all charges paid.

"Very respectfully and truly yours,

"GEORGE PEABODY."

Besides these gifts above mentioned were those of twenty-five thousand dollars to the Phillips Academy at Andover, Mass., and ten thousand dollars to the Sanitary Commission during the war. Truly the wealth God gave into George Peabody's hands was widely, and it would seem wisely, scattered.

CHAPTER XV.

Illness of Mr. Peabody. — Return to England. — Sir Curtis Lampson.

> "Adieu, adieu! my native shore
>   Fades o'er the waters blue." — CHILDE HAROLD.
>
> "And, like some low and mournful spell,
>   To whisper but the word, Farewell!" — PARK BENJAMIN.
>
> "Sorrowing most of all for the words which he spake, that they should see his face no more." — ACTS xx. 38.

IT is said that the last time Mr. Peabody spoke in public was at the National Peace Jubilee in Boston. His health was then failing; but he had a notion — a strange one, when we consider how many tons of coal-dust there are always floating about in the London atmosphere — that his life would be prolonged by remaining in London.

"On this point I am somewhat of a Cockney," he would say: "I believe in London air and London living. It is my intention to revisit America; but I shall return to England."

And he did return to England, leaving his family and

friends to feel that he had spoken to them his last fare-well. He was to be seen no more in America.

"Mr. Peabody was slightly above the medium height. His full, round face beamed with goodness. He laughed seldom, but had a smile for everybody. There was nothing ideal or poetical about his face : it was what we tritely term ' a good face.' He never spoke hurriedly. His nature was not impulsive."

But, having resolved, he carried out his purpose ; and to England, though feeble and worn, " The Scotia " carried him. Col. Forney has already described his appearance on the voyage. His friends say that he always preferred English steamers, believing them to be more safe.

" The Baltimore Sun " gives an interesting memorandum of a conversation with Mr. Peabody, furnished by Dr. J. J. Moorman, a resident physician of White Sulphur Springs, Va.; whither Mr. Peabody went for his health during his last visit to America. Dr. Moorman says, Aug. 22, 1869, —

" During my professional attendance on Mr. Peabody for the last four weeks, I have had various short but interesting conversations with him on general subjects, and to-day a more lengthy one. I note down some of his remarks, for future reference.

" On my observing to him that he had great cause of gratitude to God for having been made the instrument of doing so much for his fellow-men, Mr. Peabody replied, and with much more than usual animation, 'I never fail to take that view of it; and always, in my prayers, thank God that he has enabled me to do what I have done.' He said that the attention he receives from the world seemed strange to him; 'that he feels himself to be a very humble individual, and is enabled only by the attentions and opinions of the world in reference to his acts to regard himself as differing from others.'

"On my expressing the opinion that not the least of the great benefits that would result from the liberal distribution of his large wealth during his lifetime, for charitable objects, would be the representative character of such a course, inducing other men of wealth to do likewise, he said he assented to the sentiment; and then remarked, 'Such may not be the case during my life, as men do not generally like to seem to be influenced by their contemporaries;' but added, 'I hope and expect such an ultimate result.'

"I observed to him that the fact of his not having forgotten his relations in the distribution of his large estate, gave, in my opinion, a beautiful symmetry to his benevolence. He said, 'Yes; I should have thought I was doing very wrong if I had done so:' and then remarked, 'I have made all my near relations rich. I have given them all enough, — perhaps more than enough.' He then stated the amount he had given to each, — to Mr. George Peabody Russell, three hundred thousand dollars; to a sister, three hundred thousand dollars; to another nephew, three hundred thousand dollars ; to another, two hundred thousand dollars ; and to none less than one hundred thousand dollars.

" Mr. Peabody described the character, and what would be the operations, of his great gift for the poor of London ; contrasted it with other great schemes that had been inaugurated for the benefit of that class, that contained important reservations for the benefit of the families of the donors, while in his case he had entirely divested himself and his heirs of any ulterior benefit that might accrue ; and said, that, if the donation alluded to was 'judiciously managed for *two centuries*, its accumulations would amount to a sum sufficient to buy the city of London.'

. . . .

" Mr. Peabody was evidently much and very properly gratified at the great attention paid to him both in England and in this country ; and especially with the London statue, and its unveiling under circumstances so imposing and so honorable to him; and with the Queen's autograph-letter to him, which he showed me.

" It being absolutely necessary for Mr. Peabody to reach a warm climate before cold weather set in, that he might have the slightest chance of lengthening his days, and his mind being somewhat balanced between Florida and the south of France, he formally submitted it to me, as his physician, to decide the question. In comparing all the advantages and disadvantages of the two places for his winter residence, I preferred the south of France, and the city of Nice ; and advised that he should proceed directly there, and with as little delay as possible after leaving the mountains. He adopted my views promptly and entirely upon the subject, and immediately wrote to secure a passage on a steamer to sail the 28th of September; saying to me, he would remain a few days only with a friend in London to attend to some necessary business, and then proceed directly, by a route which he pointed out, to Nice, so as to reach there before the setting-in of cold weather."

But it was too late. The days of "the philanthropist of two worlds" were numbered, and his friends all felt this; so that his last public visit to Peabody, Mass., is thus described : —

" The last visit of a public character which Mr. Pea-'body made to his native town was in the summer of 1869, when he invited a number of personal friends, and several of the trustees of his various charities, to meet him at the Peabody Institute. An elegant lunch was served in the library, and the treasures of the Institute exhibited. Among the distinguished public characters present on that occasion were the Hon. Charles Sumner, Hon. Robert C. Winthrop, Ex-Gov. Clifford, Oliver Wendell Holmes, and others. Wealth was represented by such heavy weights as James M. Beebe and Stephen Salisbury. The aggregate wealth of the twenty or thirty gentlemen who were entertained at that board was said to be fifty million dollars. Brief remarks were made by several of the guests, and Mr. Holmes read a short poem, which was afterwards published. Later in the day, the party visited the Peabody Institute at Danvers. It was not a day of unalloyed pleasure. Mr. Peabody's health was rapidly declining; and the thought must have been suggested to all his guests, that the occasion must be to some, and might be to all, the last time they would partake of his elegant hospitality, or witness his participation in the only happiness which survives health and the ordinary blessings of life, — the happiness which is the reward of unselfish devotion in the service of mankind. It was on that occasion that he made his final gift of fifty thousand dollars to the original Peabody Institute."

Mr. Peabody never "kept house," but usually, when in London, dwelt in furnished lodgings, or made his home at the elegant residence of his friend and business-associate, Sir Curtis Lampson, an American, who, for his commendatory course in reference to the Atlantic cable, was knighted by the Queen.

CHAPTER XVI.

DEATH OF MR. PEABODY.

The Lightning News. — The Comments of the Press. — Respect shown to
Mr. Peabody's Memory. — Portraits of Mr. Peabody.

> "So live, that, when thy summons comes to join
> The innumerable caravan that moves
> To that mysterious realm where each shall take
> His chamber in the silent halls of death,
> Thou go not like the quarry-slave at night
> Scourged to his dungeon; but, sustained and soothed
> By an unfaltering trust, approach thy grave
> Like one that draws the drapery of his couch
> About him, and lies down to pleasant dreams."
>
> BRYANT's *Thanatopsis.*

> "And as we have borne the image of the earthy, we shall also bear the image of the
> heavenly." —1 COR. xv. 49.

CROSS the British cable, at the midnight hour, there came a solemn message. "George Peabody is dead!" was the report. The lightning news flies rapidly; and, before many hours, America had learned, from east to west, from north to south, that the man who had given away so many millions while he lived had gone to that world where dollars are no longer needed, but where he would find that the money given away judiciously is really saved.

" London, 4th, midnight. — George Peabody died at half-past eleven o'clock to-night, at his residence in this city," was the telegram. And forthwith the newspapers of England and America vied with each other in furnishing biographical sketches of the departed, with illustrations showing his well-known lineaments or the place of his birth. The name which Victoria wrote sounded from the lips of the little newsboy as he besought the wayfarer to learn the latest intelligence. The London papers were filled with expressions of mingled regret and respect. " The London Times " said, —

" The news of Mr. Peabody's death will be received with no common sorrow on both sides of the Atlantic. The sentiment of regret will not be a mere passing tribute of gratitude to a munificent benefactor. Mr. Peabody, through a long life, accumulated manifold titles to be lamented. He was an ardent patriot, and loved abroad as much as at home. He was no courtier; yet he was honored by sovereigns and princes. He was profuse in his charity, which pauperized nobody. He was a philanthropist, who was liked as well as honored. There was nothing hard or narrow about his philanthropy. He simply did whatever good came in his way."

" The Post," in its obituary article, said, " Mr. Peabody was one of the few whose private virtues are followed by public fame, and whose virtues may be cited as examples.

In laying the foundation of wholesome and cheerful homes for the working-classes, he acted upon a high sense of duty, and touched the mainspring of civilization. He made his means the measure of his philanthropy. Throughout his whole life, his conduct displayed a purity of character that could not fail to elevate and refine the feelings his generosity inspired."

" The Telegraph " said, " Mr. Peabody's lot was doubly happy. The inscription on his mausoleum may tell, with unquestioned truth, of the man who loved his kind, and served two countries."

" The Daily News" said, "Mr. Peabody was not a man of impulsive, emotional benevolence, but rather of judicious, widely-spread beneficence. His liberality was not posthumous. He gave from his own substance, and did not surrender what death wrested from him. His services both to his native and adopted country were fittingly and graciously recognized in royal letters and the thanks of Congress. Merchants, in passing his statue daily, do not need to learn from the consummate man of business how to gain money: his career may teach them how it may be wisely spent."

The governor of his native State did not fail to recognize the claim of Mr. Peabody to honorable mention in his inaugural address; and, after saying that he should do injustice to his own feelings if he did not notice his departure, Gov. Claflin went on to say,—

" George Peabody has been a faithful representative of

the people of his state and nation in a foreign land. His personal character and commercial success would command respect anywhere; but the nobleness of his nature, which led him to make such munificent and princely gifts for the benefit of his fellow-men in both hemispheres, without regard to rank or color, has given him world-wide fame, and no title could add lustre to his name. His remains are to rest in the soil of his native State, whose people will ever honor him as the benefactor of his race. His influence survives him in the noble institutions which he founded; and generations yet unborn will bless his name and revere his memory."

The doors of the Peabody Academy of Science in Salem were draped in mourning, and the following resolutions at once passed : —

" *Resolved*, That the trustees of the Peabody Academy of Science recognize in the death of the distinguished founder of this academy the termination of a life actuated by a noble ambition to benefit and instruct mankind.

" *Resolved*, That here in his native county, among the many noble institutions he has founded, we are keenly sensible of the greatness of his work, and the magnitude of our loss; yet a fame so pure and a life so good leave nothing to be said in praise.

" *Resolved*, That, while the people of two continents are paying their tributes to his memory, we tender our sympathies to his kindred and friends in their bereavement; and rejoice that his life was prolonged to witness so much good accomplished by his wise and munificent charities, and the assurance of their great future usefulness.

"*Resolved,* That the president be instructed, in behalf of the trustees, to co-operate with other institutions in paying proper respect to the memory of Mr. Peabody, and in making the necessary preparations for his funeral.

"*Resolved,* That a copy of these resolutions be sent to the immediate relatives of the deceased."

The Legislature of Massachusetts did not fail to notice Mr. Peabody's departure, and paid due respect to his memory by the following resolutions: —

"*Resolved,* That the Legislature of Massachusetts receives with deep regret the intelligence of the death of George Peabody, who, by the rare simplicity of his life, his constant and untiring industry, his upright and honorable career as a merchant, his broad and liberal charities as a philanthropist, and his steady devotion to republican principles, whether at home or abroad, has won for himself the admiration of his countrymen, and left his life and character to future generations as a model of the true American citizen.

"*Resolved,* That the unusual sagacity which prompted him to become the executor of his own estate, and, while living, to distribute his vast means in a way to bless the ignorant, degraded, and needy for all time to come, deserves especial approbation; while the still more remarkable spirit of catholicity which pervaded all his acts of benevolence entitle him to the grateful praises of all the people.

" *Resolved*, That a joint special committee, consisting of five on the part of the Senate, and ten on the part of the House, be appointed to attend the funeral of the deceased, as a special tribute to his memory in behalf of the Commonwealth.

" *Resolved*, That his Excellency the Governor be requested to cause a certified copy of these resolutions to be forwarded to the family of the deceased.

" *Resolved*, That, as an additional testimonial of its respect, each House do now adjourn."

Resolutions of a similar character were passed by various cities, towns, states, and by Congress itself. Salem thus testified her respect : —

" *Whereas* The death of George Peabody has been an occasion of grief to two continents, — his remains being now brought to this country under distinguished honors ; and *whereas* we desire to place upon record some testimonial of our respect for this distinguished philanthropist : therefore be it

" *Resolved*, That in the death of George Peabody the world has lost a benefactor, the nation a citizen whose acts of benevolence have reflected honor upon his native country, and our city one who has honored his place of residence by the foundation of a most useful Academy of Science.

" *Resolved*, That the City Council will signify its appreciation of the distinguished and noble services of the deceased by attending his funeral in a body.

" *Resolved*, That these resolutions be entered in full
upon the records of the City Council, and that a copy of
them be transmitted to the family of the deceased."

Peabody passed the following resolutions : —

" At a meeting of the citizens of Peabody, held last
evening, to take action in regard to the funeral obsequies
of the late George Peabody, Lewis Allen, moderator,
Hon. Benjamin C. Perkins offered the following resolutions, which were adopted : —

" *Resolved*, That we, the citizens of the birthplace of
George Peabody, deeply sympathize in the emotions of
sorrow, veneration, and love, which, on both continents,
have been occasioned by the death of the philanthropist
of the age.

" *Resolved*, That our memories associated with his life
are personal as well as public. Here was his birthplace,
and the home of his childhood; here was his first public
endowment of the Institute which bears his name, and
which will speak to generations to come of the love he
bore to his native town. To us he has confided the custody of those sacred relics which were dear to him as
tokens of the gratitude of both his native and adopted
countries.

" *Resolved*, That the munificent endowments of institutions of science and learning bear the impress of the immortal maxim which prompted his first public endowment in this town: 'Education,—a debt from the present to future generations.' Moved by the principles of this maxim, from the accumulations of his industry he has with his own hands spread the table to which he has invited future generations to partake of 'the treasures of science and the delights of learning.'

"*Resolved*, That, while we mourn his death, we unite in gratitude to God that he has given the world such a sample of practical Christianity, knowing no creed, no sect, no party; and, while death may hide from us the manly form, that is left to us which cannot be hidden,—his great example of wisdom and amiability, which will teach the world that he who seeks fame the least is most sure to gain it.

"*Resolved*, That we deeply sympathize with the relatives of Mr. Peabody, who were deprived of the sad pleasure of performing the last kind offices.

"*Resolved*, That in pursuance of the last wish of Mr. Peabody, that his funeral services should take place in his native town, we will make the necessary arrangements for the services upon the arrival of his remains; and that we choose a committee, consisting of the board of selectmen and nine others, to co-operate with the trustees of the Peabody Institute, with full powers to carry into effect the object of these resolutions.

"*Resolved*, That these resolutions be placed upon the

records of the town, and that copies be sent to the near relatives of Mr. Peabody."

By the following, it will be seen that the Congress of the United States also noticed suitably the departure of Mr. Peabody : —

"PUBLIC RESOLUTION, No. 6.

"*Joint Resolution of Tribute to the Memory of George Pea-body, deceased.*

"*Whereas*, In the death of George Peabody, a native of the United States, and late a resident of England, our country and the world have sustained an inestimable loss ; and *whereas* the Queen of Great Britain, the authorities of London, and the Emperor of France, have made extraordinary provision for the transfer of his remains to his native land: therefore

"*Be it resolved by the Senate and House of Representatives of the United States of America in Congress assembled,* That the President of the United States be authorized to make such preparation for the reception of the body of our distinguished philanthropist as is merited by his glorious deeds, and in a manner commensurate with the justice, magnanimity, and dignity of a great people.

"*And be it further resolved,* That the expenses incurred by such ceremonial as the President may adopt in the premises shall be paid by any money in the treasury not otherwise appropriated.

"Approved Dec. 23, 1869."

Portraits of Mr. Peabody became at once in great demand; and engravings and photographs of the rare giver soon multiplied. One published by B. B. Russell of Boston has received the commendation of Mr. Peabody's relatives and friends, and is adorning many homes where his name is honored.

CHAPTER XVII.

FUNERAL IN ENGLAND.

Westminster Abbey. — Transportation of the Remains to America. — Description of the Ship "Monarch." — Poem suggested by the Funeral Procession on the Ocean.

> " All flesh is grass, and all its glory fades
> Like the fair flower dishevelled in the wind;
> Riches have wings, and grandeur is a dream:
> The man we celebrate must find a tomb." — COWPER.

" A good name is rather to be chosen than great riches, and loving favor rather than silver and gold." — PROV. xxii. 1.

MR. PEABODY'S remains were embalmed; as it was his desire that his remains should be conveyed to America, to be laid in the tomb which he had built at Danvers, and in which he had placed the body of his mother. But his executors — Sir Curtis Lampson, and Mr. C. Reed, M.P. — complied with the public wish to let a funeral-service be performed over his coffin in Westminster Abbey before its removal. This ceremony, which took place on Friday week, was attended with no extraordinary pomp, saving the presence of the lord-mayor and sheriffs in their official robes, and the number of carriages, including those of the Queen and Prince of Wales, that followed the hearse from Eaton Square. But the Prime Minister and the Secretary of State for Foreign Affairs were also present among the mourners; and Gen. Grey, as representative of her Majesty. The interior of the abbey was crowded in every part by a silent and sympathizing congregation, most of whom wore mourning apparel. The multitude outside, in Broad Sanctuary and Victoria Street, consisting chiefly of workmen's wives and other poor women, seemed equally impressed with the feeling of the occasion.

The coffin, which was covered in black velvet, and surmounted by a wreath of immortelles, was carried by ten men, and deposited on a stage in front of the steps leading up to the altar. The mourners took their places on seats reserved for them on each side of the sacrarium; and inside the rails of the communion-table were seated the lord-mayor, sheriffs, and under-sheriffs, together with Mr. Gladstone and the Earl of Clarendon, and Gen. Grey in private dress, as the representative of her Majesty. The " Sentences," " I am the Resurrection," having been sung, and the ninetieth Psalm, " Lord, thou hast been our refuge," having been chanted by the choir, Archdeacon Jennings read the Lesson from 1 Cor. xv. The Lesson ended, the funeral procession was resumed; and, while an anthem was sung, the coffin was carried back, as before, into the nave, and placed by the side of an opening three feet deep, into which it was lowered, the service at the grave being read by the sub-dean, the

Rev. Lord John Thynne. At the conclusion of the service, the "Dead March in Saul" was played on the organ; while the mourners one after another stepped forward to take a parting look at the coffin as it lay in its shallow receptacle, near the third arch from the western door of the nave. The coffin-lid bore the following inscription : —

"GEORGE PEABODY, born at Danvers, Mass., Feb. 18, 1795. Died in London, England, Nov. 4, 1869."

The Bishop of London preached a funeral sermon in the abbey on Sunday morning.

The honors to Mr. Peabody on both sides of the Atlantic are as unusual and unparalleled in the case of a private individual as are exceptional the magnificent acts of benevolence which illustrated the life of this great philanthropist. It was a worthy idea, first suggested by "The London Telegraph," to convey the remains of Mr. Peabody to his native country in the first war-vessel of the United Kingdom. "The London Telegraph" says, —

"The rarely paralleled honor of sending a Queen's ship as the 'funeral-barge' of George Peabody will be enhanced by the selection of perhaps the noblest vessel at her Majesty's disposal; and he who began life as a grocer's boy will be borne to his transatlantic grave on as proud a bier as any dead king could have. The people of England will thank and applaud their sovereign and her government for this last and crowning recognition of the noble-hearted giver, whose inexhaustible love for his race has revived the almost forgotten standard of perfect charity. The people of the United States, too, will solemnly welcome to their shores the stately vessel which brings to them these sacred relics; seeing, in her, proof that we have regarded George Peabody as an ambassador of peace and unity between the Anglo-Saxon nations as well as a common benefactor, and that we restore to America the body of such an envoy with the insignia which become his grand commission and high moral embassage.

"It is not possible to put these feelings into more majestic or more emphatic language than will be conveyed by the spectacle of our great war-ship's arrival beyond the ocean, bearing this honored corpse. Words are easily written and spoken; but acts make history, and reach the hearts of men through their eyesight. And the eyes of the whole world, in a sense, will be directed upon this new employment of a first-rate ship-of-war. Humanity will note the weighing of that stern liner's anchor, with that novel freight of a trader's coffin; humanity will follow the passage of the swift engine of war across the billows upon her unaccustomed mission of peace and sad courtesy; and humanity will watch the reception of the superb chief mourner in the waters of the Western Republic. There has never really been paid, within the memory of man, so pure a tribute to virtue and to worth, apart from all those considerations which usually govern the attribution of national homage.

" It is true that the benefactions of the generous American were such and so great, that, by their mere amount, he had made two empires his debtors. But the perfect loving-kindness, and unstained integrity and benevolence, with which he gave away his gold to house and to teach the poor, sank into the hearts of his fellow-countrymen on both sides of the Atlantic more deeply than the weight of the gold itself would have done. He made his magnificent gifts richer by the simplicity and sincerity of his giving; and, being dead, we now carry him back to rest among his own kindred, as not only the friend, but also the noble examplar, of the two empires. Sailors usually object to convey the dead on board their ships; but there will be no such feeling on the present occasion. If any burden could be honorable to carry, if any freight could hallow and protect a vessel upon the sea, it would be the mortal remains of George Peabody, who was the brother and the friend of every one that speaks English, and such a man as, living or dead, it was and is good to have to do with.

" There will be left for us in England only the memory of the generous gentleman, when our mourning man-of-war sets sail and steers for the lights of Portland harbor. But they who watch for the Queen's ship upon the other side will confess that we have done all that we could do to make that memory green and beautiful among our children, and to pay the princely merchant all imaginable respect. They will have read, before the majestic vessel approaches their coast, how tender and solicitous the Queen has been in regard to Mr. Peabody's health; how she longed to see him, and chat 'quietly' with him; how she intended to call at his London home, and shake hands with ' her friend,' but that the rapid progress of the fatal illness made it impossible. They will know, too, that, yesterday, we paid to his relics the last observances of the Christian ritual; nay, at the very time when the organ was pealing the Dead March through the columns of the abbey, and the funeral-bells were rocking in its tower, strains of melodious mourning and sympathetic knells in the cities of America were responding across the expanse of the ocean. They will have heard how we gave him, so far as we could give, those obsequies of reverence and regard as an honor reserved for the greatest among our dead; nor would a resting-place in the ancient abbey have been for a moment denied to his relics, if we had had the right to lay his noble dust among that of our worthies and our sovereigns. But the dying man desired to sleep ' with his fathers;' and America has the indisputable claim to enrich her soil with those precious remains: so that it was only left to the Queen and to the people of England to show, with ' maimed rights' and such signs of affection and gratitude as were possible, what was thought of the Danvers merchant in proud and aristocratic Britain. When they reflect in Mr. Peabody's country upon what we have done, and see the great man-of-war sail into port with ensign at half-mast and minute-guns firing, they will not be dissatisfied with us, nor sorry that George Peabody breathed his last among the English half of his fellow-citizens. They will say that we have done ourselves and them and virtue honor in thus reverencing the consummate humanity which was in this king of givers; and it will happen, as we have said before, that the dead body of George Peabody will complete the work done by his living hand and heart. There will arise, out of this funeral voyage of the Queen's new fighting-ship, a thought calculated to take the trade away from fighting-ships altogether; a feeling which advances civilization with a voiceless charm of impulse. Men will be set meditating, on both sides of the Atlantic, how much wiser, better, and higher is the spirit of peace than the spirit of war; how strong must be that spirit of peace and union which can control men even from the shroud and the cerements; and, above all, how shameful and strange in the eyes of civilization the spectacle would be, if the land that sent home George Peabody's remains, and the land which received ' the noble heart that beats no more,' should ever again bandy words of menace and hatred."

Among the tributes early paid to Mr. Peabody's memory were those of Louis Blanc and Victor Hugo. The following is an extract from Victor Hugo's letter, published in " The London Times: " —

"HÁUTEVILLE, Dec. 2, 1869.

"MONSIEUR, — Your letter came to me Dec. 2. I thank you. It brings me to this *souvenir*. I forget the Empire, and think of America. I was turned toward night: I turn toward the day. You ask a word from me on George Peabody. In your sympathetic illusion, you believe me to be what I am not, — a voice from France. I am, I have said before, but a voice from exile. No matter, monsieur : a noble appeal like yours can be heard. Little as I am, I ought to respond, and do so.

"Yes, America has reason to be proud of this great citizen of the world and great brother of all men, — George Peabody. Peabody has been a happy man who would suffer in all sufferings, a rich man who would feel the cold, the hunger, and thirst of the poor. Having a place near Rothschild, he found means to change it for one nĕar Vincent de Paul. Like Jesus Christ, he had a wound in the side : this wound was the misery of others. It was not blood flowed from this wound : it was gold which now came from a heart.

"On this earth there are men of hate and men of love : Peabody was one of the latter. It is on the face of these men that we can see the smile of God. What law do they practise ? One alone, — the law of fraternity, divine law, humane law ; which varies the relief according to the distress ; which here gives precepts, and there gives millions ; and traces through the centuries in our darkness a train of light, and extends from Jesus poor to Peabody wealthy.

" May Peabody return to you, blessed by us! Our world envies yours. His fatherland will guard his ashes, and our hearts his memory. May the moving immensity of the seas bear him to you! The free American flag can never display enough stars above his coffin."

" The Times " also published the following : —

"LONDON, Dec. 9, 1869.

" SIR, — The death of so good a man as George Peabody proved himself to be is a public calamity, in which the whole civilized world ought to share. I feel, therefore, in duty bound to express, in answer to your appeal, how deeply I mourn, as a Frenchman and as a man, for the illustrious American whose life was of such value to the most needy of his fellow-men.

" It was but natural, that in a country like this, where so much is thought of long lineage, and station in life, George Peabody should receive, as the only fit token of public gratitude, the same kind of respect which is paid to kings, princes, and men of noble birth, as well as men of noble deeds ; and that his mortal remains should be committed to a temporary resting-place beneath the nave of Westminster Abbey, to be sent afterward in a ship-of-war to his native land, — the land of freedom. Nor is there any thing to complain of in this national mode of testifying to the high estimation in which the British nation held the eminent philanthropist. Yet I cannot help lamenting that there should be for men of that stamp no particular sort of homage better calculated to show how little, compared to them, are most of kings, princes, noblemen, renowned diplomatists, world-famed conquerors.

" It was not the kind-hearted republican trader who was honored by the fact of being consigned to rest in Westminster Abbey, but rather those who were considered to be worthy of sleeping there their last sleep, on account of their rank, not of their virtue.

" The number of mourners assembled within the precincts of the sacred edifice, their silent sorrow, the tears shed by so many, and, in several parts of London, the readiness of the shopkeepers to give expression to their grief by closing their shops and lowering their blinds, — these were the homages really in keeping with the affectionate admiration due to one whose title in history will be this (the highest a rich man can aspire to), — the friend of the poor.

I am, sir, obediently yours,

" LOUIS BLANC.

" Col. BERTON, Chairman American Committee."

For want of space, a full description of the war-ship " Monarch," in which Mr. Peabody's remains were forwarded to America, cannot be given. Suffice it to say, that it was one of the largest iron-plated ships in the English navy, with an armament of nine guns. The guns in " The Monarch's " turrets are said to have no peers on land or sea. The room in which the coffin of Mr. Peabody was placed was appropriately draped, and candles were kept burning throughout the voyage. " The Monarch " was convoyed by an American and a French vessel detailed for that service, to add to the honor old England was conferring on the man who gave millions away.

" The Hearth and Home " published the following poem, entitled

THE FUNERAL FLEET.

All in the winter silence,
    Rapt with a sense of awe, —
A vision half, and half a dream, —
    This was the sight I saw : —

A vision of the sea,
    And consort-vessels two :
The red cross on the flag of one ;
    And the other, red, white, and blue.

No ripple at the prows,
    No wake of shimmering spray :
Like cloudlets white in the pale moonlight
    They glided on their way.

Sentinels paced the deck
    With solemn tread and still :
" Peace " was the watchword that they gave ;
    The answering word, " Good will."

An angel at the helm
    Stood, all in garments white ;
And angels hovered o'er the keel,
    And guided through the night.

They bring no crownèd king;
  Theirs is a holier trust:
They bear a treasure from afar, —
  A good man's sacred dust,

Mourned by the rich he taught,
  Mourned by the poor he fed,
Mourned by a race with whom he broke
  A nobler food than bread.

To the soil that gave him birth
  They bring him for his rest:
Blue shall his native violets be
  Above his honored breast.

A vision of the sea,
  And consort-vessels two:
The red cross on the flag of one;
  And the other, red, white, and blue.

All in the winter silence,
  Rapt with a sense of awe, —
A vision half, and half a dream, —
  This was the sight I saw.

CHAPTER XVIII.

FUNERAL IN AMERICA.

Reception of the Remains in America. — The Funeral in Harmony Grove.
— Mr. Winthrop's Eulogy. — Prince Arthur of England.

"Unrivalled as thy merit be thy fame." — TICKELL.

"Glory, honor, and peace to every man that worketh good, — to the Jew first, and also to the Gentile." — ROM. ii. 10.

GREAT preparations were made in America for the reception of Mr. Peabody's remains. Legislatures adjourned to attend in a body. Public dignitaries paid due respect to his memory by their presence; and private individuals thronged the wharves of Portland when "The Monarch" arrived, and attended every motion of the body towards its final resting-place. The following poem by Howard Glyndon may be taken as an exponent of the sentiment of Americans who appreciated the noble deeds of the distinguished dead: it is entitled "The Coming of the Silent Guest:" —

"Lo! England sends him back to us,
    With sealèd eyes and folded palms:
He drifts across the wintry sea,
    Which chants to him its thousand psalms.

We proudly name and claim him ours ;
　We take him, England, from thy breast ;
We open wide our doors to him
　Who cometh home a silent guest.

We lent him thee to teach thy sons
　The lesson of the Open Hand,
Lest famished lips should bless them less
　Than him, — the stranger in their land.

We lent him, living, unto thee,
　To be a solace to thy pain ;
But now we want his noble dust,
　To consecrate it ours again.

England, we take him from thine arms ;
　We thank thee for thy reverent care :
If thou and we were ever friends,
　We should be so beside his bier.

His memory should be a spell
　To banish spleen and bitterness.
Have kindlier thoughts of us, — for he
　Was tender unto thy distress, —

As we have kindlier thoughts of thee
　Because of honor done to him ;
For, while we weep, we turn to see
　That English eyes with tears are dim.”

Space forbids that much should be said concerning the reception of the honored remains.　They were removed to the City Hall in Portland, and lay in state there, and afterwards in the town of Peabody, visited by thousands, who could see only, however, the catafalque and its surroundings.　Sentinels were on guard, and every possible honor paid by all to the memory of the departed. Cars were fitted by the Eastern-Railroad Company with special reference to the funeral; and bells rang while minute-guns pealed at his funeral in Danvers (or Peabody, as it is now called). According to "Zion's Herald," "The church exercises were impressive, if not solemn. Draped walls; lamps dimly burning; high pulpit, looking higher in its new robes of death; the body lifted high up before it,— the fifth of its prominent resting-places on its way to the grave; wreaths, crosses, and crowns of flowers, whose funeral fragrance sweetens and sickens the air,— these were the lifeless accessories of the event. The living ones were, first, the brother and sister of the deceased, with a score or two of relatives; next behind them sat the Prince and his suite,— he in black, they in gold and the red uniforms of the army." The Governor of Massachusetts and his suite were near, and "dignitaries of all sorts and origins followed these heads of rival States; and the old-fashioned church was speedily filled with a more solid mass of rank and fame than was probably ever gathered before in a New-England Congregational meeting-house."

Music appropriate to the occasion formed a part of the funeral-exercises. Rev. Daniel Marsh of Georgetown read the Scriptures; and Hon. Robert C. Winthrop delivered the following funeral-oration:—

"While I have been unwilling, my friends, wholly to decline the request of your committee of arrangements, or to seem wanting to any service which might perchance have gratified him, whom, in common with you all, I have so honored and loved, I have still felt deeply, and I cannot help feeling at this moment more deeply than ever before, that any words of mine might well have been spared on this occasion.

" The solemn tones of the organ, the plaintive notes of the funeral-chant, the consoling lessons of the Sacred Scriptures, the fervent utterances of prayer and praise, — these would seem to me the only appropriate, I had almost said the only endurable, interruptions of the silent sorrow which befits a scene like this.

" Even were it possible for me to add any thing worth adding to the tributes, on both sides of the ocean, which already have well-nigh exhausted the language of eulogy, the formal phrases of a detailed memoir or of a protracted and studied panegyric would congeal upon my lips, and fall frozen upon the ears and hearts of all whom I address, in presence of the lifeless form of one who has so long been the support, the ornament, the dear delight, of this village of his nativity.

" We cannot, indeed, any of us, gather around these cherished remains, and prepare to commit them tenderly and affectionately to their mother-earth, without a keen sense of personal affliction and bereavement.   He was too devoted and loving a brother, he was too kind and thoughtful a kinsman, he was too genial and steadfast a friend, not to be missed and mourned by those around me as few others have ever been missed and mourned here before. I am not insensible to my own full share of the private and public grief which pervades this community.

" And yet, my friends, it is by no means sorrow alone which may well be indulged by us all at such an hour as this. Other emotions — I hazard nothing in saying, far other emotions — besides those of grief are even now rising and swelling in all our hearts, — emotions of pride, emotions of joy, emotions of triumph.

" Am I not right? How could it be otherwise? What a career has that been, of which the final scene is now, at length, before us! Who can contemplate its rise and progress, from the lowly cradle in this South Parish of old Danvers — henceforth to be known of all men by his name — to the temporary repose in Westminster Abbey, followed by that august procession across the Atlantic, whose wake upon the waters will glow and sparkle to the end of time, growing more and more luminous with the lapse of years, — who, I say, can contemplate that career, from its humble commencement to its magnificent completion, without an irrepressible thrill of admiration, and almost of rapture?

" Who, certainly, can contemplate the immediate close of this extraordinary life, without rejoicing, not only that it was so painless, so peaceful, so happy in itself; not only that it was so providentially postponed until he had been enabled once more to revisit his native land to complete his great American benefactions, to hold personal intercourse with those friends at the South for whose welfare the largest and most cherished of these benefactions was designed, and to take solemn leave of those to whom he was bound by so many ties of affection or of blood, — but that it occurred at a time and under circumstances so peculiarly fortunate for attracting the largest attention, and for giving the widest impression and influence, to his great and inspiring example ?

" For this, precisely this, as I believe, would have been the most gratifying consideration to our lamented friend himself, could he have distinctly foreseen all that has happened since he left you a few months since. Could it have been foretold him, as he embarked with feeble strength and faltering steps on board his favorite ' Scotia ' at New York on the 23d of September last, not merely that he was leaving kinsfolk and friends and native land for the last time, but that hardly four weeks would have elapsed after his arrival at Liverpool before he should be the subject of funeral honors by command of the Queen of England, and should lie down for a time beneath the consecrated arches of that far-famed minster, among the kings and counsellors of the earth ; could it have been foretold him that his acts would be the theme of eloquent tributes from high prelates of the Church, and from the highest minister of the Crown, and that Great Britain and the United States — not always, nor often, alas ! in perfect accord — should vie with each other in furnishing their proudest national ships to escort his remains over the ocean, exhibiting such a funeral-fleet as the world in all its history had never witnessed before, — could all this have been whispered in his ear as it was catching those last farewells of relatives and friends, he must indeed have been more than mortal not to have experienced some unwonted emotions of personal gratification and pride.

"But I do believe, from all I have ever seen or known of him, — and few others, at home or abroad, have of late enjoyed more of his confidence, — that far, far above any feelings of this sort, his great heart would have throbbed as it never throbbed before with gratitude to God and man, that the example which he had given to the world by employing the wealth which he had accumulated during a long life of industry and integrity in relieving the wants of his fellow-men wherever they were most apparent to him; in providing lodgings for the poor of London; in providing education for the children of our own desolated South; in building a memorial-church for the parish in which his mother had worshipped; in founding or endowing institutes and libraries, and academies of science, in the town in which he was born, in the city in which he had longest resided, and in so many other places with which, for a longer or a shorter time, he had been connected, — that this grand and glorious example of munificence and beneficence would thus be so signally held up to the contemplation of mankind in a way not only to commend it to their remembrance and regard, but to command for it their respect and imitation. This, I feel assured, he would have felt to be the accomplishment of the warmest wish of his heart, the consummation of the most cherished object of his life.

" Our lamented friend was not, indeed, without ambition. He not only liked to do grand things, but he liked to do them in a grand way. We all remember those sumptuous and princely banquets with which he sometimes diversified the habitual simplicity and frugality of his daily life. He was not without a decided taste for occasional display, — call it even ostentation, if you will. We certainly may not ascribe to him a pre-eminent measure of that sort of charity which shuns publicity, which shrinks from observation, and which, according to one of our Saviour's well-remembered injunctions, ' doeth its alms in secret.' He may or he may not have exercised as much of this kind of beneficence as any of those in similar condition around him : I fully believe that he did. We all understand, however, that

> ' Of that best portion of a good man's life, —
> His little, nameless, unremembered acts
> Of kindness and of love,' —

there can be no record except on high, or in the grateful hearts of those who have been aided and relieved. That record shall be revealed hereafter. The world can know little or nothing of it now.

" But any one must perceive at a glance that the sort

of charity which our lamented friend illustrated and exercised was wholly incompatible with concealment or reserve. The great trusts which he established, the great institutions which he founded, the capacious and costly edifices which he erected, were things that could not be hid, which could not be done in a corner. They were, in their own intrinsic and essential nature, patent to the world's eye. He could not have performed these noble acts in his lifetime, as it was his peculiar choice to do, and as it will be his peculiar distinction and glory to have done, without suffering himself ' to be seen of men ; ' without being known and recognized and celebrated as their author. He must have postponed them all, as others have done, for posthumous execution, he must have refrained from parting with his millions until death should have wrested them from a reluctant grasp, had he shrunk from the notoriety and celebrity which inevitably attend upon such a career.

" He did not fail to remember, however, — for he was no stranger to the Bible, — that there were at least two modes of doing good commended in Holy Writ. He did not forget that the same glorious gospel, nay, that the same incomparable Sermon on the Mount, which said, ' Let not thy left hand know what thy right hand doeth,' said also, ' Let your light so shine before men, that they may see your good works, and glorify your Father which is in heaven.' This, this, might almost be regarded as the chosen motto of his later life, and might not inappropriately be inscribed as such on his tombstone.

" Certainly, my friends, his light has shone before men. Certainly they have seen his good works. And who shall doubt that they have glorified his Father which is in heaven? Yes, glory to God, glory to God in the highest, has, I am persuaded, swollen up from the hearts of millions in both hemispheres with a new fervor as they have followed him in his grand circumnavigation of benevolence, and as they have witnessed, one after another, his multifold and magnificent endowments. And his own heart, I repeat, would have throbbed and thrilled as it never thrilled or throbbed before with gratitude to God and man, could he have foreseen that the matchless example of munificence which it had been the cherished aim of his later years to exhibit would be rendered, as it has now been rendered, so signal, so inspiring, so enduring, so immortal, by the homage which has been paid to his memory by the princes and potentates, as well as by the poor, of the Old World, and by the government and the whole people of his own beloved country.

" I have spoken of the exhibition of this example as having been the cherished aim of his later years ; but I am not without authority for saying that it was among the fondest wishes of his whole mature life. I cannot forget, that in one of those confidential consultations with which he honored me some years since, after unfolding his plans, and telling me substantially all that he designed to do, — for almost every thing he did was of his own original designing, — and when I was filled with admiration and amazement at the magnitude and sublimity of his purposes, he said to me, with that guileless simplicity which characterized so much of his social intercourse and conversation, ' Why, Mr. Winthrop, this is no new idea to me. From the earliest years of my manhood, I have contemplated some such disposition of my property; and I have prayed my heavenly Father, day by day, that I might be enabled, before I died, to show my gratitude for the blessings which he has bestowed upon me by doing some great good to my fellow-men.'

" Well has the living laureate of England sung, in one of his latest published poems, —

> ' More things are wrought by prayer
> Than this world dreams of.'

That prayer has been heard and answered; that noble aspiration has been more than fulfilled. The judgment of the future will confirm the opinion of the hour; and History, instead of contenting herself with merely enrolling his name in chronological or alphabetical order as one among the many benefactors of mankind, will assign him, unless I greatly mistake her verdict, a place by himself, far above all competition or comparison, first without a second, as having done the greatest good for the greatest number of his fellow-men — so far, at least, as pecuniary means could accomplish such a result — of which there has thus far been any authentic record in merely human annals.

" It would afford a most inadequate measure of his munificence were I to sum up the dollars or the pounds he has distributed, or the number of persons whom his perennial provisions for dwellings or for schools will have included, in years to come, on one side of the Atlantic or the other. Tried even by this narrow test, his beneficence has neither precedent nor parallel. But it is as having attracted and compelled the attention of mankind to the beauty, the nobleness, the true glory, of living and doing for others ; it is as having raised the standard of munificence to a degree which has almost made it a new thing in the world ; it is as having exhibited a wisdom and a discrimination in selecting the objects and in arranging the machinery of his bounty, which almost entitle him to the credit of an inventor ; it is as having, in the words of the brilliant Gladstone, ' taught us how a man may be the master of his fortune, and not its slave ; ' it is as having discarded all considerations of caste, creed, condition, nationality, in his world-wide philanthropy, regarding nothing human as alien to him ; it is as having deliberately stripped himself in his lifetime of the property he had so laboriously acquired, delighting as much in devising modes of bestowing his wealth as he had ever done in contriving plans for its increase and accumulation, — literally throwing his bags like some adventurous aeronaut who would mount higher and higher to the skies, and really exulting as he calculated, from time to time, how little of all his laborious earnings he had at last left for himself; it is as having furnished this new and living and magnetic example, which can never be lost to history, never be lost to the interests of humanity, never fail to attract, inspire, and stimulate the lovers of their fellow-men, as long as human wants and human wealth shall co-exist upon the earth, — it is in this way that our lamented friend has attained a pre-eminence among the benefactors of his age and race, like that of Washington among patriots, or that of Shakspeare or Milton among poets.

"I do not altogether forget those Mæcenases of old whom philosophers and poets have so delighted to extol. I do not forget the passing tribute of the great Roman orator to one of the publicans of his own period, as having displayed an incredible benignity in amassing a vast fortune, not 'as the prey of avarice, but as the instrument of doing good.' I do not forget the founders of the Royal Exchange in London, and of the noble hospital in Edinburgh, the princely merchant of Queen Elizabeth's day, or the 'Jingling Geordie' of England's first King James. I do not forget how strikingly Edmund Burke foreshadowed our lamented friend, when he said of one of his own contemporaries, 'His fortune is among the largest, — a fortune, which, wholly unencumbered as it is, without one single change from luxury, vanity, or excess, sinks under the benevolence of its dispenser: this private benevolence, expanding itself into patriotism, renders his whole being the estate of the public, in which he has not reserved a *peculium* for himself of profit, diversion, or relaxation.' I do not forget the Baron de Monthyon of France, whose noble benefactions are annually distributed by the Imperial Academy, and whose portrait has been combined with that of our own Franklin on a medal commemorative of their kindred beneficence. I recall, too, the refrain of an ode to a late munificent English duke on the erection of his statue at Belvoir Castle, which might well have been sung again when Story's statue of our friend was recently unveiled by the Prince of Wales : —

> ' O my brethren ! what a glory
> To the world is one good man ! '

Nor do I fail to remember the long roll of benefactors, dead and living, of whom our own age and our own country and our mother-country — New England and Old England — may so justly boast. But no one imagines that either Caius Curius, or Sir Thomas Gresham, or George Heriot, or Sir George Savile, or any Duke of Rutland, or Monthyon, or Franklin, or any of the later and larger benefactors of our own time or land, can ever vie in historic celebrity, as a practical philanthropist, with him whom we bury here to-day.

" Think me not unmindful, my friends, that, for the manifestation of a true spirit of benevolence, two mites will suffice as well as untold millions ; a cup of cold water as well as a treasure-house of silver and gold. Think me not unmindful, either, of the grand and glorious results for the welfare of mankind which have been accomplished by purely moral or religious influences; by personal toil and trust; by the force of Christian character and example; by the exercise of some great gifts of intellect or eloquence; by simple self-devotion and self-sacrifice, without any employment whatever of pecuniary means; by missionaries in the cause of Christ; by reformers of prisons,. and organizers of hospitals; by Sisters of Charity; by visitors of the poor; by champions of the oppressed; by such women as Elizabeth Fry and Florence Nightingale, and such men as John Howard and William Wilberforce; or, to go farther back in history, by men like our own John Eliot, the early apostle to the Indians; or like the sainted Vincent de Paul, whose memory has been so justly honored in France for more than two centuries. But philanthropy of this sort, I need not say, stands on a somewhat different plane, and cannot fairly enter into this comparison.

" It is enough to say of our lamented friend, as we have seen and known him of late, that in him were united — as rarely if ever before — the largest desire and the largest ability to do good; that his will was, at least, commensurate with his wealth; and that nothing but the limited extent of even the most considerable earthly estate prevented his enjoying the very antepast of celestial bliss : —

'For, when the power of imparting good
Is equal to the will, the human soul
Requires no other heaven.'

" And now, my friends, what wonder is it that all that was mortal of such a man has come back to us to-day with such a convoy and with such accompanying honors as well might have befitted some mighty conqueror or some princely hero? Was he not indeed a conqueror? Was he not indeed a hero? Oh! it is not on the battle-field or on the blood-stained ocean alone that conquests are achieved and victories won. There are battles to be fought, there is a life-long warfare to be waged, by each one of us, in our own breasts, and against our own selfish natures. And what conflict is harder than that which awaits the accumulator of great wealth? Who can ever forget, or remember without a shudder, the emphatic testimony to the character of that conflict which was borne by our blessed Saviour — who knew what was in man better than any man knows it for himself — when he said, ' How hardly shall they that have riches enter into the kingdom of God!' and when he bade that rich young man sell all that he had, and distribute to the poor, and then come and follow him?

" It would be doing grievous injustice to our lamented friend, were we to deny or conceal that there were elements in his character which made his own warfare in this respect a stern one. He was no stranger to the love of accumulation. He was no stranger to the passion for gaining and saving and hoarding. There were in his nature the germs, and more than the germs, of economy, and even of parsimony ; and sometimes they would sprout and spring up in spite of himself. Nothing less strong than his own will, nothing less indomitable than his own courage, could have enabled him, by the grace of God, to strive successfully against that greedy, grudging, avaricious spirit which so often besets the talent for acquisition. In a thousand little ways, you might perceive to the last how much within him he had overcome and vanquished. All the more glorious and signal was the victory. All the more deserved and appropriate are these trappings of triumph with which his remains have been restored to us. You rob him of his richest laurel, you refuse him his brightest crown, when you attempt to cover up or disguise any of those innate tendencies, any of those acquired habits, any of those besetting temptations, against which he struggled so bravely and so triumphantly. Recount, if you please, every penurious or mercenary act of his earlier or his later life which friends have ever witnessed (if they have ever witnessed any), or which malice has ever whispered or hinted at (and malice, we know, has not spared him in more ways than one), and you have only added to his titles to be received and remembered as a hero and a conqueror.

"As such a conqueror, then, you have received him from that majestic turreted iron-clad which the gracious monarch of our mother-land has deputed as her own messenger to bear him back to his home. As such a conqueror, you have canopied his funeral-car with the flag of his country; ay, with the flags of both his countries, between whom I pray God that his memory may ever be a pledge of mutual forbearance and affectionate regard ! As such a conqueror, you mark the day and the hour of his burial by minute-guns, and fire a farewell shot, it may be, as the clods of his native soil are heaped upon his breast.

"We do not forget, however, amidst all this martial pomp, how eminently he was a man of peace; or how earnestly he desired, or how much he has done, to inculcate a spirit of peace, national and international. I may not attempt to enter here, to-day, into any consideration of the influence of his specific endowments, at home or abroad, American or English; but I may say, in a single word, that I think history will be searched in vain for the record of any merely human acts, recent or remote, which have been more in harmony with that angelic chorus, which, just as the fleet with this sad freight had entered on its funeral-voyage across the Atlantic, the whole Christian world was uniting to ring back again to the skies from which it first was heard; any merely human acts, which, while, as I have said, they have waked a fresh and more fervent echo of ' Glory to God in the highest,' have done more to promote 'peace on earth, and good will towards men.'

"Here, then, my friends, in this home of his infancy, where, seventy years ago, he attended the common village school, and served his first apprenticeship as a humble shop-boy; here, where, seventeen years ago, his first large public donation was made, accompanied by that memorable sentiment, ' Education, — a debt due from present to future generations;' here, where the monuments and memorials of his affection and his munificence surround us on every side, and where he had chosen to deposit that unique enamelled portrait of the Queen, that exquisite gold medal the gift of his country, that charming little autograph-note from the Empress of France, that imperial photograph of the Pope inscribed by his own hand, and whatever other tributes had been most precious to him in life; here, where he has desired that his own remains should finally repose, near to the graves of his father and mother, enforcing that desire by those touching words, almost the last which he uttered, ' Danvers, Danvers! don't forget!' — here let us thank God for his transcendent example; and here let us resolve that it shall neither fail to be treasured up in our hearts, and sacredly transmitted to our children and our children's children, nor be wholly without an influence upon our own immediate lives. Let it never be said that the tomb and the trophies are remembered and cherished, but the example forgotten or neglected.

" I may not longer detain you, my friends, from the sad ceremonies which remain to be performed by us; yet I cannot quite release you until I have alluded, in the simplest and briefest manner, to an incident of the last days and almost the last hours of this noble life which has come to me from a source which cannot be questioned. While he was lying, seemingly unconscious, on his deathbed in London, at the house of his kind friend, Sir Curtis Lamp son, and when all direct communication with him had been for a time suspended, it was mentioned aloud in his presence, in a manner and with a purpose to test his .consciousness, that a highly-valued acquaintance had called to see him; but he took no notice of the remark. Not long afterwards, it was stated, in a tone loud enough for him to hear, that the Queen herself had sent a special telegram of inquiry and sympathy; but even that failed to arouse him. Once more, at no long interval, it was remarked that a faithful minister of the gospel, with whom he had once made a voyage to America, was at the door; and his attention was instantly attracted. That 'good man,' as he called him with his latest breath, was received by him, and prayed with him more than once. 'It is a great mystery,' he feebly observed; 'but I shall know all soon:' while his repeated 'amens' gave audible and abundant evidence that those prayers were not lost upon his ear or upon his heart. The friendships of earth could no longer soothe him; the highest honors of the world, the kind attentions of a sovereign whom he knew how to respect, admire, and love, could no longer satisfy him: the ambassador of Christ was the only visitor for that hour.

"Thus, we may humbly hope, was at last explained and fulfilled for him that mysterious saying of one of the ancient prophets of Israel, which he had heard many years before as the text of a sermon by one whom he knew and valued, which had long lingered in his memory, and which, by some force of association or reflection, had again and again been recalled to his mind, and more than once, in my own hearing, been made the subject of his remark: ‘And it shall come to pass in that day, that the light shall not be clear nor dark; but it shall be one day which shall be known to the Lord, not day, nor night: but it shall come to pass, that at evening-time it shall be light.’

“At evening time it was indeed light for him. And who shall doubt, that, when another morning shall break upon his brow, it shall be a morning without clouds, — all light and love and joy? ‘for the glory of God shall lighten it, and the Lamb shall be the light thereof.’

“And so I bid farewell to thee, — brave, honest, noble-hearted friend! The village of thy birth weeps to-day for one who never caused her pain before. The ‘flower of Essex’ is gathered at thy grave. Massachusetts mourns thee as a son who has given new lustre to her historic page; and Maine, not unmindful of her joint inheritance in the earlier glories of the parent State, has opened her noblest harbor, and draped her municipal halls with richest, saddest robes, to do honor to thy remains. New England, from mountain-top to farthest cape, is in sympathy with the scene, and feels the fitness that the hallowed memories of ‘Leyden’ and ‘Plymouth’ — the refuge and the rock of her Pilgrim Fathers — should be associated with thy obsequies. This great and glorious nation, in all its restored and vindicated union, partakes the pride of thy life and the sorrow of thy loss. In hundreds of schools of the desolated South, the children even now are chanting thy requiem, and weaving chaplets around thy name.   In hundreds of comfortable homes provided by thy bounty, the poor of the grandest city of the world even now are breathing blessings on thy memory.   The proudest shrine of Old England has unlocked its consecrated vaults for thy repose.   The bravest ship of a navy ' whose march is on the mountain-wave, whose home is on the deep,' has borne thee as a conqueror to thy chosen rest ; and as it passed from isle to isle, and from sea to sea, in a circumnavigation almost as wide as thy own charity, has given new significance to the memorable saying of the great funeral orator of antiquity : ' Of illustrious men, the whole earth is the sepulchre ; and not only does the inscription upon columns in their own land point it out, but in that, also, which is not their own, there dwells with every one an unwritten memorial of the heart.'   And now around thee are assembled not only surviving schoolmates and old companions of thy youth, and neighbors and friends of thy maturer years, but votaries of science, ornaments of literature, heads of universities and academies, foremost men of commerce and the arts, ministers of the gospel, delegates from distant States, and rulers of thy own State, all eager to unite in paying such homage to a career of grand but simple beneficence as neither rank nor fortune nor learning nor genius could ever have commanded. Chiefs of the Republic, representatives and more than representatives of royalty, are not absent from thy bier. Nothing is wanting to give emphasis to thy example ;

nothing is wanting to fill up the measure of thy fame. But what earthly honor, what accumulation of earthly honors, shall compare for a moment with the supreme hope and trust which we all humbly and devoutly cherish at this hour, that when the struggles and the victories, the pangs and pageants, of time shall be ended, and the great awards of eternity shall be made up, thou mayst be found amongst those who are 'more than conquerors through Him who loved us'?

"And so we bid thee farewell, — brave, honest, noble-hearted friend of mankind ! "

After Mr. Winthrop had concluded his remarks, the anthem,

"Their sun shall no more go down,"

was sung by the choir, and the Rev. Mr. Marsh offered a solemn prayer. The services were closed with Watts's hymn, commencing,

"Unveil thy bosom, faithful tomb; "

and the benediction was then pronounced by Rev. Mr. Marsh.

The congregation were most devout throughout the service. The greatest attention was paid by Prince Arthur to the eulogy, and at some portions of it he was observed to be deeply affected.

It was a touching tribute of respect to the royal mother

of Prince Arthur that he should be found among the mourners at the funeral of London's benefactor, in his far-off native land; and his princely bearing while on his late visit to the United States has won the esteem of the nation, and reflected credit upon the mother whom England and America delight to honor.

CHAPTER XIX.

DESERVED TRIBUTES.

Newman Hall on George Peabody. — Tributes from Various Sources. — The Pulpit's Voice in Praise of his Beneficence. — List of his Donations.

> "Nor let thy noble spirit grieve
> Its life of glorious fame to leave:
> A life of honor and of worth
> Has no eternity on earth." — LONGFELLOW.

> "Render therefore, to all, their dues." — ROM. xiii. 7.

THE mortal remains of the great benefactor now repose in Harmony Grove, — the spot selected by himself. This is a beautifully wooded rising ground near Salem, and bordering upon that part of Danvers now known as Peabody. " Upon the principal street of the latter, the visitor still sees the house, with its small shop-front, in which, as the boy of the village-store, many of the youthful days of the great philanthropist were spent. The little window of its narrow attic is that of his bedroom." From it, doubtless, he often looked out on the green spot where his body rests. He has gone to the grave with the highest honors two great nations could pay. England and America buried him, and France looked on with sympathy at the funeral.

Eulogies fell from eloquent lips on both sides of the sea. Rev. Newman Hall preached a sermon in reference to his departure, from which the following extracts are taken : —

"The old arches of Westminster Abbey never looked down on a spectacle more solemnly impressive, more touchingly eloquent, more sublime in its simplicity, than when, two days ago, the remains of George Peabody were deposited beneath its sacred pavement. What a sermon did that ancient cathedral preach to the assembled thousands, as they waited in sorrowful silence the arrival of all that was mortal of the deceased philanthropist! . . . All the centuries of England's grand old history were looking down upon us. Spirits of Saxons and Normans, of steel-clad kings and feudal chiefs, of sturdy barons and mitred prelates, of mailed crusaders and shaven monks, of Cavaliers and Roundheads, of statesmen and jurists, of poets and orators, of philosophers and philanthropists, seemed to gather round, intent to watch the accession which this day would bring to those venerated vaults. . . . .

"Many a scene of pomp and splendor has that abbey witnessed; but far more in harmony with its solemn architecture, impressive antiquity, and monuments of death, was such a scene as last Friday witnessed. The spacious building was crowded in every part by a multi-

tude clad in mourning attire, and bearing in their features
and demeanor the expression of a reverential sorrow. If
any spoke, while waiting till the appointed hour, it was
with bated breath, so as not to disturb the expressive
silence which was broken only by the solemn knell from
the old tower pealing ever and anon through the arches
so long familiar with the sound. . . .

" The funeral now solemnized was of a private citizen,
who had sought no distinction of rank or title, but who,
by industry and sagacity, accumulated vast treasures,
which it was his delight to employ for the benefit of the
poor. His was a warfare against want, in waging which
he built many homes, and desolated none. His was a
statesmanship which simply looked at suffering, and at
once mitigated it by a generosity which could give no
occasion to party difference, by a law of love which none
would ever wish to repeal. An American citizen, his
business and home were for many years in London.
Here he beheld the miseries of the teeming multitudes of
the poor, often crowded together in unhealthy abodes,
forbidding comfort, cleanliness, and decency. Blessed by
Divine Providence with great prosperity in business, he
felt it his pleasure to distribute of his treasures to the poor,
rather than to go on augmenting the heap, so as to have
the questionable credit of dying richer than most of his
compeers. Besides large benefactions in his own country,
successive donations have reached the sum of half a million sterling, invested in trustees, to be employed for the

benefit of the poor of the metropolis throughout future generations. Noble was his gift, and just has been the nation's appreciation. The Queen, some time since, sent him a special mark of her personal honor and regard, and earnestly desired to see him; inviting him to Windsor to meet her quietly for personal intercourse, and then proposing to visit him at his own residence. But, alas! illness and death frustrated the monarch's graceful and characteristic purpose. And now, though his body was finally to rest in the land of his birth, all that could be done in honor of him dead was done, — a funeral in Westminster Abbey.

" And now the solemn procession is entering from the cloisters; and from afar we hear the wailing notes of the choristers, as in long array they slowly move up the nave between the multitudes of sympathizing spectators. Very slowly they pass along; their plaintive voices — now most sad, now swelling forth in tones of hope — mingling with the notes of the great organ. The coffin is borne along, followed by mourners of both nations, into the choir, where every seat had long been occupied by representatives of all parties in the State, waiting thus to do homage to the memory of the poor man's friend. The chanted psalm is now heard ringing in the vaulted roof, and the sublime words which tell of victory over death through Jesus Christ our Lord. Again the solemn procession is seen emerging from the choir, and traversing the cathedral, till it reaches the grave, where the concluding prayers are

offered up, and the final anthem sung, — 'His body.
Then the principal mourners stood for a while gazing into
the grave. The Premier of England, as representing the
government and the nation, stood there, thoughtful and
devout, rendering the willing homage of his great and
sympathizing nature. And the Secretary for Foreign Affairs was there, as representing the empire in its relations
with all other lands, and especially with the great nation
to which the deceased belonged. And beside him was the
Queen's chamberlain, as representing her own personal
admiration, and paying her own personal tribute to the
deceased benefactor of her people. And the lord-mayor
and magistrates of London were there, to testify their
obligations to so princely a benefactor to their city.
And amongst these, and others of varying celebrity, was
the American ambassador, his keen eye taking in every
feature of the scene, his high intelligence marking well its
significance. And what did it mean? It meant something more potent than his diplomacy, or that of any statesman of either country, anxious as they may be to remove
all misunderstanding, and consolidate a lasting peace.
More than conferences, protocols, treaties, explanations,
compensations, — far more is done by such deeds as those of
Peabody, and such appreciation as was witnessed that day,
to cement together our two nations. George Peabody,
the American, amassing a princely fortune to bequeath to
the poor of Great Britain; George Peabody, the American, buried with a nation's lamentation among her princes

18

and statesmen in Westminster Abbey; George Peabody, his body, after the highest honors Great Britain could pay it, carried across the ocean in a British ship-of-war, there to be interred for its final resting-place in his own land, — George Peabody is a link of peace and love between the two nations, which must never be broken. And as American and British statesmen stood around that open grave; as American and British citizens blended their voices in the prayer to ' our Father in heaven ' to forgive us our trespasses as we forgive each other; as, at the same hour when this solemn service was performing in Westminster Abbey, the cradle of both nations, similar services were being conducted in America, while flags were lowered and bells were tolled, — I felt, that, whether diplomacy has yet finally and formally completed its business or not, there never again can be a question about the maintenance of friendship. All thoughts of the possibility of quarrel must forever pass away; and in the grave of Peabody, both at Westminster and at Danvers, must every remaining suspicion and memory of evil be buried; both nations resolving that no deeds or words of menace or ill will shall again be exchanged, and that not mere rigid justice, but generous love, shall settle all matters still in debate. The interests of civilization, the cause of liberty, the claims of religion, the welfare of the world, demand, that as we are essentially one nation, so we shall ever be bound together in the closest ties of brotherhood, each seeking the honor and welfare of the other, and both

co-operating to lead the van in the triumphant march of
universal civilization, freedom, and peace. Other thoughts
then crowded on my mind. The first was this: How
wise, yet how rare, the course which Mr. Peabody pur-
sued! Having attended to personal claims, he had vast
wealth remaining, — far beyond what he needed for himself. He did not care to squander it in idle ostentation. It
was impossible to exhaust it on his own wants or luxuries,
had he been so disposed. Where would be the advantage
of leaving behind him, to be disposed of by others, so vast
a sum, when he might have the happiness of being his
own almoner? How petty the ambition of dying worth a
fabulous sum of money! As we can take nothing with
us, we cannot die worth any thing. Rich and poor alike
came naked into the world, and naked they must leave it.
It is certain we can carry nothing out. Why not, then,
use it while we may, and enjoy the luxury of making
others happy? How awful it is to die rich, when such
riches have been accumulated by neglecting the claims of
religion and charity! With a thousand claimants for
help; with philanthropic machinery of all kinds standing
still, or working inefficiently, for want of the fuel we
possess and cannot use ourselves; with the hungry crying
for food, and the ignorant claiming instruction, and sinners
needing the gospel, 'perishing for lack of knowledge,' —
it is a fearful responsibility to possess great wealth, an awful crime to die rich, after a life of ' covetousness which is
idolatry.' All honor to Mr. Peabody, that, in his lifetime,

he recognized the responsibility, as well as enjoyed the privileges, of wealth ; and that he derived greater satisfaction in scattering his possessions amongst the poor than in indefinitely augmenting his store !"

"The London Evening Standard" contained the following poetical tribute while the remains of Mr. Peabody were taking their solemn way across the deep : —

REQUIESCAT IN PACE.

We send him home.
England sends home her son, — her son (for he
Is yours, and ye our first-born) ; sends him home
As nations send the men they honor most, —
In pride and state and pomp of splendid death.

We send him home.
The land he loved to his own loving land, —
The loan to the lender ; and we add thereto
A royal usury, — a people's tears.

We send him home, —
The good, kind heart, the simple gentleman, —
And, sending, say, " This body spans the gulf.
We stretch across as with a fleshly arm,
And our own flesh (oh, never doubt !) will clasp
The hand of brotherhood with strong right hand.
Wipe out the past, — all but the old kind years
Before an oft-regretted harshness snapt
The filial link ; the years when England still
Was ' home ' to far-off hearths, and saw with pride
Her Titan offspring towering into strength. . . .

Wipe out the past, — the wrongs, the unnatural strife,
And the red blood that English hands have poured
From English veins.   War is a curse; but war
Betwixt one race, one kindred, doubly cursed."

What gain in war?   No gain; but loss of much
Of life, of treasure.   Gain of honor, then?
The weaker falls : what honor to the strong?
O war! what honor hast thou?   Honor none.
But war treads down the blossoming rose of peace;
With iron heel stamps out the smouldering sparks
Of spiritual fire, and the strugglings faint
Of poor, blind, dumb humanity for light.

We send him home
Who showed a better way.   With good, not ill,
He nobly conquered, and, where darkness reigns
Amidst the abodes of night, made day, himself
Illumined by the brightness that he gave.

He taught us love; and let us learn the theme, —
Prelude alike and close of all that is.
And whilst with stooping flag and muffled march
The great ship bears the lowly to his rest;
Whilst twice ten thousand brazen lips ring woe,
And thousand thousand hearts re-echo it;
Yea, whilst the funeral-peal is thundering forth
Even from the black cannon-mouths agape for war, —
Join we our hands above the gracious dead,
And, mingling tears in one long sorrow, swear
To write this epitaph above him, — PEACE.   H. O. P.

The pulpit on both sides of the Atlantic gave its voice
in favor of his beneficence, and made the name of GEORGE
PEABODY a household word.

The following is a list of his donations, in a convenient form for reference ; and it embraces all the more important public gifts of Mr. Peabody to various institutions and charities during his lifetime, including the bequests contained in his last will and testament : —

To the State of Maryland, for negotiating the loan of $8,000,000,	$60,000
To the Peabody Institute, Baltimore, Md., including accrued interest	1,500,000
To the Southern Education Fund	3,000,000
To Yale College	150,000
To Harvard College	150,000
To Peabody Academy, Massachusetts	140,000
To Phillips Academy, Massachusetts	25,000
To Peabody Institute, &c., at Peabody, Mass.	250,000
To Kenyon College, Ohio	25,000
To Memorial Church in Georgetown, Mass.	100,000
To Homes for the Poor in London	3,000,000
To Libraries in Georgetown, Mass., and Thetford, Vt.	10,000
To Kane's Arctic Expedition	10,000
To different Sanitary Fairs	10,000
To unpaid moneys advanced to uphold the credit of States	40,000
Total	$8,470,000

In addition to the above, Mr. Peabody made a large number of donations for various public purposes, ranging in sums from two hundred and fifty to one thousand dollars, and extending back as far as the year 1835.

The amount of property left by him at his death is estimated at about four million dollars in value. With the exception of a few bequests in the will, this amount is directed to be distributed among his relatives, including one brother, one sister, and about fourteen nephews and nieces. On his last visit to this country, he divided among them one million five hundred thousand dollars; and the property left at his death is to be distributed in the same proportions to each as were awarded by him in that gift.

CHAPTER XX.

THOUGHTS SUGGESTED.

The Lessons of George Peabody's Life. — Money is Power. — A Consecrated Purse is that of Fortunatus.

> "We tell thy doom without a sigh;
> For thou art Freedom's now, and Fame's, —
> One of the few, the immortal names
> That were not born to die." — HALLECK.

"Be not overcome of evil; but overcome evil with good." — ROM. xii. 21.

GRACE GREENWOOD paid a beautiful tribute to Mr. Peabody in an article entitled
"The Good Giver." We have only space for
a part of her true words. She said, —

"The honors paid to the memory of the late George
Peabody are a cheering sign of the state of moral sentiment in England. The English people, from the Queen
to her humblest subject, reverenced this good giver as
no other American citizen was ever reverenced in the
mother-country. It shows that deeds of benevolence are
getting to be more esteemed than deeds of valor, even in
that land of military heroes. . . .

" When *this* man died, as he had lived, a simple American citizen, the honors paid him by the great of his adopted country were personal rather than national tributes, altogether voluntary and loving ; while his sincerest mourners were among the humblest of the poor. ' The blessing of those ready to perish ' canopied his hearse. We may almost think of angels as walking in his funeral-procession. . . .

" Would that our rich capitalists might take home the lesson of George Peabody's wise and generous benefactions, and allow themselves the almost divine luxury of distributing their own charities of *giving*, not *willing !*

" Who can doubt that the rich banker found a sweeter happiness, if not a keener pleasure, in scattering abroad, than he had ever found in amassing his splendid fortune ? He cast his bread on the waters with a liberal hand ; and though he had here no return in kind, and needed none, amid the pleasant pastures of the better land, on the green banks of the river of life, it will all come back to him."

The following poetical tribute appeared in " The New-York Independent : " —

> " Nations have vied to do him honor, — him
>   Whose royal heart went out to all his kind ;
>   Whose hand e'er proved the princely almoner
>   To do its generous bidding. Now in death
>   Each throbbing pulse is stilled. Fold the white hands
>   Upon the quiet breast : their work is done !

Give him brief place 'mongst England's titled dead,
Where kings and warriors, borne with regal pomp
And rites imposing, lie in gilded state,
While o'er them banners wave, and music swells;
Where, wreathed with fadeless laurel, poets sleep.
Vain are these empty pageants! Better far
The widow's blessing and the orphan's tear,
In grateful memory of such kindly acts
As graced *his* life, and crowned it at its close.

Blow gently, gales! and waft o'er summer seas
The gallant convoy with its precious freight.
In his far childhood's home, 'mid rural scenes,
In sweet seclusion from the world's turmoil,
There let the good man rest!
                              No costly pile,
Graven with the shining record of his deeds,
Shall tell the world that here a conqueror lies:
His cenotaph is reared in every clime;
On every shore where sweeps the ocean-surge
Lingers the echo of his nobler fame."

The lessons of his life are before the people of England
and America. They are indicated on every page of this
volume. Introduction and Memoir teach the same great
lessons; and, while his eulogist at the final funeral allowed
that he had faults, the hearts of all who remember his
benefaction will gladly echo the words of large-souled
Gilbert Haven: " The great snow monument piled up
by the hands of Heaven over his grave on the very night
of his burial is a felicitous symbol of the whiteness of his
fame. Cleaned of all spots by the washing of death and
grace and time, it shall stand forth in the future, pure as

the driven snow, an incentive to all men of wealth so to use their acquisitions, that when they fail, as fail they must, these shall receive them into everlasting habitations. . . . Will not such an example aid the man of wealth in conquering this demon, and making it his slave, and not his master? Begin young, O man of business! as he began, to devise liberal things. Let not your money insnare you, or ruin yours. Give to your brother, the church, the poor, the ignorant; and ye shall have treasure in heaven."

Money is power, for good or for evil. George Peabody made it an instrument for good. He made "friends of the mammon of unrighteousness" by using his great gains for the benefit of humanity. The following is a copy of the main provisions of his will, as taken from the books of Doctors' Commons, London: —

"I, George Peabody, gentleman, do make this my last will and testament: —

"Firstly, I direct that my remains shall be sent to my native town of Danvers, now incorporated by the name of Peabody, in the County of Essex, and Commonwealth of Massachusetts, in that part of the United States of America called New England, and be deposited in the ground appropriated to that purpose in the cemetery of Harmony Grove in Salem, in said county, near the Peabody town-line, under the direction of my executors hereinafter named.

"Secondly, I give and bequeath to Henry West, of 22,

Old Broad Street, London, £2,200; and, in the event of his decease, to his wife, Louisa West; and, in the event of her decease, to his surviving children.

"Thirdly, I give and bequeath to Thomas Perman, of 22, Old Broad Street, London, the sum of £1,000; and, in the event of his decease, to his wife, Annette Emma Perman; and, in the event of her decease, to his surviving children. And I empower my executors to pay the above-named legacies within six months after my decease, and free from any tax, duty, or charges, whatever.

"Fourthly, I give and bequeath to the Right Hon. Lord Stanley, the American minister at the court of St. James for the time being, the Right Hon. Stafford Northcote, Bart., Sir Curtis Miranda Lampson, Bart., and Junius Spencer Morgan, Esq., trustees of the Peabody Donation Fund, and their successors, trustees of the said fund, the sum of £150,000, upon trust, for the building of lodging-houses for the laboring poor of London, as defined in my late letters to said trustees; and I direct that this legacy be considered a part of the second trust, and disposed of in accordance with the said trust. And I direct that my London executors shall, of the said sum of £150,000, pay to said trustees of the Peabody Donation Fund £100,000 on the first Monday of October, 1873; and the sum of £50,000 at any time during said year of 1873. As this work progresses, the labor and responsibility increase; and I therefore deem it essential that another trustee be added, who will have the necessary time, and possess the requisite knowledge of all that may be needed for the successful prosecution of the trust. Without assuming to dictate to the trustees, I would mention the name of Charles Reed, Esq., M.P., who is well known to me for his high and most honorable character, as a most suitable person to fill that office.

" Fifthly, I nominate, constitute, and appoint Sir Curtis Miranda Lampson, of 80, Eaton Square, Pimlico, Middlesex, and of Rowfant, in the parish of Worth, Sussex, Bart., Charles Reed of Erlmead House, Hackney, Middlesex, Esq., M.P., George Peabody Russell, Esq., of Salem, Essex County, State of Massachusetts, U.S., R. Singleton Peabody of Rutland, in the State of Vermont, counsellor, and Charles W. Chandler of Zanesville, in the State of Ohio, counsellor, executors of this my last will and testament; fully authorizing the said Sir Curtis Miranda Lampson and said Charles Reed, called my London executors, to act independently of said George Peabody Russell, said R. Singleton Peabody, and said Charles W. Chandler, called my American executors. And I also authorize my American executors to act independently of my said London executors: that is to say, my London executors to have full management and control of my personal estate in England; and my American executors to have full management and control of my real and personal estate in America. But it is my wish and hope that all my executors, both London and American, may act together with the utmost harmony for the best interests of the estate.

"Sixthly, I direct that all and each of my executors aforesaid be exempt and excused from giving bonds to any court or magistrate, or otherwise, for the performance of their duties or offices as my executors.

"Seventhly, I give and bequeath to the said Sir Curtis Miranda Lampson and said Charles Reed £5,000 each for their services.

"Eighthly, I give and bequeath to the said George Peabody Russell, R. Singleton Peabody, and Charles W. Chandler, my American executors, £5,000 each.

"Ninthly, I give and bequeath to the said George Peabody Russell, R. Singleton Peabody, and Charles W. Chandler, all the rest, residue, and remainder of the property, both real and personal, of which I shall be possessed at my decease, or which may afterwards come or fall into my estate, upon trust to sell, exchange, or retain, and the interest accruing on the same to divide semi-annually (re-investing the same in the case of minor children) among the parties named as beneficiaries in the family-trust, of which Messrs. J. M. Beebe, S. T. Dana, and S. Endicott Peabody, are trustees, according to the proportions of the sums allotted to each in said trust, or such other proportions as I may hereafter prescribe to them, my said American executors.

"In witness whereof, I, the said George Peabody, declaring this to be my last will and testament, written on seven pages of paper, have hereto set my hand and seal, this ninth day of September, 1869.

"GEORGE PEABODY."

By this will, it is seen that Mr. Peabody sought to exert his power as a man of wealth to induce harmonious action between Americans and Englishmen. This desire to promote peace between the two nations was very evident in Mr. Peabody's life and character; and the wealth used for such a purpose may certainly be deemed consecrated. A writer declares that " the munificent charities that have made the name of PEABODY a household word in two hemispheres were not the promptings of temporary vanity, or a sudden freak of old age to win the applause of mankind: on the contrary, they were but the fulfilment of a long-cherished design formed in his own mind, as a matter of duty, more than a quarter of a century ago, and which had constituted his chief incentive to the acquisition of wealth. While in this city, last summer, he said to his old partner in business, who had known him intimately for thirty-five years, ' Mr. J——, it has been my constant prayer to God for upwards of twenty years, that I might be enabled to accumulate a large sum of money to bestow in charity to the poor.' It will scarcely surprise those who believe in the efficacy of prayer to be told, that, during all those years, there was not a single business enterprise which he undertook that did not prove successful, and hardly a thing which he touched that did not turn to gold in his hands."

It was this effort to spend his money for the good of others that secured him the applause of the public. Not the wealthy merchant, but the benevolent man, did his fellow-citizens and townsmen delight to honor. It may not be amiss to place on record a report rather more extensive of the honors paid to the remains of Mr. Peabody in his native town. "The Boston Post" thus describes the scene : —

"The arrival of the train was the signal for the tolling of the bells and the firing of minute-guns. The citizens of the surrounding towns seemed to have come to witness the ceremonies, and the vicinity of the dépôt was packed with people. The body was first taken from the train, and placed upon the funeral-car. This was a structure about eleven feet in length, seven feet in width, and ten feet high, covered with black velvet appropriately festooned, and trimmed with silver lace and fringe studded with stars. On the top rested the casket containing the remains. Underneath the casket were winged cherubs in silver; on each corner an elaborate bronze vase, two feet and a half high; on the front and back ends the coat of arms of the deceased, and on one side the English, and on the opposite the American coat of arms, in gold; on each corner the monogram of the deceased, in silver, enclosed with laurel-wreaths. The car was drawn by six horses covered with black housings trimmed with silver. The four companies of United-States Artillery which accompanied the remains then disembarked, and escorted the procession; the Sutton Guard acting as a guard of honor, and the different committees who came on the train following in double files. A direct route was taken for the Institute, which was reached about sunset. The artillery drew up in line, and the civic portion of the procession passed into the hall, which was appropriately draped as below described. Soon after all had entered, the body was brought in and placed in its proper position, and a guard posted; and the procession passed around the head of the catafalque, and out of the hall.

" The funeral decorations in the Institute building at Peabody were arranged with taste and beauty. On entering the library-room, the emblems of mourning were seen at once; the windows and railing having been heavily draped with black, with a white border on either edge, and tastefully trimmed with rosettes of black and white. At the end of the room, seen through the catafalque, is the picture of her Majesty, and above it the royal flag of England and the American flag, both artistically draped with crape. At the other end of the room, the bust of the deceased, that occupies the space above the door, is also draped with the sombre hues of mourning. Above, in the lecture-room, the portrait of the deceased is draped in black and white, with the cross of St. George and the stars and stripes on either side, covered with crape; and above them an elegant original fresco representing Britannia and Columbia by female figures reclining over an urn containing the ashes of the dead, and guarded by the British lion and American eagle on either side.

19

"The catafalque is a raised dais, ten feet in length and six feet in width, covered with black velvet. From each corner rises a standard, supporting a framework of the same size as the base, and about six inches in width. Pendent from this are heavy black-velvet hangings, artistically cut, and trimmed with a wreath of silvery stars enclosing a large star on each of the four sides, and heavy silver-bullion fringe, with wide silver braid above it, and massive silver tassels appropriately placed. Above the hangings, a neat silver moulding on a black-velvet groundwork meets the eye. Above this is a row of silver stars, and another moulding that rises to a peak on each of the four sides, containing emblems of mourning, in silver. The one on the front end has two reversed torches crossed; on the rear, the hour-glass, with the wings of Time, are to be seen; and on either side a large silver star, encircled by its emblem of eternity, — an endless snake. On each corner arises an elegant arabesque ornament in silver, surmounted with handsome funeral-plumes. In front, on the base, is the monogram of the deceased, in silver letters, on a black-velvet groundwork, enclosed in a laurel-wreath in silver, pendent from a leaning pole, surmounted by a knot and rosette of silver. On each corner of the base are cherubs' heads with angels' wings in silver; the whole being arranged in the ancient Grecian style, that is at once elegant and artistic."

We have already referred to the funeral-services, and need add no more here in regard to those unrivalled obsequies. Further services in honor of Mr. Peabody took place a few evenings afterward at the Peabody Institute in Danvers, which was appropriately decorated for the occasion by Mrs. E. G. Berry. The exercises began at seven o'clock with the singing of the anthem, " Blessed is he that considereth the poor," by the united choirs of the town, under direction of Mr. John S. Learoyd. Prayer was then offered by Rev. George J. Sanger. It was followed by another anthem, reading of the Scriptures by Rev. S. I. Evans, and a choral song by the choir. Rev. James Fletcher then delivered an elegant eulogy on the deceased. He began by a reference to the traits of character developed by Mr. Peabody in early life, when entering upon his business-career, amid circumstances of great discouragement and trial. During that period of several years, he displayed the tough fibres of his nature, — his hardihood, perseverance, unbending integrity, high sense of honor, and commanding traits as a business-man. These qualities shone all through his mercantile career. He was undismayed by danger, and preserved his integrity and manliness of character in the severest of trials. His great services in upholding American credit abroad were referred to, and then his deportment in the time of prosperity depicted. He felt that God had bestowed his great wealth upon him that he might do good with it; and, with that feeling and purpose,

he distributed his riches with more than princely munificence for the benefit of his fellow-men. He believed
that God raised him up to accomplish some grand benefit
for his race. Unlike many others, when his wealth came
to him, he had the elevation of spirit and the affluence of
soul to give it away, instead of adding to it. He gave in
the full tide of a prosperous life, and for purposes which
displayed benevolence of the highest order.

The simplicity and modesty of Mr. Peabody's character were next touched upon. He never boasted of his
success, or sought the applause of men. His devotion to
his mother and sisters, and his love to his birthplace, were
alluded to in feeling terms ; and the reverend gentleman
concluded with a fine tribute to the breadth of Mr. Peabody's character, the benignity of his life, and the blessings he had conferred on his fellow-men on both sides of
the ocean.

The services closed with an ode by Rev. James Brand,
and the benediction.

Among the tributes already mentioned was that of Rev.
Newman Hall; and a further quotation from it will show
that the London preacher rightly apprehended the value
of that power which accompanies money. He said,
" There is danger, lest, in admiration of Mr. Peabody's
princely gifts, some may suppose that such liberality, of
itself, is religion. Even the teachers and preachers of
Christianity may unintentionally mislead the public by too
unqualified and indiscriminating admiration. I yield to

none in appreciation and honor of Mr. Peabody's noble gifts and life of benevolence. Nor have I any reason to doubt that such generosity sprang from the very highest motives. But it is the duty, at such a time, of Christian teachers to brave the possibility of being misunderstood, and to testify, in the midst of all this well-deserved applause, that we are not saved by our benefactions either to relieve the poor or to promote religion. We are rebels against God, and can only be saved by being reconciled to him through Jesus Christ. We must preach repentance towards God, and faith in our Lord Jesus Christ, as the only way of salvation. He taught us, that, if we should do all our duty, we should still be 'unprofitable servants,' — only just doing what is required. But, as none of us do this, how plain it is that 'by grace we are saved, through faith'! 'If I give all my goods to feed the poor, and have not charity, it profiteth me nothing.'

"Then came the other thought, — that, with faith in Christ, and reconciliation to God, as the foundation, there must be, and will always be, the superstructure of good works. . . . Certainly, of the two, it would be better to have good works of charity, however defective their motive, and without true Christian faith, than to have only the pretence of possessing faith and no good works. The former case has something to show, which, at least, may benefit our fellow-men : the latter case has absolutely nothing ; for 'faith, if it have not works, is dead, being alone.'

" Then came this thought, — that the privilege of performing good works and serving Christ is not confined to the wealthy. A large gift strikes our imagination because its obvious benefit is large. Thus man judges of beneficence. But God looks to the motive, measures the means, sees the amount of self-sacrifice, and approves and rewards accordingly. He who has only a shilling in the world, and gives away sixpence, thereby depriving himself of half a meal, may be as acceptable in the eye of God as he who gives half a million, but has half a million left. Jesus said that the poor widow who threw into the treasury her two mites had actually given more than the rich who cast in liberally, but did it out of their abundance. This is not to disparage great and liberal benefactors ; but it is to encourage all, however poor, — even so that they can give merely a cup of cold water, — that they shall not be unrewarded ; and that if the smallest sum is given in a right spirit, and in proportion to our ability, and with self-sacrifice, as he that receiveth a prophet in the name of a prophet shall receive a prophet's reward, so he that gives away a penny in the spirit of a benevolent millionnaire shall receive a benevolent millionnaire's reward.

" And then a concluding thought was this : Two nations — yea, the civilized world — are admiring the gifts of the rich man, who was still rich in spite of his benefactions. How should we esteem Him, who, though he was rich, yet for our sakes became poor, that we by his poverty might be made rich " !

A correspondent of " The New-York Tribune " tells the
following anecdote concerning Mr. Peabody's use of that
money which gave him power, and of the way in which
he liked to have others use money : —

" When Mr. Peabody was in the United States last
year, he visited the Institute at South Danvers which
bears his name, and inquired particularly into its operations ; going over the accounts, and discussing with the
trustees the cost of its maintenance and the annual income
from the fund.   I suppose I am telling no secret, and
hurting nobody's feelings, when I say that even so good
and benevolent a man as George Peabody was not exempt
from the misfortunes of age and bodily infirmity, and that
he consequently allowed himself at times to criticise pretty
freely — not to say unjustly — the policy of the custodians
of his benefactions.   On this occasion, he is said to have
fretted a great deal.   From various causes, not necessary
to mention, and certainly not easy to avoid, the revenue
from the endowments had not kept pace with the increased expenses which followed the general rise of prices
during the war ; and the benevolent founder felt more
keenly how far the Institute fell short of his expectations
than how much it really had accomplished.   ' You spend
too much money,' he complained ; ' you spend too much
money.   You pay your lecturers too much.   You must
get them cheaper.'   And so he went on for a while, until
the momentary irritation passed away.   His face soon

brightened, and a soft expression began to play about his mouth. ' Well, well,' said he, drawing something from his pocket, ' I must give you fifty thousand dollars more, and get you out of trouble. And I must say,' he continued, ' that none of my foundations have been so admirably administered and given me so much satisfaction as this one at my native place.' So the good old man continued for a long time praising every thing connected with the Institute, and assuring his delighted friends that they had fulfilled his wishes in the smallest particulars. It is well known that the South-Danvers foundation was his favorite child."

" The Boston Journal " expressed its idea of the public feeling in regard to the Peabody obsequies, saying that those who regarded his life as useful and noble were expressing sincere respect for his memory, and adding, —

" George Peabody was a representative man of his era and of his country. We would not adopt the curious idea of Victor Hugo, that John Brown and George Peabody are America's characteristic contributions to the historic figures of this age. It is true, however, that the one did not more truly embody the Puritanic conscientiousness and dauntlessness of our country than the other exemplified its thrift, animated by pure motives, and ending in boundless but well-directed philanthropy. The latter showed the world that the phrase, ' the almighty dollar,' supposed to carry with it an American stigma, really included a full share of those attributes of beneficence as well as of power which belonged to the epithet. Set down amid an aristocracy whose accumulated wealth dated from the middle ages, George Peabody set them a lesson in the act of true benevolence. The poor of London to-day know his name better than they do the names of those who have in their veins ' all the blood of all the Howards.' Like a true American, also, he remembered most fondly his own countrymen; and his benefactions, completely unexampled in amount and extent of application, will send their enriching influences down to future generations. Let all honor, then, be paid to the memory of one who founded his fame on the great good he has done to his fellow-men."

" The New-York Albion " speaks in highly eulogistic terms of Mr. Peabody, saying without reserve, —

" George Peabody was, in a wider sense than is often applicable, a new type of manhood. In him were combined in finely, almost perfectly, balanced proportions, three qualities seldom found in close association, — the shrewd intuitive perception necessary to the acquisition of great riches, the moral impulses which prompt to a beneficent distribution of them, and the masculine judgment which exercises such a mastery over both as to prevent their running into mischievous excess. A life which exhibits to us these characteristics on a colossal scale furnishes scope for highly profitable study ; but, in order to this, we need to see it in·its internal development rather than in its external incidents; or, rather, we should be more correct in saying that any knowledge we may obtain of the latter will be valuable only as it may help to disclose the former. Whence originated this felicitous opposition of qualities so rarely to be seen in conjunction? To what extent were they due to natural constitution or to ancestral history? How much of their strength did they derive from early training? and of what sort was that training? In what respects were they owing to circumstances? and what were the circumstances, if any, which account for the extraordinary bias of this man's will? We want to observe his character in its first manifestations, in its growth, and in the influences which fused into unity tendencies so commonly antagonistic to each other. Of course, we cannot expect to find what we want in the bare compilations which appear in the columns of a newspaper. The biography of the late George Peabody, to be written as it well deserves to be, would demand a high order of intellectual and sympathetic skill and an indefatigable spirit of research, and would undoubtedly present to the world one of those contributions to psychological study which give a new direction and a powerful stimulus to human motive and effort.

"Of Mr. Peabody's business aptitudes, his commercial success is the best proof. It is not by any means impossible to find his parallels as to this feature of his character. Modern times have been peculiarly favorable to the production of millionnaires. The sudden expansion of the means of locomotion, the marvellous facilities provided for quick and frequent intercourse, and the stupendous works which the application of science to industrial pursuits had made not merely feasible, but almost indispensable, have opened the way to many men endowed with competent abilities to acquire for themselves fortunes which in any previous age would have been deemed fabulous. In regard to this matter, Mr. Peabody had a considerable number of compeers. But it is worthy of note, that the grand moral traits of his character stood out in high relief before the world, in connection with his pursuit of wealth, long before they were publicly displayed in the distribution of it. That he was rapidly amassing riches in the country of his adoption was not more widely surmised, perhaps, than it was known, that, in all the methods of acquisition employed by his house, the soul of mercantile integrity and honor was eminently conspicuous. His rectitude, like the granite of his native State, was immovable. It invited trust, and never gave way under any weight of responsibility resting upon it. It armed him with a reputation which enabled him to negotiate loans for public bodies, even when their credit had been tainted. His own name amply sufficed as a guaranty for the fulfilment of engagements entered into, not merely on his own behalf, but on behalf of defaulting legislatures. Wherever he saw fit to pledge it, men built their speculations upon it with a sense of security. . To be true was one of the necessities of his being.

" To his remarkable talent for acquiring wealth was conjoined a noble purpose in the daily pursuit of it. He cared little for the selfish and garish pleasures for which affluent means are commonly desired. His tastes were simple. They had been formed, probably, upon the traditions of his Puritanic forefathers, and by that atmosphere of opinion which surrounded him in his younger days. His personal wants were few and inexpensive. He hated the very semblance of ostentation. As he had not been born into a system which made extravagant expenditure a duty owing to his station, so he aspired not to be identified with it. He preferred to occupy the position of a tenant in trust. His gains were sought and obtained, not as an end, but as means to an end; not with a view to himself, but with a view to others. He held himself to be a debtor to his kind; and his accumulations were used in the faithful discharge of that debt. This moral conviction was evidently deeply rooted in his heart. It withstood all the influences which would otherwise have destroyed it. When vast wealth is only in prospect, it is not at all uncommon, because not at all difficult, to entertain the most generous intentions as to what shall be done with it, and to lose sight of them in proportion to the extent to which that prospect is realized. Mr. Peabody, on the contrary, instead of allowing the inflowing tide of his riches to submerge his sense of responsibility, thought and purposed and lived so as to keep it evermore uppermost; and, as his means increased, his anxiety to make them subservient to the well-being of others increased also. Great prosperity, instead of closing his hand, opened it the wider; and, in reverse of the usual order of things, age, enlarged rather than contracted the scope of his liberality.

" But impulsive benevolence, oftentimes the offspring of weakness and indolence, seems to have had no power to guide the career of this truly remarkable man. No one knew better than he how to say ' No ' to applications for aid which did not commend the approbation of his reason. He spared no pains to ascertain how he could direct his beneficence into the most serviceable channels. He laid out his immense wealth with as conscientious a carefulness as he might have done if he had expected to be called upon to account for and justify every shilling of his expenditure. Rarely has the life of a plutocrat exhibited so perfect an illustration of the idea of stewardship as did George Peabody's. Few intelligent men of this generation will forget the letter in which he sketched, for the intended trustees of his bounty to the poor of London, his own views of the object to which it might be usefully devoted. Pauperism had no attractions for him : industrious and struggling poverty chiefly engrossed his sympathies. Indeed, it was a marked feature of his beneficence, that it almost invariably had respect to something beyond and better and more enduring than the immediate benefit it might confer. Sometimes patriotism, sometimes international amity, gave direction to his liberality. He set the highest store upon education; and, in applying his resources for the advantage of his own countrymen, he selected precisely those modes of assisting them which were most peculiarly adapted to their position and wants. The Peabody Institute at Danvers, the Literary and Scientific Institute at Baltimore, and his munificent contribution to the Southern Educational Fund, bear testimony to his quick appreciation of the special needs of the times. The means of intellectual refinement, where they could become available, and of elementary instruction where they were most lacking and most urgently required, drew forth his readiest and largest bounty. London presented a different claim upon his purse. Even education could do but little for the industrious poor of the English metropolis until they were better housed. His penetrating glance fastened at once upon the special need of the capital; and, in supplying the remedy, his head and heart united in doing the very best that could be done.

" Mr. Peabody's life was an impressive homily from beginning to end. It was full of the most timely lessons, enforced upon society not by words, but by deeds. He has rebuked the narrow sectarianism of the day by his display of ' good will to men,' quite irrespectively of their religious differences. He has illustrated in his own history how it is possible to combine with ardent patriotism a breadth of sympathy extending beyond merely national limits. He has set an example of wise philanthropy, capable of being initiated on the largest scale without undermining the self-reliant spirit of the poor. Above all, he has taught us the true uses of wealth, on what conditions it should be held by its proprietors, in what ways it may be fruitfully employed, and what durable honor and happiness it may be made to achieve for the comparative few to whom it is given. Rich and poor alike may contemplate his career with practical advantage. London, especially, will keep alive his memory with grateful admiration ; and, let us trust, his name, emblazoned by his works, will exercise a talismanic influence in persuading the prosperous to recognize their responsibilities, and to do what good their hands can find to do whilst they yet live to superintend and rejoice in the effects of their beneficence."

While these pages were passing through the press, a writer in " The New-York Tribune " furnished an account of the Peabody homestead and the birthplace of the great giver, which is so graphic, and in many respects so interesting, that, although it did not appear in season for the early chapters of this memoir, it may, perhaps, be allowed to appear at the close : —

" The town of South Danvers, in which George Peabody was born, in which he served his apprenticeship to a country shopkeeper, in which he founded one of the noble institutes of popular education that bear his name, and in which, after this magnificent funeral-procession of a whole month's duration, his remains will at last repose, is, to all intents and purposes, a part of Salem, and in some of its features not unlike that ancient and ghost-haunted seaport. I speak of it as South Danvers; for it has come so lately into its new name of Peabody, adopting, after a fashion not uncommon with legatees, the family appellation which belongs with the property, that the change has not yet renewed the faces of the sign-boards, and is only half recognized in the talk of the inhabitants. The main street of Salem runs out along the crest of a hill, with a general determination toward the north-west, but with erratic impulses now and then to the right and left. It never gets into the country; and its broad, quaint, comfortable old houses are scarcely far enough apart to have even a suburban look, before up the elm-shaded street comes a persistent smell of leather. The road pitches down into a little valley full of tanneries; then up another hill whose slopes are mostly hung with hides, and upon whose crest stands the brick-and-granite building of the Peabody Institute; down once more into a second hollow, likewise given up to leather; and there you are in the heart of South Danvers. A single-track horse-railway, with infrequent turnouts and still more infrequent cars, stretches from here through Salem. You may come that way if you are in no particular hurry; but, if pressed for time, you had better walk.

"It is not natural to look for beauty in a village which devotes itself to tanning hides and spreading tan-bark

around its door-yards, only varying these useful pursuits
by the cognate industry of manufacturing glue; but Peabody, in spite of unsavory smells, is a pretty place, and the
pilgrims who visit it during the approaching ceremonies
will find the Massachusetts Mecca not unworthy of its
shrine. A Massachusetts village — especially an *old* Massachusetts village, in which the shade-trees have had years
enough to develop their beautiful proportions, and spread
their arms across the wide roadway, and whose best
houses were built before the day of staring white clap-
boards and prim green blinds (you know the kind of
house I mean, — front-door close to the street, holly-
hocks, phlox, and prince's-feather under the parlor windows) — is always a pleasant sight; and even in this
gloomy season, with bare trees and muddy roads, Peabody
has a clean, thrifty, substantial, and, withal, tasteful appearance. It is pretty well stricken in years for an American
village. The old houses are many enough and prominent
enough to give it an antique aspect, in spite of the factories;
and flavors of the half-forgotten past, such as hung around
Hawthorne's custom-house down at the port, are wafted
along its quiet road. Off to the right, at the foot of the
ridge, there is a pond or inlet of brackish water: a steam-
railway runs along there, and there most of the factories
are built. But in the main street on the hill there is little
to break the stillness. Just by the side of the road there
is an old graveyard. Right opposite, on the other side of
the water, lies Harmony Grove, a newer and more fash-

20

ionable place of sepulture, where the upper classes may be interred with all the modern improvements, including a patent burial-case and a granite monument. Mr. Peabody's remains will be placed in this grove; but the precise spot for their permanent resting-place has not yet been selected."

THE HOUSE IN WHICH MR. PEABODY WAS BORN.

"In company with Mr. Poole, the courteous librarian of the Institute, I went to see the house in which Mr. Peabody was born. It is on the outskirts of the village, and, eighty years ago, was probably quite in the country. What it was eighty years ago it is not now in any respect, save that most of the old building remains and can be identified. A long L has been added; a small kitchen, which was anciently attached to the rear like an excrescence, has been moved away; and improvements, enlargements, and alterations have been made to such an extent, that the old place has all the external appearance of a modern Yankee-village house. A few rods in the rear is a tannery: a few rods away, at one side, is a glue-factory; and the owner of the factory, Mr. Upton, is also the owner, though not the occupier, of the house. We met the lady of the house near the door; and she very kindly gave us permission to enter, and showed us all that remains of the old house where Thomas Peabody lived, and his son George was born. It was a two-story house, with a short hall and narrow stairway in the middle, and on each floor a single small room on each side of the hall, — four rooms in all. These, with the kitchen-outhouse, now removed, comprised the whole. The front-door opens close to the ground, and only a foot or two from the street railing. There is no porch; and the front of the house is almost as bare as if it had been shaved off with a plane. Bare and ugly enough the place must have been when the old Peabody family held it; though now, with its enlarged proportions, bright paint, and neat appearance, it is so far improved, that a sensitive man might, perhaps, live in it without absolute unhappiness. The original rooms have not been altered. On the first floor, they are only a little over six feet high ; and across the middle of the ceiling runs a beam, which tall visitors must stoop to pass. The heavy timbers of the framework are also conspicuous at the corners. But for these, with the fresh wall-paper, bright carpets, and modern furniture, there would be nothing in the appearance of the rooms to remind you of their age. 'I have tried everywhere,' said Mrs. ——, ' to get some furniture which belonged to the old place ; but not a bit can be found. I would like, above all things, to make at least one of these rooms look as it did when the Peabodys had it.'

" ' You must be very much annoyed with visitors,' said I ; 'and I am ashamed of my own intrusion upon your patience.'

" ' Oh, not at all ! I know that strangers like to see the house, and I am very happy to show it.' But, before the funeral is over, I fear the kind lady's good nature will be taxed to its uttermost limits."

" America gratefully receives back the ashes of her distinguished son and citizen, and commits them to the earth. They are to mingle with the soil on which he was born, and for which he had such an affection. There is not a citizen of this country whose ear is not open to catch every syllable of the funeral-words. There is not a heart in the land that is not present at his open grave. He comes home to be enshrined. If we of this time would henceforth undertake a new pilgrimage, let it be to the burial-place of the man who has taught the world anew, as never man taught it before, how much more blessed it is to give than to receive. The name of Peabody is to stand, for the future, synonymous with Philanthropy. This single word shall be his lasting monument."

THE END.

www.ingramcontent.com/pod-product-compliance
Lightning Source LLC
Chambersburg PA
CBHW031029120726
47905CB00007B/2098